LANDON

LIGHTHOUSE SECURITY INVESTIGATIONS
MONTANA

MARYANN JORDAN

Landon (Lighthouse Security Investigation Montana) Copyright 2025

All rights reserved. No part of this book may be reproduced or transmitted in any form or by any means, electronic or mechanical, including photocopying, recording, or by any information storage and retrieval system without the written permission of the author, except where permitted by law.

If you are reading this book and did not purchase it, then you are reading an illegal pirated copy. If you would be concerned about working for no pay, then please respect the author's work! Make sure that you are only reading a copy that has been officially released by the author.

This book is a work of fiction. Names, characters, places, and incidents are either products of the author's imagination or are used fictitiously. Any resemblance to actual persons, living or dead, events, or locales is entirely coincidental.

Cover by: Graphics by Stacy

Cover photograph: Eric McKinney 612Covered Photography

ISBN ebook: 978-1-965847-03-9

ISBN print: 978-1-965847-04-6

❦ Created with Vellum

ABOUT THE AUTHOR

I am an avid reader of romance novels, often joking that I cut my teeth on historical romances. I have been reading and reviewing for years. In 2013, I finally gave in to the characters in my head, screaming for their story to be told. From these musings, my first novel, Emma's Home, The Fairfield Series, was born.

I was a high school counselor, having worked in education for thirty years. I live in Virginia, having also lived in four states and two foreign countries. I have been married to a wonderfully patient man for forty-three years. When writing, my dog or one of my cats can generally be found in the same room if not on my lap.

Please take the time to leave a review of this book. Feel free to contact me, especially if you enjoyed my book. I love to hear from readers!

Facebook

Join my Facebook group: Maryann Jordan's Protector Fans

Sign up for my emails by visiting my Website!

Website

AUTHOR NOTES

When writing fiction, I research topics so the reader can enjoy the story and feel as though it is as real as possible. I often change the names of cities and places. Choosing to do so allows me creative license to write the places as I see them and not become bogged down in trying to re-create a real place. This is fiction—enjoy!

And for those of you who say, "But there are no lighthouses in Montana!" You will discover how it all works out as you read this story!

All books have errors, no matter how many author, editors, proofers, and readers have looked at the manuscript. If the errors are minor and do not affect the story, please forgive and ignore. But, if you find errors that you deem necessary to report, please send me an email with your notations and do not try to report to Amazon.

Be kind to authors… we are human!
authormaryannjordan@gmail.com

1

Stan stared at the woman in front of him. Her perfectly made-up face was marred by the sneer twisting her red lips. Her long dark hair shimmered as she tossed it over her shoulder with a practiced flick. He'd once found it attractive. Now, it was just a distraction. Her hands were planted on her hips in a stance meant for maximum intimidation. Her towering heels elevated her height, making her legs appear endless, while the snug cashmere turtleneck sweater clung to the curves she loved to flaunt.

"You'll be sorry!" she spat, her voice sharp.

He recognized the pre-tantrum tone, and his jaw tightened. "I already am! I was sorry years ago!"

As the words tumbled out, he remembered how his feelings had changed over the years. She had counted on her allure to draw him in from the beginning. She was captivating, and he was the dumb fuck who fell for her practiced charms.

She continued to lead him by his dick for a long

time. A new designer bag after every argument. Designer clothes when she felt down, which, now that he thought about it, was more often than not. Jewelry for whenever business took him away for a few nights and she had to care for their children... which meant his mom and the help they hired did all the caring just like they had since the children were born.

His mind drifted to their early days, wondering if she was like this when he first started dating her. Back then, he'd been more interested in her beauty... hell, just a chance to bang her rocking body drew him to her. His parents warned him. *"She's a gold digger, Son."*

And when she got pregnant, they'd murmured, "Told you so." But he'd still been so excited about impending fatherhood that he placed a ring on her finger and thought he'd hit the jackpot. But it was Pamela who'd hit the jackpot.

She gave birth to twins, then declared she was done having more children. But his son and daughter were the light of his life... something else she resented. She never liked how much affection he showered on the children and demanded that she be given the same attention.

For years, it was easy to satisfy her with gifts, giving her the lifestyle she craved—the house, the cars, and the status of being in the Fugate family in Montana. After all, with his father owning a massive ranch, she had married into wealth. Over the past thirteen years, she allowed her true self to shine through more and more. She was never satisfied.

The final blow had come when he discovered her

latest boy toy had been in the house with her while Stan was gone, and the children were just down the hall. Stan filed for divorce. Even though she had been pregnant when they were married, his father and their family attorney had insisted on a prenuptial agreement. It was very generous to her, so she'd readily signed it.

Now, she was back, wanting more. Stan had given in when she'd cried about needing more child support even though there was joint custody. He'd added generously when she declared that their daughter needed designer dresses for a school dance even though Penny was only ten years old at the time. And when their son, Tad, was eleven, she'd insisted that his growth spurt meant he needed all new clothes. Of course, Stan had already taken Tad out shopping and bought an entire wardrobe that would last until the next growth spurt. However, Pamela insisted that their son needed equal clothes to be kept at her place. According to Tad, he still had to carry clothes back and forth since that money was never spent on him.

Even her expensive condo overlooking a golf course and lake was paid for by Stan in the divorce agreement. He wanted the kids to have a nice place to stay when they were with her.

And now, she was back, wanting more. The words of his father rang in his ears. *"As long as you keep giving, she'll keep taking. You've got to put a stop to it at some point."* Stan had argued that with the twins now being twelve, he only had six more years, and then he'd cut out all the child support, just paying for everything Tad and Penny needed without giving Pamela anything.

She wanted to take the kids out of school for a weeklong trip to the Caribbean—paid for by Stan, of course. The kids would be at her condo for the weekend, so she'd hurried to the family ranch house to argue with him about more money.

"Enough. I'm done," he said quietly, but his words shook with resolve. "Tad has soccer, and there's an upcoming game he won't want to miss. Penny is the first chair violinist for the school orchestra, and taking a week off during school could cost her the honored placement."

"I don't know what the big deal is," Pamela fumed, arching a perfectly shaped eyebrow. "It's just a vacation. Don't you think the kids deserve a vacation?"

Stan sighed as he pinched the bridge of his nose, trying to stave off the blooming headache. Sucking in a deep breath, he steeled his expression as he pinned her with his stare. "The kids have vacations we plan when their school is out—not in the middle of their education and activities."

She huffed, then surprisingly stopped glaring. "Fine. Have it your way. I'll just tell the kids you won't allow them to have a Caribbean vacation. You can deal with their despondency."

"Christ, Pamela. Why do you have to make everything so complicated? If you want to plan something for the kids, do it when they're out of school. And if it's when they're with me, I'll be more than happy to let them go with you."

The tight, fake smile she aimed his way bounced off, like most of her expressions and words nowadays. He'd spent ten years trying to make things work for the sake of the children, but now, he cared more about them than trying to keep her satisfied. Thank God, with the help of his parents and other good people in their lives, Penny and Tad were down to earth and not obsessed with designer shit.

Pamela flounced out of the office in the family home on the ranch. He moved to the window and watched as she stomped in her heels to her sedan and settled behind the wheel. He slowly shook his head as she gunned the car down the long driveway.

"Woman's a mess. Always has been."

The words came from a familiar deep voice approaching from the doorway. He nodded, then turned to see his father enter the room. "You're not wrong, Dad. But then, if I hadn't met her, I'd never have Penny and Tad."

His dad nodded slowly. "You're right. They're worth everything… even putting up with that moneygrubbing —" He sighed. "Sorry, Son. I never say anything about her when the kids are around."

"I know, Dad. It's fine. You and Mom were right all those years ago. I was young… thinking with my dick and not realizing that what she was after had nothing to do with me."

A deep chuckle came from Thurston Fugate as he looked at his son. "You aren't the first man to fall into that particular trap."

"No, I guess not." Stan glanced out the window again, the sedan of his ex-wife long gone. But his gaze moved over the ranch with the mountains in the background, and he couldn't help but smile. This was his heritage. Passed down for several generations. And would be passed down to Tad and Penny at some point. Without the prenup his parents insisted on when he'd married Pamela, he could have jeopardized the whole ranch.

"She'll ask again to take the kids when they have their next vacation from school," he said, then shook his head. "Actually, forget that. She wants a vacation now and wants me to pay for it. She probably promised her latest side piece that she'd take him. She'll want something else by the time the kids have a break."

His father clapped his hand on Stan's shoulder. "Your mom had Janelle fix a good lunch. Harvey is joining us, so let's eat. Good food and good company... it'll take your mind off what Pamela is up to."

With that, the two men walked out of the office and headed toward the dining room.

Pamela's eagle eye stared at the clothes she had packed and nodded with a sly grin.

"Hey, babe, you ready?"

She looked over her shoulder at the man walking into her bedroom. Roger. Tall, tanned, muscular. His blond hair was just a few weeks beyond needing a haircut, curling slightly over his ears and the back of his neck. His blue eyes never left hers, and his smile quirked upward on one side. He didn't stop until he was directly in front of her, and his arms snaked around her waist. He jerked her sharply to him until her breasts were crushed against his chest. His lips slammed down onto hers, and his tongue thrust deeply.

Roger worked for the condo association. She'd had no problem catching his eye the previous year as she learned to be at the pool on the days he handled the maintenance. The boob job was worth the money.

Of course, their relationship would never become serious, considering he had no money, but she liked the adoring attention he was willing to offer. As their kiss ended, she wondered if she could keep him around once she found her next money honey. Besides Roger, she'd latched onto an older gentleman, Henry, who lived in one of the larger condos. He was stuffy, but she could have the best of both worlds since he willingly spent freely on her.

Henry split his time between his home in Montana and a Jamaican resort, having invited her several times. The last time, she'd flown down with Roger after Henry's plans fell through, but he'd already arranged for her to have a vacation on the island. It had been glorious… a private resort house, Roger sharing her bed, and not having to pretend to be enthusiastic about sex with Henry.

Taking Roger had been sneaky, but she'd paid the housekeeper extra to make sure she didn't say anything to Henry.

Looking up at Roger, she said, "The kids will be home from school in a few minutes, and I'll spring the surprise trip on them."

"And our plans?"

Her smile faltered, but she straightened her spine. "Don't worry… once we get there, it will be fine." She wrapped her hand around his neck and pulled him closer until their lips met. Sucking on his bottom lip, she felt his cock thicken. Her free hand snaked downward, but the front door opening and her children's voices made her pull back. Seeing Roger's narrowed eyes, she placed a forefinger on his lips. "No pouting, baby," she cooed. "Let's get ready for a vacation."

Stepping back, she walked out of her bedroom and met Tad and Penny at the bottom of the stairs. She swung her hands wide to the side, her eyes bright with anticipation. "I have a surprise for you. We're taking a trip for the weekend. Who wants to go where it's warm and has sandy beaches?"

"Seriously?" Penny asked, eyes wide. "We're going to the beach?"

Tad tilted his head to the side. "What's up? You didn't tell us about this earlier."

"It's a surprise," she huffed. "Can't a mom surprise her children?"

"We haven't packed—" Penny began.

"I had the housekeeper do it for you. Your suitcases are being loaded into the car as we speak."

A dubious expression remained on Tad's face. "Does Dad—"

"Who do you think had the idea for this retreat?" Pamela quickly said, her smile still wide.

"What about our homework?" Penny continued.

"Bring all your books with you. You'll have plenty of

time on the airplane. Let's hurry, and we can start our weekend getaway to Florida!"

Penny and Tad shared a look, then shrugged. They grabbed their backpacks from where they had been tossed onto the floor near the front door and headed to their mom's car.

Pamela winked at Roger, then inclined her head toward her luggage. "Don't forget to carry that last one down. After all, we need to keep up the appearance of you coming as our assistant." With that, she made sure to offer him a close-up view of her ass showcased in her tight skirt as she sashayed out of the room.

2

Landon Sommers sprinted up the hillside, his lungs burning as he pushed his body harder and rounded the corner of the dirt path. His boots crunched over the gravel, sending a few small rocks skittering into a narrow ravine. He shifted his weight to keep from sliding down the slope. Suddenly, a blur of movement shot past him. "Shit, Sadie," he cursed under his breath.

Sadie Hargrove was a coworker who used her smaller size to round the curves and hug the side of the hill to keep her balance. "Catch up, Landon." She laughed. "Don't make me label you an old man."

Old man. He knew she was joking, but he had to admit that the words stung slightly more than he cared to admit. He sure as hell felt older than his thirty-seven years some days. He had been in the military, then special ops. Then he'd worked as an FBI agent for years, last stationed in California. He was currently employed with a private security company. Some might wonder about the numerous employment changes, but he'd gotten closer to perfection with each career move. Now, he was a Keeper for Lighthouse Security Investigations Montana. If a more perfect job existed for him, he couldn't imagine it.

He caught up to Sadie, and as they rounded the last curve together, he spied several other Keepers already at the rendezvous point. Within a moment, the others arrived. Their boss, Logan Bishop, handed out water bottles and protein bars as they plopped down on the hard-packed dirt and watched the sun glide over the mountains to the west. He twisted the cap off and took a long, refreshing gulp.

He sat between Sisco Aguilar and Jim Devlin, known as Devil. Both men had served with Logan, joining him in the successful endeavor of LSIMT. Their pilot, Cole Iverson, sat across from him, along with brothers Frazier and Dalton Dolby. Aldo Caspani, known as Casper, was the quiet one of the group, sitting slightly to the side. While light on conversation, he made up for it with stealth. Todd Blake and Cory Brighton sat nearby, their backs against the large boulders and their eyes trained on the sky. Timothy Clemons's gaze was upward, but he appeared to be staring at the light tower on the mountaintop.

The light tower was an old throwback to when airplanes needed to be warned of mountain ranges in the dark to be guided safely over the tops, much like the old lighthouse keepers near the water. Hence, the original name of Lighthouse Security Investigation. Mace Hanover, who started the original LSI in Maine, expanded to the West Coast, where Carson Dyer ran that branch. Now, the latest LSI operation was based in Montana.

After their rest, Logan stood, and everyone gave their attention to their leader as the LSIMT manager, Bert Tomlison, rode into view on a four-wheeled Gator. As they watched, he swept the canvas off the back of the vehicle, allowing them to see it was filled with T15 paintball guns, replicas of the US Army's M4 assault rifle.

"Hell yeah!" The shouts rang out as Landon and the others took to their feet, each hustling over to claim their weapons. There was playful jostling while the Keepers still maintained competitiveness. One thing Landon knew about the Keepers from all three localities was that the bosses liked to encourage cooperation as well as competitiveness, and training was essential for both.

The trip down the mountain involved dodging paintball hits, ducking behind boulders, racing around curves, and even a few skids down into small ravines. By the time Landon arrived back at headquarters for the group to be dismissed, he was ready to hit the showers before heading home for the evening. Calling out his goodbye, he climbed into his SUV and rumbled down the road.

He had purchased land not far from the compound and built a house. Since he was living alone, it would have been easy to keep the structure small, and at times, he wondered why he didn't. He'd watched when the men and women from the LSI West Coast had fallen in love, married, and started families. Logan was now married to Vivian, a woman he'd met on an assignment. Even Sisco was now married to a single mom and had adopted their little girl.

When Landon planned his house, he liked the idea of single-story living with extra bedrooms upstairs. The large living room and owner's bedroom faced the mountains, with windows allowing easy viewing. The eat-in kitchen, dining room, and office faced the east and offered panoramic scenes of the sunrise. A two-story garage led through a laundry room that led into the kitchen.

The two large bedrooms upstairs both had en suite bathrooms. Those were for guests, which, except for his parents, he'd never had. But one day, he hoped to have someone to share his house with. Snorting, he wondered if Montana wasn't the place for him to find a forever someone.

That night, he willed sleep to come, but his mind roamed to the other Keepers he'd worked with while in California. Each of them had found great women, perfect for them to fall in love with. *So when will it be my turn? And if not, why the fuck did I build this big house?*

The dawn streaked across the Montana sky as Landon stood by the sliding glass door, the early light casting a gentle glow over the kitchen. His gaze lingered on the stone patio, where the morning stillness was broken only by the faint chirping of birds. He lifted his mug, the rich aroma of coffee mingling with the crisp air, warming him from the inside out. His mind was still on the thoughts from last night. While he was comfortable with solitude, he wanted someone to share his life with.

His phone vibrated, and he grinned at seeing the caller ID. "Hey, Mom. How's the sunshine?" His parents had moved from their longtime home in Pennsylvania to South Carolina several years ago. They were desperate for warmer weather and no more snow to contend with.

"Good morning, sweetheart," she said. "I wanted to check in since I figured you would be heading to work soon."

"Everything okay?"

"Oh, everything's fine," she assured him, her tone laced with fond exasperation. "Though your father decided he could fix the garage door by himself. He nearly toppled off the stepladder. I told him it was a terrible idea, but you know how he is. 'I'm not paying someone to fix something I can do myself!'" She snorted, the sound both loving and resigned. "I did manage to convince him to get some help. Next thing I know, our seventy-five-year-old neighbor is out there in the garage, trying to help. I finally left them to it. If those two old coots want to strain their backs, who am I to stop them?"

Landon chuckled, the image of his father and their spirited elderly neighbor bumbling around the garage vividly playing in his mind. His parents' dynamic, filled with humor and unwavering partnership, was something he deeply admired. They had built a marriage on love, laughter, and teamwork, setting a shining example for him and his brother.

"I spoke to Robert the other day," his mother mentioned casually.

"How's he doing?"

"If you'd ever call him, then you'd know," she teased with a playful huff. Before Landon could respond, she continued, "He's fine. Says work is going well, although I never really understood what on earth he actually does."

Landon smirked. His brother was seven years younger and was a software engineer for a tech company in California. Landon and his brother enjoyed each other's company when they met at their parents' house for the holidays but only talked about once a month on the phone. "I'm glad he's good. I'll call him in a couple of weeks."

"I won't keep you, but I just missed hearing your voice," she said, her affection evident. "Now, I need to get your father's breakfast going before my book club luncheon later."

"Love to you and Dad, Mom. Talk soon." He ended the call, the lingering warmth of their conversation settling over him. Finishing the last sip of his coffee, he rinsed the cup and set it in the sink. With a deep breath, he grabbed his keys and stepped into the garage, the echo of his mother's voice still wrapping around him like a comforting embrace. It didn't take long to drive to the LSIMT compound. Walking into the main building, he passed through the security Logan had built in and headed down the hall.

He smiled at the woman in a wheelchair rolling past him with her tablet and several files on her lap. "Good morning, Mary," he greeted.

She smiled and nodded. "Logan is about ready to start once everyone gets here."

"Think he's got something for me?"

She winked. "Go on in and find out. Then come see me."

With that bit of encouragement, he grinned and headed inside. Greeting the others, he sat at the conference table with the other Keepers at the compound.

Logan looked up and said, "Okay, let's get started. Cory, you and Dalton have a security design to work on. You'll fly to Michigan, leaving the day after tomorrow. Casper… you've got a security detail to prepare for. It'll take you to Canada, so Mary will have all your travel arrangements ready for next week. And Landon, you'll make a trip to the Caribbean."

The room buzzed with energy, the voices erupting in fake protestations, all clamoring for the assignment. Logan, sitting at the head of the table, let out a deep laugh and shook his head. "Sorry… this one is for Landon. It's a slow burn but needs someone with a steady hand. Someone not as scary to kids as the rest of you."

"Hey!" Sisco protested, lowering his brow. "My little Evie thinks I'm a teddy bear!"

Landon grinned at his friend whose last big assignment brought the beautiful Lenore and her daughter, Evie, into Sisco's life. Turning his attention back toward his boss, Logan's expression gave nothing away as he continued to review open and upcoming cases, then dismissed the meeting. Chairs scraped against the floor as the team dispersed, each retreating to various computer stations and desks around the room. Landon walked over to sit beside Logan, his curiosity piqued. He dropped into the seat beside his boss, feeling the weight of something unspoken hanging in the air.

"This just came in," Logan said, his tone low. "Thurston Fugate reached out. He and his wife, Margaret, own one of the largest ranches in Montana. There's a situation involving their son, Stan, his ex-wife, Pamela, and their twin grandchildren."

Landon looked down at his tablet as the information and photographs filled the screen before lifting his gaze back to his boss.

"Thurston came to us because he wants to keep the situation out of the press. The risk of public exposure is high. A friend of his from the FBI referred him to us, and he requested you specifically when he heard about your background—FBI and special ops."

Landon gave a curt nod, focusing on the unfolding story.

"Stan and Pamela have joint custody of the twins, but Stan has physical custody. The kids live with him on the ranch. They spend two weekends a month with their mom, who has a condo outside of Helena. According to the custody agreement, they also spend spring break and a month in the summer with her. She was unhappy with this arrangement since she gets almost no child support money, but her alimony is way over the top, so when her attorney petitioned the court the last time for more money, the judge shut her down. According to Thurston, her alimony helps support her latest boy toy and lifestyle, but he says it's worth it to keep her interaction with them at a minimum."

Landon's lips tightened. "She sounds charming."

Logan snorted. "Yeah, a real piece of work. The latest issue? Pamela wanted to whisk the kids off on a Caribbean vacation during school. Stan refused. He didn't see why he should foot the bill for what he believed was her excuse for a free holiday with her latest fling. But she had them for the weekend and decided to do it anyway. She packed them up, got on a plane, and the next call Stan received was her demanding a new alimony agreement. She dropped the bomb that they were already in the Caribbean."

Landon blew out a breath, his jaw tightening. "And she's using the kids as leverage?"

"To get the kids back safely, Stan has had his attorney draw up new agreements, but she refuses to put the kids on a plane until she knows it's ironclad. She isn't coming back, afraid that she'll be arrested. To make matters worse, a storm is brewing in the Atlantic, and it's approaching Jamaica, where they discovered she and the kids are staying. The Fugates are fast-tracking the agreement but want the kids escorted back home safely. A Montana social worker recommended by the judge will accompany you to ensure the kids are safe and their rights are protected during this process."

"So the social worker and I fly to Jamaica, get her signature on the new documents, pick up the twins, and then accompany them back to Montana?"

"And transport a $500,000 for her. That's the plan to pay her off. No money exchanged with her until you are there to take the children back home."

"What if she refuses to hand the kids over?"

Logan's expression hardened, his voice like steel. "Then you do whatever it takes to bring them home. She'll sign away her visitation agreement for the payout. That's part of the deal."

Landon's eyes narrowed further, his mind already working through the logistics. "Do I meet the Fugates first?"

"Yes. They want to go over everything with you personally. You'll fly out on their private jet. The social worker will be there, too. The twins have been kept in the dark. They think their dad approved the trip."

Landon exhaled, the weight of responsibility settling over him. "Understood. I'll get it done."

Logan gave him a firm nod. "I knew you would."

"I'll head home and be ready to leave in less than an hour."

"Mary will have your info. Bert will have the equipment and weapons bags for you. You can drive to the ranch to meet with the Fugates. We'll be here for any backup or any problems you encounter."

"Sounds straightforward," Landon said.

Logan snorted. "Famous last words. You know as well as I do… any mission can get fucked when you least expect it."

Landon nodded but prayed that the mother would play nice and just do what she'd agreed for the kids' sake. In-and-out mission. Just the way he liked.

3

A few hours later, Landon was driving down the winding, tree-lined driveway that stretched through the sprawling Fugate Ranch. The land rolled out before him in waves of golden pastures and sturdy wooden fences, the scent of fresh hay and earth wafting through the open window. The main house loomed ahead, a stately yet rustic structure that spoke of both wealth and a deep connection to the land.

A ranch hand escorted him through a side door, leading him into a large, comfortable family room that appeared well-lived in. The scent of wood smoke lingered faintly, mixing with the aroma of leather. Photographs adorned the mantel above the stone fireplace—snapshots of holidays, milestones, and candid moments that spoke of love and togetherness. His eyes caught a familiar image of the twins, Tad and Penny, their youthful faces beaming with innocence.

The murmur of voices preceded the entrance of a man who exuded authority and approachability in equal measure. Barrel-chested, with steel-gray hair and piercing blue eyes, he walked with the confidence of someone who had spent a lifetime commanding respect without demanding it. His rolled-up sleeves revealed strong, weathered forearms, and his jeans, though worn, were spotless. This was Thurston Fugate, a man who worked alongside his ranch hands, never above them.

At his side was a woman who carried herself with quiet grace. Her blond hair, streaked with silver, was pulled into a no-fuss ponytail. She wasn't attempting to cover the strands of gray that attractively streaked through the blond. She was in jeans, a long-sleeved blouse, and flat shoes. Bare makeup allowed her features to show the tension in her face. Despite this, she radiated a natural beauty, her features softened by the light filtering through the windows. Thurston's hand rested gently on her back as they moved forward in a silent gesture of support.

Introductions were quick, the formalities dispensed with ease. "We don't stand on ceremony here," Thurston said with a small smile. "Call me Thurston, and this is Margaret."

Landon nodded, his gaze steady. "Pleasure to meet you both. And Landon is also fine."

Next came a man who strode into the room in a similar manner as the elder Fugate. He resembled his dad, but Stan had his mother's blond hair. He also wore jeans paired with a navy polo with the Fugate Ranch logo over the left side of the chest. "Sorry to be late. I was just on the phone with Roy, our attorney. I wanted to make sure nothing could go wrong."

After Stan and Landon shook hands, Thurston said, "We'll wait just a few minutes before we begin. The social worker is on her way."

Landon nodded and then turned back to the photographs. He felt a presence beside him, and he wasn't surprised when Margaret Fugate said, "I know I'm biased, but my grandchildren are beautiful."

"I'd have to agree, ma'am." Tad was on the cusp of manhood, with blond hair and blue eyes. His sister's hair was also blond but darker. He'd seen a photograph of Pamela, and while she was beautiful, he had no idea what she would have looked like at Penny's age.

"They're not only physically beautiful, Landon, but they have managed to come out of this mess of a divorce as well-adjusted and sweet kids. Their mother is a snake in the grass, but considering she's had little to do with them since they were born, her influence has thankfully been limited." She sighed and shook her head. "I don't want them upset. I don't want them afraid."

He turned to face her fully. "Margaret, it's my job to ensure their safe return. I'll do everything possible to take care of them during the exchange."

The tension in her face eased slightly. Reaching out, she placed her hand on his arm. "Thank you—"

The housekeeper entered, keeping her voice low. "Ms. Lennox is here."

All eyes turned as a woman stepped into the room. Dressed in khaki pants and a deep green blouse, she exuded quiet confidence. Her brown hair, streaked with hints of red and gold, was pulled back with a simple headband, the soft waves falling past her shoulders. He couldn't help but stare. He had expected the social worker to be older, perhaps with seniority status, for the judge to have personally recommended her.

Ms. Lennox smiled as she moved first to Margaret, who had slid to her husband's side. The smile was professionally reserved, and Landon wondered if it was due to the situation. A flash of desire to see her smile brighten enough to reach her eyes filled him. He jerked slightly at the unbidden idea.

"I'm Noel Lennox." She shook hands with Thurston and Margaret, then moved to Stan. "You must be Tad and Penny's father. It's nice to meet you, but I'm sorry for the circumstances."

After the Fugates welcomed her, she turned her gaze to Landon. She hesitated, her eyes widening slightly as though surprised. He liked that she was caught off guard and no longer reserved. He had no idea of her age, but upon closer observation, she was older than he'd initially thought if the little crinkles around her eyes were any indication.

As he walked straight to her and offered his hand, her cool professionalism slid back into place. The word brown for her eyes was too limiting. Like her hair, her eyes were multicolored... brown and hazel with gold flecks.

Blinking away the ridiculous musing, he managed to find his voice. "I'm Landon Sommers with Lighthouse Security Investigations."

"Of course." She nodded. "I was told that someone

from a security company would be traveling with us. It's nice to meet you, Mr. Sommers."

"Please, call me Landon."

"And I'm Noel." Her lips quirked upward ever so slightly. "My mother's favorite holiday will explain my name."

He inclined his head and then realized he was still holding her hand. He let it go just as Thurston said, "Let's sit and get down to business. Stan wants to make sure you have all the information you need to deal with Pamela when you get down there."

Thurston waited until his wife was seated on one of the sofas and Noel on the other before he took his place sitting next to Margaret. Stan perched on the end of the armchair, and Landon moved to sit beside Noel. Thurston then nodded toward Stan.

Stan leaned forward, the tension from his body palpable. "Pamela and I met at an event in Billings about fifteen years ago. She was beautiful, seemed sweet, and everything I thought I wanted in a girlfriend. She never asked how much the family was worth nor indicated she was a gold digger."

Thurston huffed, but Margaret shushed him. "None of us thought that at the beginning."

Stan sighed, then continued, "Looking back, I realize there were subtle signs, such as hinting for specific pieces of jewelry or gifts, especially when we had a disagreement. I hadn't proposed, and to be perfectly honest, I wasn't ready to be engaged. And then she became pregnant."

"In case you're wondering," Thurston interrupted,

"we told Stan that he needed to insist on a paternity test. My wife and I were unconvinced that her nature wasn't mercenary by that time."

"She agreed, and yes, I was the father," Stan admitted. "I was thrilled with impending fatherhood. All Pamela seemed to care about was our wedding, marred by the prenup agreement we insisted on. She wanted to hold the fact that she was pregnant over my head to keep from signing. Our attorney explained that without it and no marriage, she would be entitled to child support but no alimony. She signed, but not without a lot of headaches on all our parts. She wanted to get married quickly after finding out she was having twins since her figure would change faster. She wanted big and lavish, and since her parents were deceased, we handled the costs. After the wedding, Pamela quickly became more frustrated when her body changed so much due to having twins. I assumed her maternal instinct would kick in when Tad and Penny were born, but it never did. She wanted to hire a nanny immediately."

Margaret's voice hardened with resolve. "There was no way I'd let a stranger raise my grandchildren. So we brought in someone we trusted, a woman we'd known for years. Plus, we were always around to help."

Noel leaned forward, her expression thoughtful. "There wasn't any mention of neglect or abuse in the documents. Did Pamela ever mistreat the children?"

Stan exhaled heavily, rubbing a hand over his face. "No, not in the traditional sense. Pamela wasn't neglectful, exactly. She loved the kids... in her way. As they grew older, she enjoyed the social aspects of motherhood—taking Penny shopping and attending Tad's soccer games. But it felt more about appearances than genuine support."

Thurston's face darkened, his voice a low growl. "She cared more about being seen than actually being there for them."

Noel nodded, absorbing the weight of his words. "And the divorce? How did that impact Tad and Penny?"

Stan's shoulders sagged slightly, the weight of past decisions pressing down on him. "By the time they were nine, the kids had already turned to my mom for the nurturing they craved. They knew Pamela wasn't that kind of mother. Around that time, I found out she was having an affair—not her first. I confronted her, and when it was clear she wasn't going to change, I filed for divorce. Despite the custody arrangement, I had enough evidence to ensure physical custody of the kids."

Landon, who had been silently observing, raised an eyebrow. "And the prenup?"

Stan's lips thinned into a grim line. "Because of her infidelity, her alimony was minimal. In court, I laid everything bare. Even with joint custody, I got physical custody. She sees them every other weekend and during specific holidays and summer weeks. But every visit comes with her asking for more money. She claims she spends it on the kids—restaurants, shopping—but the kids tell me otherwise. I've stopped giving her anything extra."

Margaret's voice cracked, raw emotion bleeding through her composed exterior. "Her financial lifeline is drying up, and now she's stooped to holding her own children hostage. I knew she was greedy, but this... this is beyond anything I could have imagined."

Thurston pulled her into a comforting embrace, his strength steadying her trembling form. Landon watched the scene unfold. He had seen humanity at its worst, witnessed the depths people could sink to. A mother using her children as pawns wasn't the most heinous act he'd encountered, but for the Fugates, it was a personal hell.

"When did you realize the kids were missing?" Noel asked.

Landon turned his attention to the soft-spoken social worker. He appreciated how Noel gently shifted the Fugates' focus from their emotional to practical needs.

"They were spending the weekend with her, but she had come by to ask me to let them skip a week of school, and she'd take them to the Caribbean... all on my dime, of course. I said hell no! The kids have scheduled holidays, and they need to be in school. As you can imagine, she was pissed."

"So they went to her place after school on Friday?" Noel prodded, and Landon wondered how much she knew ahead of this meeting.

"She called late last night to tell me they were in Jamaica, and she was keeping the kids unless I agreed to up the alimony."

Thurston's jaw clenched, his fists tightening on the arms of his chair. "We won't bog you down with all the back-and-forth—threats, pleas, lawyers getting involved. She thought she was untouchable down there, but she started negotiating once she realized we had the means to have her arrested and extradited. She handed us a list of demands. When we talked with Tad and Penny, they let it slip that a young man accompanied them to the Caribbean. Penny said it was her boyfriend, but Tad thought she was dating an older man. Anyway, just letting you know there is someone else down there with them who is probably hoping to cash in on her gains."

Landon nodded, absorbing the information. "I've reviewed her demands. You've come to an agreement?"

Stan's mouth twisted in disgust. "Yes. She's agreed to sign away her parental visitations." He paused, rubbing his temples. "Christ... who the hell does that?"

A heavy silence filled the room, the weight of Stan's words pressing down on everyone. Noel's gaze met his, a silent understanding passing between them. Her lips tightened, but she offered a small, encouraging smile before turning back to the Fugates.

Landon took a breath, knowing they needed to move forward. "Is she expecting us?"

Stan nodded, leaning forward. "Yes. She knows you'll arrive with the new alimony agreements and money. The kids are supposed to be ready to leave with you."

"We want this handled quietly," Thurston added, his eyes sharp. "No press. It would only make things worse for everyone, especially Tad and Penny. They know their mom took them on an unsanctioned trip, but when they come home tomorrow, we'll manage the story. They don't need to know the full extent of their mom's betrayal."

Noel nodded in agreement. "That's the right approach. Keeping their well-being at the forefront is crucial."

Thurston leaned forward. "My longtime friend, Judge Samuel Waterford, recommended you both. He said Lighthouse Security would be a good choice to protect my grandchildren and that a social worker would ensure their mental and emotional well-being during this time."

Noel glanced at Landon again, a small smile playing on her lips, a mix of reassurance and camaraderie. "We'll do everything we can."

Landon's eyes lingered on her for a moment before he turned back to the Fugates. "Absolutely," he said firmly. "We'll bring them home safely."

4

With little left to say beyond goodbyes, Noel found herself swiftly escorted outside. The late afternoon sun cast a golden glow over the expansive Fugate Ranch, the light reflecting off the sleek black SUV waiting for her. The ranch's logo was subtly emblazoned on the door. Landon walked beside her, his stride confident yet unassuming. Without a word, he reached for the door handle, holding it open with a practiced ease. His hand extended, offering her a steadying grip as she climbed into the back seat.

The touch was brief but firm, his fingers warm against hers, sending a tiny spark through her skin. As she settled into her seat, her gaze drifted to the back of the vehicle, where her overnight bag sat alongside another—presumably Landon's.

As they pulled away from the sprawling ranch, she cast a sideways glance, drawn once more to the man beside her. Landon's commanding presence had struck her the moment she'd entered the Fugate's family room.

Even standing near the imposing, ruggedly handsome figures of Thurston and Stan Fugate, her awareness had gone straight to Landon—tall and dark-haired, with a quiet intensity that seemed to radiate from him. His looks were almost movie-star striking yet rugged, his thick hair trimmed neatly on the sides and slightly tousled on top. She imagined he was the kind of man who rarely bothered with grooming products and likely did just a quick run of his fingers through his hair before moving on, practical and effortless.

His black T-shirt stretched across broad shoulders, and the leather jacket added a roughness that hinted he was ready to handle anything that came his way. Landon carried a sense of professional control and capability but also a ruggedness that made her heart beat just a little faster. Their introduction had been brief, but when their hands met, she felt a rare connection. His handshake was firm, warm, and lingering, a touch that conveyed strength without overpowering, as though he was holding back something deeper, a gentleness underneath the hard edges. She didn't mind that he hadn't let go right away.

Landon closed his door, and the driver pulled away from the ranch house as soon as he was buckled. Giving her head a slight shake, she wondered why her thoughts had strayed to the man sitting beside her. It wasn't like her to be distracted during a case, and she forced her mind back to the task.

Landon was on his phone, but he looked toward her and apologized. "I'm sorry. I'm not trying to be rude, but I wanted to let my office know that we were on our way."

Noel waved a hand, brushing off his concern. "No worries," she replied softly. "I understand. We both have jobs to do." She turned her gaze to the window, watching as the sprawling pastures and wooden fences of the ranch faded into the distance. Her mind drifted back to the mission ahead—the delicate handoff of Tad and Penny. The weight of responsibility pressed down on her, the importance of keeping the children safe and easing their transition back home. They would have questions and want to know what was happening.

"Is this common for you?"

Her head swung around, finding Landon's intense gaze on her. She shook her head. "No, not like this." Seeing his head tilt slightly, she continued. "I have often participated in the handoff of children who have been caught between two warring parents going through a divorce and custody issues. There are cases where the child or children are taken by a parent and hidden away from the other parent, but those are usually handled by law enforcement, and then I step in for evaluation."

She paused, glancing out the window at the passing landscape, before adding, "I've never been part of a case where a parent took children out of the country. It's… different."

"Why do you think you were asked to do this?"

Her lips quirked upward. "I could ask you the same.

You represent a private investigation and security company, not law enforcement."

Suddenly, his lips twitched. "Touché." Nodding, he said, "The Fugates wanted this handled with discretion."

She nodded, then sighed. "These situations suck."

His eyes widened slightly.

She chuckled, then lifted a brow. "I'm sorry... that wasn't professional. But does the word *suck* offend you? If so, you'll probably be shocked when I use words like *shit, damn, asshole, bitch,* and *fuck.*"

Landon barked out laughter. "Okay, that wasn't what I expected."

"Sorry, again." She laughed as her shoulders shook, glad for the distraction of seeing his face when it wasn't set in stone. The smile was welcome, although it transformed his face from handsome to gorgeous. "I tend to let my mouth run rampant at times. My dad had been in the Navy and always said he owed his colorful language to his time in the military. It drove my mom nuts." She leaned closer and whispered, "But I promise, I'll be professional on the job, even if this is completely out of my realm of usual."

"I'm sure." He nodded.

She couldn't tell if he believed her or not. "Really, my life is very boring."

This brought a lifted brow, and he shook his head. "I'm not sure I believe that at all."

She smiled as his attention shifted to his phone, and his fingers began tapping. It was strange to miss having his attention suddenly. His deep-set gray-blue eyes were mesmerizing when aimed at her—almost like the sky before a storm. She was hardly a blushing schoolgirl, but it had been a while since her insides flip-flopped at the sight of a handsome man. *It's a good thing this trip will be over quickly... I might not be able to keep my composure while being around him for longer than a few days.* Dismissing her wandering thoughts, she looked down at her phone and sent a message to her mom.

Getting ready to fly to Jamaica. Let you know when I land. Met the accompanying security. Nice man.

Her fingers hesitated. *Nice man.* She snorted and then quickly coughed to cover the first sound. She refused to see if Landon's attention had shifted back to her with the ridiculous sounds she emitted. Continuing to text, she let her fingers fly over the keyboard once again.

Should be home the day after tomorrow. Love to all of you.

"Tell me what you know about the family."

Landon's softly spoken request surprised her. After hitting send on her text, she swung her head around to look at him. "I don't know the family other than what I've been told since this morning. My boss got a call from Judge Waterford last night, and I was called later. Honestly, I had already gone to bed. He said I was on this case, and here I am." She shrugged and added, "I have been in front of Judge Waterford with custody dispute cases to ensure the child's best interest was presented, so I suppose he thought of me when the Fugates contacted him."

"You'd never met the Fugates before?"

"No, but I have heard of them—from occasional pieces in the press. Wealthy Montana rancher donates to various causes and backs politicians... that kind of thing. I've never heard anything bad about them." She cocked her head to the side. "What about you?"

"No. Just when my boss also assigned the case to me earlier today. With my background at the FBI, I seemed to be the right person for the job."

Her eyes widened in surprise. "You used to work for the FBI?" When he nodded, she added, "I can see that."

He remained quiet but lifted his brows in silent question.

"You have this... serious air about you," she admitted, her voice soft but laced with curiosity.

His brows arched even higher, a hint of amusement flickering in his eyes. "You think FBI agents are serious all the time?"

She scrunched her nose, suddenly worried she might have overstepped. "It's just... in my experience, they usually are. I've met a few during cases—mostly when they interviewed me or the children I was working with. They never seemed like the kind of people who smiled easily."

Landon held her gaze, his expression unreadable, but after a moment, he gave a slow nod, acknowledging her observation without offering much in return. The silence between them stretched, but it wasn't uncomfortable. Instead, it seemed to pulse with unspoken thoughts and questions.

Her natural curiosity sparked again, and she found herself wanting to ask why he left the Bureau. But she held back, recognizing that the question would be too personal for someone she'd just met. Still, the mystery surrounding him only deepened, making her wonder about the stories hidden behind those serious, watchful eyes.

Landon's steady gaze remained fixed on her, a quiet intensity that made Noel feel both exposed and compelled to keep talking. The silence stretched between them, pressing down until she found herself filling it, almost against her will. "So, um… I remember reading about Stan and Pamela Fugate in the gossip columns once. There was this big scene outside a charity event." His brow lifted slightly, prompting her to continue.

Noel rushed to explain, her words tumbling out in a hurried stream. "Apparently, Pamela had too much to drink, and when Stan tried to escort her outside, she caused a scene. She was screaming, yelling… it became such a spectacle that some nearby journalists snapped photos and wrote a pretty damning article."

Landon nodded, offering no verbal response, his silence a steady undercurrent that seemed to draw more out of her.

Noel wondered if that was requisite for agents… or former agents—to stay silent until the other person blabbed all their secrets. Blowing out her breath, she added, "After that, the next thing in the papers was that they were getting a divorce. I obviously don't run in the same circles, so that's all I know."

She was saved from her continued gossip column recitation when interrupted as the vehicle turned down a road leading to the private section of the airport. The SUV bypassed the bustling main terminal, heading toward a secluded area where sleek jets stood ready for departure.

Once parked, Landon alighted, and by the time the driver opened her door, Landon was there with an outstretched hand to assist her down. Noel placed her hand in his, and her breath caught in her throat at the feel of his long fingers wrapping around hers. The same surge of warmth she felt earlier coursed through her again, confirming it wasn't a one-off reaction.

The moment her feet touched the ground, the connection broke, but not before she noticed the slight furrow in Landon's brow, as if he, too, was puzzled by the lingering sensation. He turned away, heading toward the back of the SUV. Noel followed, her heart still fluttering slightly. The driver opened the trunk, and Landon grabbed their bags before she could even offer to help.

"I've got it," he said, his tone leaving no room for argument. He nodded toward the small, sleek jet parked nearby. "This is their jet."

"Oh," Noel muttered, the word slipping out before she could stop it. As they walked toward the jet, a giggle bubbled up unexpectedly.

Landon glanced back over his shoulder with a quizzical look in his eyes.

She shook her head quickly. "Sorry. It's just... I've never flown on anything other than a commercial airline. You know, crammed in with a hundred strangers, usually stuck between two people who invade my personal space." She gestured toward the jet. "This? This is way out of my league."

His gaze held hers for a moment longer, and she felt the heat of his attention. Even as they walked, she fought the urge to squirm under his scrutiny.

Landon stepped aside at the base of the jet's steps, gesturing for her to go first. As she climbed, she couldn't help but think of the romance novels she read at night. The thought made her wince, her cheeks heating.

She shook her head, trying to banish the thought. Romance novels were a secret love of hers, a guilty pleasure that offered a refuge from the harsh realities of her job. People often dismissed them as fluff, but she knew better. They provided hope, a reminder of the beauty in connection and the possibility of a happily ever after, even in a world often filled with pain and hardship. And in her business, sometimes seeing the worst of what can be done to a child, her evening escape into romance helped to balance the scales of emotions in her weary mind.

As she entered the plane and looked around the interior, she tried to cover her wide-eyed expression of awe. *Toto... I'm sure as hell not in Kansas anymore.* She chalked up her wavering attention to finding herself in an unusual and exceptionally different atmosphere than she was accustomed to.

Her job was either spent in a cramped office, the courtroom, or various homes that ranged from the wealthy to the poor. Flying on a private jet was not something she'd ever expected to do, much less on the job. She had seen photographs of ultra-rich jets before. This one was probably modest compared to many, but the plush leather seats facing each other with small tables between were a luxury she had never experienced.

"Hello, I'm Jana. You must be Ms. Lennox and Mr. Sommers." An attractive woman in a flight attendant uniform walked from the front with a pleasant smile. She looked at Landon and indicated where he could stow their bags. He stepped around the two women, placed their bags into a bin, then turned toward Noel.

Uncertain where to sit, she hesitated, her gaze moving between Jana and Landon. "Do I sit somewhere special?" she asked.

Jana smiled. "No. Sit anywhere you like. I'll bring out refreshments when we're in the air."

Nodding her thanks, Noel moved to the closest chair, ensuring it was near a window, and sat down. The plush leather seat was contoured to fit the human body, and she felt cradled. Even the seat belt buckle was shiny.

She glanced up, curious to see where Landon would sit, when another man walked through the doorway, his gaze circling the interior.

"Mr. Westerly," Jana greeted. She showed him where to stow his bags and asked what he'd like to drink once they were in the air.

His gaze didn't return to Noel but held Landon's with a steely expression. The two men shook hands as they introduced themselves.

"Mike Westerly. I'm the chief ranch manager for Mr. Fugate. Been with the family for a long time. Stan and his parents wanted the kids to see a familiar face. They figured that'd make them more at ease."

"Hello," she greeted. "I'm Noel Lennox."

He inclined his head. His broad shoulders and sturdy frame bore the mark of a life spent tending to the land. Deep lines etched his sun-kissed skin, offering evidence of countless days spent under the relentless sun and in the biting cold of early mornings. His thick and neatly combed silver hair framed a face that exuded quiet authority and wisdom. He dressed in jeans and a long-sleeved shirt with the Fugate logo stitched over his heart.

Landon lifted a brow. "We didn't meet you at the ranch—"

"No, no... sorry about that. I was trying to make sure everything would run smoothly while I was away. Just made it back to say goodbye to Thurston and the family before I came here. It's real nice to meet you two. It'll be good to get those kids away from that bitch."

Before Mike could claim a place to sit, Landon deftly moved to the seat closest to Noel. He sat facing her, with only the small table between them. Mike turned, moved to the opposite side of the plane, and settled into a seat.

Stunned at the added person to their group and surprised that the Fugates didn't mention someone else coming with them, she noticed Landon's assessing gaze on her. She made bug eyes at him as her lips curved. His gaze dropped to her mouth, and his lips twitched. The situation was surreal, and she wondered what other surprises were ahead.

She mouthed, "Anyone else coming with us?" Landon shook his head and pulled out his phone. Noel wondered if he was checking in with his employer. She sighed as his attention stayed on his phone and pulled out her e-reader. It appeared her flight to Jamaica would be spent reading since, so far, Landon had seemed to be a man of few words. When she glanced to the side, Mike had earbuds in, and his fingers flew over his phone keyboard.

As the jet taxied down the runway, the hum of the engines grew louder, and Noel instinctively gripped the armrests. Her knuckles whitened as the plane surged forward, lifting off the ground with a rush of power. The sensation of being propelled skyward made her stomach lurch, leaving her feeling momentarily untethered. It wasn't until she noticed Landon's steady gaze on her hands that she realized how tightly she was holding on.

"Sorry," she muttered, forcing her fingers to relax, though her heart still raced. "I don't fly often. It always feels like my stomach stays on the ground while the rest of me hurtles down the runway."

Landon gave a small nod, his expression softening, a hint of understanding in his eyes. "No problem. Would ginger ale help?" Before she could respond, he turned his head and called over his shoulder. "Jana? Can you bring some ginger ale for Ms. Lennox?"

"Certainly," the efficient attendant agreed, disappearing behind the deep blue and gold curtain that separated her area from the passengers' sight. Moments later, she returned, gliding gracefully through the slight sway of the aircraft. In her hands, she carried a crystal tumbler filled with amber liquid.

Noel accepted the drink with a murmured thanks, noting the elegance of the glass as well as the thoughtful gesture. Jana also served drinks to Mike and brought water for Landon, each served in beautiful cut-glass tumblers that added a touch of sophistication to the journey.

Sipping the cool ginger ale, Noel felt the soothing bubbles ease her unsettled stomach. After a few moments, she glanced at Landon and gave him a grateful nod. "Thanks. This is perfect."

The corners of his lips curved ever so slightly in a subtle gesture but enough to transform his typically stoic demeanor. That almost smile sent a flutter through her chest, a small triumph that felt oddly significant. She couldn't help but wonder if she might see that expression more often, maybe even a full smile, once the mission was complete and they had the children safely on their way home.

A sudden realization struck her. Why exactly was someone like Landon necessary for this trip? The Fugates had kept things vague when briefing her, and she hadn't had much time to process the full scope of her role before being whisked away.

Leaning slightly forward, she met Landon's steady gaze, her curiosity piqued. "Tell me… why do the Fugates need a security specialist on this trip? What do you think will happen?"

5

Despite his earlier efforts to keep his attention elsewhere, Landon's gaze lingered on the woman sitting across from him. At the Fugates' house, he'd tried to focus solely on the mission, but Noel Lennox's presence was impossible to ignore. He had been caught off guard, expecting an older, more seasoned social worker for a judge to have recommended. Instead, she was young, strikingly attractive, and carried herself with a quiet confidence that hinted at depth beyond her years. Upon reflection, he realized his original assumption that she would be older was ridiculous.

Her gaze was filled with intelligent curiosity, not idle curiosity. Landon had seen that same look during his years with the Bureau, usually from the people who offered the most valuable insights. Noel was clearly more than capable, and her questions were precise, cutting to the heart of the matter.

And her question was well-founded. The demands from Pamela were being met. He was carrying the signed paperwork. A copy had already been sent to her to review. The need for the social worker made sense, considering Pamela wouldn't allow anyone from the family to come, and they wanted to ensure the children's emotional well-being was being met.

But Landon knew better than to underestimate human unpredictability, especially when emotions were running high. Despite getting what she wanted, Pamela had already shown herself to be manipulative and mercenary, willing to use her children as bargaining chips. That kind of unpredictability warranted extra caution.

Glancing to the other side of the plane, he spied Mike with his eyes closed and earbuds in place. The man may be listening to their conversation. Landon had sent the name and a quickly snapped photograph of Mike to the LSIMT compound. He hoped to hear back soon to confirm Mike's story. While the reason was plausible, Landon didn't trust the man and feared there might be another reason behind his accompanying them on the trip.

Looking across the small table at Noel, he said, "I'm here because the Fugates don't trust Pamela and are more comfortable ensuring security on the trip."

Her lips pressed together into a thin line. "You anticipate problems?"

"I hope not," he replied, his tone calm but firm. "But it's always better to be safe than sorry." He offered a tight-lipped smile, hoping to ease her concerns, but her expression remained serious.

Noel nodded slowly but didn't smile. Her expression

vividly showed her thoughts. She was obviously pondering his words, reading between the lines. She opened her mouth as though to speak, but her gaze darted to the side. Her mouth snapped shut, and her brow lowered as she kept her attention on Mike for almost a minute. Even from the side, Landon could tell where her thoughts had gone. She was suspicious of their cabinmate.

Looking back at Landon, she mouthed, "What about him?"

He simply shrugged, giving no verbal response. She must have understood his desire not to speak in front of the unknown man. The edge of her bottom lip caught between her teeth as she nodded slowly. He had to admit that it was hard not to stare at the reddened flesh but keep his gaze squarely on her eyes.

Noel leaned back, seemingly deciding to let the topic drop for now. "I won't keep you from your work," she said softly. "I have some reading to catch up on, and considering my boss called in the middle of the night, I could use a bit of rest."

She turned slightly in her chair, facing the window, and pulled out her e-reader. Landon should have felt relieved at the prospect of a quiet flight, free from further questions. But as Noel's voice faded and she turned her attention to her book, a surprising realization settled over him—he already missed the sound of her voice.

She read for a few moments, then rested the device in her lap, leaned her head back, and closed her eyes. The cabin fell into a gentle hush, the hum of the plane the only sound filling the space. And for the first time in a long while, Landon, a man who thrived in solitude, felt an unfamiliar pang of loneliness.

It didn't take long before he received the awaited message from LSIMT. Looking down at his phone, he read the message twice. Mike Westerly. Fifty-four years old. Employed with the Fugate Ranch for almost forty years. Started as a stable boy when he was a teenager. Moved up to ranch hand. Then he continued over the years to progress until he became Thurston's right-hand man. From all accounts, loyal. Nothing suggested he was there for any other reason than to be precisely what he said... a familiar face to the kids to make their journey back home less stressful.

Taking advantage of Noel and Mike sleeping while Jana was behind her curtain, he used his handheld device for detecting bugs. Slowly rotating the device around the interior, he looked down at the indicator, glad to discover no listening devices were planted inside the cabin of the plane. That included anything on Mike's person.

It struck him odd that Mike wasn't introduced to them inside the ranch home. *Was there a reason Thurston wanted Mike's presence on the trip to be unknown until they were almost in the air?* He tapped out more questions to the Keepers back at the compound. While he waited for the answers, Landon's gaze drifted to the woman sitting across from him, unable to pinpoint exactly what it was about her that commanded his attention. She wasn't just pretty; she had a kind of understated allure, the type of beauty that sneaks up on you, familiar and comforting, like the girl next door. Yet there was more beneath the surface. She smiled easily, a warmth that seemed genuine, but he'd also seen her maintain a serious focus, the kind that suggested a mind that didn't miss much.

With her eyes closed and her face softened in sleep, Landon allowed himself to observe her without interruption. Her features were delicate yet strong—an intriguing contrast. The faint lines at the corners of her eyes, barely noticeable, spoke of experience, not just years.

Subtly, he tapped into his phone, waiting for the information he'd requested. It didn't take long for Sadie to respond.

Noel Lennox. Thirty-two years old. Single, never married. Born and raised in Billings, Montana. Parents still living, one brother. Graduated from the University of Montana with a degree in psychology, and then earned a master's degree in social work. Employed by the Helena Department of Social Services for nine years. Lives alone in a small apartment. Pays her bills on time, no criminal record—not even a parking ticket.

A faint smile tugged at Landon's lips. A spotless record wasn't unexpected for someone in her profession, but not even a parking ticket? That hinted at someone who played by the rules. He couldn't help but wonder how she'd react to the kind of rules his line of work often required him to bend—or break.

Strangely, as he stared at her gentle features as she slept, he wished she had been the one to reveal her background to him. Digging into her life felt invasive even though it was standard procedure. Knowing all the players was essential for any mission, but something about prying into her life left a sour taste.

Shifting his focus, he skimmed over the details Sadie had sent about Mike. A few run-ins with the law—bar fights, public intoxication—all handled discreetly by the Fugates' attorney, Roy Barton. Nothing that raised any red flags. Ranch life was tough, and Thurston Fugate likely saw no harm in a man blowing off steam now and then as long as he remained fiercely loyal to the family. Landon could understand why Thurston trusted Mike enough to send him along.

Satisfied for now, Landon leaned back in his seat. So far, nothing alarming had come up. Maybe, just maybe, this mission would go smoothly. In and out. A clean retrieval.

Yet as his gaze drifted back to Noel's serene face, a niggling feeling lingered. Missions like these rarely remained simple.

Noel stirred in her seat and lifted her head, blinking as she looked around, confusion written on her face. She met his gaze, and a blush rose from her blouse to her neck before settling over her cheeks. "Oh God, I hope I didn't drool."

His lips twitched as he shook his head. "No drooling noted."

"Good." She sat up and smiled at him. "How long was I out?"

"About thirty minutes."

She blinked again, her mouth dropping open. "No way. Seriously? I thought we must be almost to Jamaica by now."

"Sorry to disappoint, but we still have about five hours to go."

Noel blew out a soft breath, a playful smile curving her lips. "I've been a rather boring flight partner so far, haven't I?" she said, her tone light and teasing. Before Landon could respond, she tilted her head, a spark of mischief in her eyes. "But you probably don't need someone prattling while plotting and planning."

His brows shot upward. "Prattling. Plotting. Planning. That was a mouthful for someone who just woke up."

Her laughter rang out, and he couldn't hold back a smile. Her gaze dropped to his mouth, and he immediately adopted a severe expression.

"Are you afraid of smiling?" she asked, a crinkle forming between her brows.

Surprised, he jerked slightly. "No."

"Hmm," she murmured.

If she was going to say something else, their attention was diverted by Jana returning to the cabin. She placed a tray of fruit, cheese, crackers, cookies, and various other delights onto the table between Landon and Noel. "What would you like to drink?"

"Just another water for me," he replied.

"Do you have cranberry juice?" Noel asked.

"Yes."

"Then I'd like cranberry juice and ginger ale, please."

"Of course," Jana said, smiling. She disappeared and soon arrived with two more cut-glass tumblers filled with their drinks.

Jana glanced at the other side of the plane before

disappearing again. Noel swiveled her seat from facing the window to face Landon and looked over to see Mike still sleeping.

Noel grinned, plucking up a grape. "I guess he'll miss the snack. Maybe he's waiting for the main course." She popped the fruit into her mouth, her lips still curving.

Landon followed her lead, and they soon nibbled their way through the food.

"Tell me about this security company you work for. Thurston mentioned Lighthouse Security. That's a rather fascinating name for a company in Montana."

"The original company was located near a lighthouse in Maine."

She continued to hold his gaze, waiting as though his lone sentence explanation wasn't enough.

"Another one is located on the coast of California. And while we are in Montana, where there are no lighthouses, there are light towers."

Her eyes widened, and so did her smile. "Guiding to safety. I get it."

It took a lot for Landon to be surprised, but for her to so quickly understand the meaning of the LSI company's name caught him off guard. And once again, in her presence, his lips curved. "You're right. Different places, but essentially the same mission."

"You asked me if this was a usual job for me. What about you? I know your assignments are probably private, but is this normally what you do?"

He hesitated, the instinct to deflect rising to the surface. But something about the way she looked at him —her eyes bright with genuine curiosity—made him want to share more than he usually would. "No, this isn't usual for me," he admitted. "Though my job covers a wide range of tasks."

"Vague answer, but I get it," she said with a soft chuckle, her smile inviting him to continue.

He considered her for a moment longer, then decided to give her a glimpse into his world. "The tasks can be anything from designing intricate security systems to escorting high-profile clients out of the country and conducting investigations. We work with government contracts as well as private clients."

"Like the Fugates."

"Yes." He nodded.

She studied him, her gaze searching but not invasive. "You like what you do."

It wasn't a question, just a quiet observation, but it hit him with surprising accuracy. He realized she had been reading him, peeling back the layers with a perceptiveness that felt both unsettling and oddly comforting. For a man used to being the one observing, being on the other side was a rare experience.

Staring into her eyes, he felt an unexpected sense of ease. She didn't press him for details he couldn't share nor did she make assumptions about his work—no clichéd ideas of glamorous bodyguarding or action-packed missions. She simply saw him, and that recognition stirred something deep within him.

Jana came back around with dinner trays. He grinned as Noel's eyes widened at the fare. "Better than the meals served when squished in your seat?"

Laughter burst forth from her. "I've never flown far

enough to get a meal on an airplane. I always had to buy my snacks from the airport before the flight. But then, I often didn't have any room to get them out of my bag. This is… well, let's just say I've never had a case where I was offered this treatment. I might get spoiled."

Mike had woken up, and though they sat on opposite sides of the plane, he followed Noel's lead by swiveling his seat toward the center, making conversation easier for the three of them. Landon leaned back, opting to mostly listen as Mike launched into a series of animated ranching stories.

Noel, ever the gracious conversationalist, smiled warmly, asking thoughtful questions about the ranch and showing genuine interest in the details Mike shared. Her eyes sparkled as she listened, her soft laughter punctuating his more humorous anecdotes. Landon admired her ability to engage, even as Mike's tales grew more repetitive and overly enthusiastic.

After finishing his meal, Landon grew weary of Mike's effusive chatter. Thankfully, the older man finally leaned back and soon drifted off to sleep, his snores filling the cabin.

Despite the tediousness of Mike's stories, Landon had managed to glean a few valuable insights about the Fugates that could impact the mission. Mike had been summoned to the ranch house in the middle of the night and had been present for the family discussions about Pamela's latest manipulative scheme—holding her own children hostage to extract more from Stan. It struck Landon as peculiar that the head ranch manager would be involved in such a sensitive, personal matter.

Mike's familiarity with Tad and Penny was evident. He had known them since birth and clearly cared for them. But his loathing for Pamela was equally palpable. His face twisted with a sneer every time her name was mentioned, the disdain in his voice unmistakable.

Landon couldn't help but question how impartial Mike could be when they eventually faced Pamela. The family might have intended to send a familiar face to comfort the kids, but Mike's personal feelings could easily complicate things. Landon glanced across the cabin at the snoring man, and his mind churned with possibilities. He needed this mission to go smoothly—no unexpected confrontations or emotional outbursts.

But as he watched Mike, sprawled out and oblivious to the world, Landon couldn't shake the unease settling in his gut. He had seen too many missions take unexpected turns when emotions ran high, and Mike was a wild card he couldn't fully predict.

Noel's eyes were closed, and he heard the slow, rhythmic breathing of sleep and smiled. He quietly stood and then walked toward the front of the plane. After using the restroom, he stepped out to see Jana putting away some of the food.

She twisted her head and smiled. "Is there anything I can do for you, Mr. Sommers?"

"I wondered if you knew anything about the storm approaching?"

"I'm afraid not, but I can have the pilot talk to you. I know we're supposed to have a quick turnaround in Jamaica."

"I'd appreciate any information the pilot can offer.

That will help with my planning to know how much time we'll have on the ground before we need to get back into the air."

Jana contacted the cockpit, and momentarily, a woman in a pilot uniform stepped out. "Hello, Mr. Sommers. I'm the copilot. I was going to talk to you when we were closer, but now is a good time. I'm sure you're aware of the hurricane approaching the Caribbean. The worst should be north of Jamaica. We hope that the time you will need to get from the airport to where you'll take charge of the children won't be more than three hours. That will give you time to return to the airport, and we can safely get into the air ahead of the storm. If not, we may have to depart to safety and come back to pick you up later."

He nodded, glad to hear they would have that much time. "Okay, that should be doable. The children's mother is supposed to have everything ready. I don't know what the internet will be like for electronic documents, so I'll need a few minutes with her, but then we should be ready for you to take off well within your timeframe."

"Excellent, sir."

He thanked the copilot and Jana, then returned to his seat. For the next few hours, he tried to focus on the upcoming transaction but found his attention continually glancing over to see Noel sleeping peacefully.

6

"Oh God, how long was I out this time?" Noel blinked rapidly, her vision clearing to find Landon's eyes on her, his lips twitching in the barest hint of a smile. She couldn't help but feel a surge of satisfaction. She was determined to coax a full smile from him before their trip ended.

"Not too long," he replied smoothly. "And don't worry—no snoring, no drooling. Although," he added with a mischievous glint in his eyes, "you might have mumbled a bit while sleeping."

Her eyes widened in alarm. "Really? What did I say?" A wave of anxiety rushed through her. *Please, God, don't let it be about how ridiculously attractive I find him.*

A deep chuckle escaped him, a rich, warm sound that settled in her chest, making her heart skip a beat. She still yearned for a wide smile, but this laugh—oh, she'd take that any day.

"No," he admitted, his amusement evident. "I was just messing with you. No mumbling."

"Hmm, a real jokester, aren't you?" she teased, feigning annoyance.

"Not usually," he confessed, the hint of a grin lingering.

Noel sat up straighter, running her fingers through her hair in an attempt to smooth it, ensuring she didn't look too disheveled. "I guess I bring out the humor in you," she quipped, smoothing her hands over her pants to straighten them.

Landon's gaze remained fixed on her, his eyes filled with something softer, something contemplative. "You always seem to carry a good sense of humor. Maybe it's contagious."

She lifted her gaze to meet his, the sincerity in his expression catching her off guard. "Life's too short not to find humor wherever you can," she replied softly.

"Even in your job?" he asked, his tone almost reverent.

Her breath hitched, and she nodded slowly. "Yes. Especially in my job."

"I suppose you've seen the worst in humanity."

"I've spent my entire career in child protective services. I've seen things no one should ever have to see—abuse and neglect. But I've also witnessed the kind of courage and resilience in children that would put the bravest soldier to shame."

Landon's eyes softened. "I'd bet that to many of those kids, you're the hero."

His words caught her off guard. She cocked her head to the side as she stared, taking him in. "This comes from the man who works for a security firm after having been an FBI agent. I have a feeling between the two of us, you would be considered the hero."

He held her gaze, his expression serious. "I've had moments in my career when I felt that my mission or my actions were heroic," he admitted. "But that's not the same as being a hero."

Smiling, she shook her head. "I have a feeling you and I could argue the definition of heroism all day."

He chuckled again, and just as before, she allowed the sound to wash over her, warm and comforting. She glanced at his phone, held casually in his hand, and thought of how he tapped on the keyboard after Mike Westerly climbed aboard. "So," she asked, her tone playful, "what did you find out about me?"

Landon's eyes widened, clearly caught off guard by her question. His mouth opened, but no words came out.

Noel couldn't suppress her laughter, though she quickly clamped a hand over her mouth, glancing over to ensure Mike was still snoring away.

Landon's gaze sharpened, narrowing slightly as he leaned in. "What makes you think I needed to learn anything about you?"

She didn't flinch, meeting his intense gaze with equal resolve. Leaning forward, she lowered her voice. "You strike me as the kind of man who doesn't leave anything to chance. This assignment came together fast—Pamela and the kids flew to Jamaica yesterday, and her demands hit Stan last night. The Fugates worked with their attorney to set the plan in motion, and thanks to their judge friend, both of our agencies were on board by morning. I figure you'd want to know exactly who you were partnering with."

Landon pulled his bottom lip inward, biting down slightly, clearly weighing his response. The flicker of admiration in his eyes didn't go unnoticed, and Noel waited patiently, knowing he was calculating the best way to answer.

She waved her hand dismissively. "It's okay, Landon. I'm not offended. Believe me, there are no skeletons in my closet for you to find. But I am curious what you already know about me."

The air left his lungs in a long, slow exhalation. "I found out that you are who you say you are. Noel Lennox. Thirty-two years old, and no police record."

"Considering I work in social work with children, it's paramount that I have a clean record."

"Understood. I wondered why the judge recommended you specifically," Landon said, his voice calm yet probing. "Especially since you don't seem to have any prior connection to the Fugates. I had my team look into a few of the cases you've worked on."

A soft gasp escaped her lips. The thought of her private cases being scrutinized unsettled her.

As though he understood her concerns, he said, "I don't know the particulars. I just know what was part of the public record."

"What did you discover?"

"You worked on the high-profile case in the news

last year. Where the children witnessed their father killing their mother and then threatened to kill them."

Her body remained still, though her heart raced. She had no words to add to his straightforward summary.

"You also spent two years in one of the toughest areas of Billings, working with homeless children, some of whom were being trafficked."

With each revelation, it became harder to keep her emotions in check, and her hands clenched in her lap as Landon continued.

"You're frequently called to hospitals to assess suspected child abuse cases. And your experience presenting evidence to the courts—especially when parental rights are in question—is well-documented."

"I take parental rights very seriously," she finally said, unsure why she defended herself when he made no accusation. "It's one of the most critical decisions we make as social workers. If we return a child to their birth parents and the abuse or neglect continues, we've failed that child. But if we're too quick to sever parental rights from someone who's genuinely trying to change, we've failed them too. It's a delicate balance... one we always want to get right."

Her eyes flickered with emotion. "But sometimes mistakes can be made. I've had to go back and change recommendations when that happens. Thank God there haven't been many over the years."

He leaned forward, resting his forearms on the small table, his face now inches from hers. The proximity made her pulse quicken. "How do you handle those mistakes?" he asked, his voice a low murmur.

Noel's lips curved into a faint smile, though her eyes remained serious. "I could joke about needing a bottle of wine, but humor feels wrong here. Truthfully, I always focus on what's best for the child. It's the guiding principle in every recommendation I make."

He nodded slowly, his gaze never wavering, but she had no idea what he thought of her.

"Then I stand by my earlier comment. To those children, you are a hero." His words were softly spoken, and the warmth she felt when he chuckled was nothing compared to the intensity of this man speaking with such care. She'd only known him for hours, and while their journey would soon end, she wanted more time with him. More time to talk. To share. To learn. "Can I confess something to you?" she asked, her voice soft but sincere.

His brow furrowed, but he immediately nodded. "Yes. Of course."

"I take every situation seriously. In this case, we have a parent essentially holding her children hostage to make demands on the father. The reality is that they are staying in a luxury beach house in Jamaica. I have no reason to fear for the children's health or safety, yet I have a job to make sure that their needs are met during this transition. But"—she sighed and wrinkled her nose—"this almost feels more like a vacation trip out of the office. Granted, I won't be lounging on the Jamaican beach while drinking fruity cocktails with an umbrella sticking out of the top, but I'm being flown in a private jet with amazing accommodations, basically at the whim of a powerful family who reached out to a judge, who tapped my boss for me."

"You feel guilty."

His words stated precisely what she was experiencing. She exhaled slowly, nodding. "Yes."

"The circumstances might not be as dire as you've experienced in the past, but in the end, you still have a job to do. You have a parent willing to hold and then *bargain* her children to get money from their dad. They may not know it now, but if they have a clue of what's happening, they'll be upset."

"I imagine the kids will have questions," she said, thinking about what she had been told. "If we stick to the Fugates' script, they should be okay—that their mom decided to stay in Jamaica, and their dad sent Mike and a couple of people he trusted to ensure they got home safely." She shrugged, adding, "It will be up to their dad and grandparents to explain what their mom did."

She returned his gaze, a silent understanding passing between them. At that moment, she felt less burdened by the guilt, knowing she wasn't facing this alone.

She leaned back, needing a little distance between them, feeling the heat of his intensity in her lady parts that had been sorely neglected. Her lips curved. "You know a lot about me, Landon Sommers. I feel like I should know something about you since I don't have secret ways to find out about people. It looks like you're going to have to talk."

He scoffed and leaned back in his seat. "What do you want to know?"

"Anything," she shot back. Looking down at the time on her phone, she said, "We only have another hour. Tell me what makes you tick before we land."

"I'm afraid I have no idea what makes me tick."

"I don't believe that. I think you don't like talking about what makes you tick."

He opened and closed his mouth a few times, then twisted his head to look first at Mike, and then out the window. She looked over her shoulder to see Mike still snoring. Turning back to Landon, she found his gaze on her.

"I was born and raised outside of Philadelphia. My dad was a police officer. My mom worked in estate sales. I have a younger brother who works for a tech firm in California. My parents moved to South Carolina several years ago, after my dad retired, wanting warmer weather."

"Tell me about the estate sales," she prodded.

His eyes widened, and his chin jerked back. "You're not going to ask about my dad's police career and how that affected my choices?"

She smiled, and a chuckle slipped out. "No, I'd rather hear about the estate sales and what drew your mom to that career."

His lips twitched, and she waited, wanting to know more.

"It happened organically. My mom's parents had her when they were older, and my grandfather died when she was in her twenties. Her mom didn't want to live in the house anymore, so she moved in with us for a while. It was tough for my grandmother to clean out her family home. She agonized over every piece of paper, so Mom finally stepped in and said she would handle it all. My grandmother trusted her. Mom looked at every object and decided what to keep, what to sell, what to give away, and what to trash."

Leaning back in her seat, Noel discovered she was fascinated. "Please, keep going."

"Eventually, she learned how to empty the house quicker, and that was the start of her new career. She helps people clean out their houses when someone has died or is unable to live alone anymore and the relatives need assistance. Sometimes she just consults, and other times, she handles the entire work herself."

Landon seemed at ease talking about his mom, and Noel was finally gifted with a small smile. "Your mom loves her job, and she's helping people."

He held her gaze as he nodded. "I never thought about it that way, but you're right. Usually, the praise is heaped on Dad because of being a police officer, but Mom has always been a helper."

"She meets people when they're desperate and takes over so they can deal with the emotions of clearing out a family home."

He continued to nod, seeming to ponder her words.

"What about—"

Jana walked back through the cabin, interrupting Noel's question.

"We'll be landing soon," she said. "Please make sure everything is stowed away." She efficiently cleared away the remaining glasses and plates from the latest snack she served.

"I guess we'll have to save more of the Landon Sommers' story for another time," Noel said, smiling. As soon as the words left her mouth, she realized that while she meant for another time on their trip, it could be interpreted as seeing him after the trip. *Would that be so bad?* She looked down and fiddled with her seat belt, not wanting him to see the emotions on her face. Because, no... seeing more of him would not be bad.

Jana gently woke up Mike, and he snorted several times as he emerged from a deep sleep. He looked over and grinned. "My mom used to say I could sleep anywhere. I've worked on a ranch my whole life. I've slept outdoors, in barns, on wooden floors. Have to say, this was a luxury. Can't believe we're almost there."

He hurried to the front to use the restroom, then sat down as they descended into Jamaica.

Landon looked at her, then over at Mike, and said, "A hurricane is approaching from the northeast and will skirt past Jamaica probably as a tropical storm. I spoke to the copilot, and she wants us to handle our business in only about three hours. I will deal with Pamela. The kids will know you, so they'll be comfortable. Noel, you can talk with them once we are aboard. The last thing we want is to get stuck on the island with a major storm."

Mike agreed, adding, "If Pamela gives us any problems, I'll deal with her. It wouldn't be the first time."

Noel wondered about his meaning, but if Pamela had lived on the ranch with Stan and the children for eleven years before the divorce, she was sure Mike had plenty of experience being around Pamela.

She glanced at Landon, noticing the shift in his demeanor. The easygoing man she'd been chatting with had vanished, replaced by someone focused on the task ahead. His posture was rigid, his expression sharp and serious. While she understood the necessity, she couldn't help but miss the more relaxed Landon she had been getting to know.

Sucking in a deep breath, she tried to steady herself as the plane began its descent. Her stomach flip-flopped, and a familiar unease washed over her. Her hands instinctively pressed tightly on the tabletop, her knuckles whitening as she braced against the turbulence.

Closing her eyes, she willed herself to stay calm, but the jarring sensation of the descent made her heart race. Then unexpectedly, she felt the gentle warmth of fingers wrapping around her hand. Her eyes flew open, and she found Landon having leaned closer.

His hand was clasped firmly over hers, anchoring her in the moment. His grip was strong yet reassuring, a silent offering of comfort. He didn't say a word, and his face remained serious, but his eyes—those steady, deep-set eyes—held a warmth that made her breath catch.

For a moment, the tension in her body eased. The turbulence still rocked the plane, but the panic that had taken hold of her began to dissolve under the quiet strength of his touch. She held his gaze, finding solace not in words but in their unspoken connection.

7

As the wheels touched down, Landon's mind wasn't on the upcoming assignment. Not on Pamela nor the legal papers he carried for her to sign. Not on Mike or the kids that they would escort back to Montana.

Instead, his focus was solely on the woman sitting with him—and the unexpected warmth of her hand in his.

Reaching out to her had been instinctive, a gesture born of an urge to provide comfort. He hadn't planned it, hadn't even thought about it. But now, as he stared down at their linked hands, he questioned why he had acted so impulsively. It wasn't like him to act without calculation, yet here he was, his thumb lightly brushing over her soft skin, feeling the steady thrum of her pulse beneath his fingers.

Her hand curled gently around his, her grip soft yet grounding. His breath hitched, shallow and uneven, as her gaze lifted to meet his. Those expressive eyes seemed to lock onto his, holding him in place, making the rest of the world blur around them.

"I think we've stopped," she murmured softly, her voice pulling him back to the present.

He blinked, momentarily disoriented. "What?"

Noel's tongue darted out and moistened her lips, a nervous gesture that sent a spark of awareness through him. "The plane... it's stopped."

Realizing how tightly he'd been holding her, he abruptly released her hand as if it had burned him. "Yeah," he mumbled, scrambling for composure. "I knew that. I was just..."

"Thank you," she said, her gentle smile filled with gratitude. "You made me forget how terrifying landing can be."

Landon stood quickly, desperate to put some distance between them before the moment's intensity overwhelmed him. "No problem," he replied, his voice gruff as he reached for their bags from the overhead bin.

He moved toward the front of the plane, pausing to gesture for her to go ahead. Noel offered a quick smile and briefly thanked the pilots before stepping out of the plane. Landon followed, his mind still reeling from the unexpected intimacy of the moment they'd shared, wondering what exactly about Noel that so thoroughly unraveled him.

"Oh my God, it's so warm!"

Landon chuckled at her enthusiasm as he almost plowed into her at the top of the open stairway leading to the tarmac. "Yeah, it's going to be. Caribbean... remember?"

She looked over her shoulder and narrowed her eyes. "I know, I know, smart-ass. But I've never been to a tropical island." She sighed. "Damn, and we have to head straight back. Too bad we couldn't spend a few days with the kids at a resort."

Suddenly, the idea of Noel in a bathing suit lying on a lounger with a tropical drink filled his mind. Blowing out a long breath, he forced his thoughts back to the assignment. Just as he expected, a roomy SUV waited down below. The dark-skinned driver smiled as he approached.

"Mr. Sommers?"

"Yes."

"Excellent. I'm Jonathan, your driver. Mr. Fugate arranged for me to meet and take you wherever you need. If you will allow, I'll take your bags." He turned to Noel. "You must be Ms. Lennox."

Noel greeted Jonathan as Landon handed him their two small bags. The driver then assisted Mike, and they quickly settled into the vehicle. Landon and Noel were in the back, while Mike sat in the passenger seat beside Jonathan.

Driving along palm-lined streets, Landon noted Noel's head swung back and forth as though she didn't want to miss anything. On either side of the streets were brightly painted shops, but many were in the process of having their windows boarded.

"Big storm is coming," Jonathan said. "But don't worry. It won't hit us directly. Just have lots of wind and rain. Mr. Fugate said your business on the island will be dealt with quickly, and I'll take you back to the airport. Yes?"

"Yes, that's the plan," Landon confirmed.

"Good, good. I am sorry you will not be here long enough to enjoy all the beauty of Jamaica, but you will come back... yes?"

A soft giggle slipped from Noel's lips. "Yes, I hope so," she replied.

Landon looked to the side and found her smiling at him, and suddenly, he wanted to promise Jonathan they would be back.

"Where're we headin'?"

Mike's words pulled Landon out of his random musings, and he grimaced, vowing to regain and retain his focus.

"Mr. Fugate said I was to take you to the resort where you are to pick up your charges. They are staying in a house on the beach there."

"Must be nice," Mike grumbled, his tone thick with resentment. "Pamela never had a problem burning through Stan's hard-earned money even though she didn't lift a finger to earn any of it."

Noel's eyes sharpened, a distinct edge creeping into her voice. "You won't talk about her like that when Tad and Penny are with us, will you?"

Mike chuckled, shaking his head. "No, ma'am, I won't. Trust me, we're all careful about what we say around the kids. They don't need to hear the worst from us. But they'll figure it out soon enough. Their mom just sold them to their dad, after all."

Landon watched as Noel's lips pressed into a tight line, her displeasure clear. He understood Mike's anger—years of loyalty to the Fugates had likely built up a well of frustration. But he also knew Noel was fiercely protective of the children's emotional well-being. She wanted to shield them from the harsh truths for as long as possible. Scrubbing a hand over his face, Landon felt the weight of the assignment pressing down on him. He wanted this mission wrapped up, but at the same time, a part of him wasn't ready to let go of the time he'd been spending with Noel.

The SUV turned onto a smooth, paved lane flanked by vibrant flower beds. Stone gates loomed ahead, opening into a stunning resort. Once inside, they passed through meticulously maintained private gardens. Golf carts zipped along narrow paths, ferrying residents and visitors between secluded beaches, elegant houses, condos, and a handful of charming shops and restaurants.

Jonathan navigated the winding paths with ease, revealing a collection of cream-colored houses and condos that seemed to glow against the turquoise blue of the ocean and the lush green of the surrounding gardens. Unlike the sprawling high-rise resorts, this place offered privacy and tranquility, each residence spaced out to give its occupants a sense of seclusion.

Landon had studied every detail of the resort—the layout, the photographs, the house where Pamela was staying. It was part of his nature to be over-prepared, a lesson drilled into him through years of experience. He hoped Pamela would be ready for them so he could obtain the necessary signatures and leave with Tad and Penny without delay.

Mike's presence would offer familiarity and comfort. And Noel, with her kind eyes, gentle smile, and soft-spoken demeanor, would easily win their trust.

As the SUV rolled to a stop, Landon glanced out his window, taking in the sight of the multistory house nestled among the vibrant greenery, the white sand beach just beyond. The photographs he'd studied didn't do it justice. The place was breathtaking, a paradise draped in shades of blue and green.

Lost in thought, he suddenly became acutely aware of Noel's presence. She leaned closer, her gaze fixed out his window, completely engrossed in the view. Her hand rested lightly on his thigh. The seemingly absent-minded gesture sent a jolt through him. Every nerve in his body came alive, heightened by her proximity.

She seemed unaware of her effect on him, her attention entirely captured by the scenery outside. But Landon couldn't ignore it. The warmth of her touch and the subtle scent of her perfume mingling with the sea breeze wrapped around him, making it hard to focus on anything else.

They approached the front door, and Landon lifted his hand to ring the bell. The chime had barely echoed inside when the door flew open with surprising force. Standing before them was Pamela—but not the composed, polished woman he'd expected.

Instead, Pamela looked disheveled, almost frantic. Her eyes, wide and glassy, darted between them, a wild glint catching the light. The expertly applied makeup from earlier in the day had smudged into dark streaks beneath her eyes, giving her a raccoon-like appearance. Her long blond hair, usually styled to perfection, was now hastily pulled back into a low ponytail, stray strands framing her face in messy waves. The elegance suggested in her photos was replaced by a chaotic edge.

Her outfit was a strange blend of luxury and disarray. She wore silky, flared pants—likely made of actual silk—that clung to her form, matching a top that should have screamed sophistication. But over it all, she had thrown on a man's shirt, rumpled and in need of both a wash and an iron. The odd combination only added to her frazzled appearance.

Pamela's gaze flickered rapidly between them. First, she locked eyes with Landon, then her attention dropped to Noel, lingering for a few seconds before finally settling on Mike. At the sight of him, her composed facade shattered.

Dropping to her knees on the cold, tiled entryway, she buried her face in her hands. Her sobs echoed around them, raw and uncontrollable, filling the air with a heavy, unsettling tension. "They're gone!" she cried.

8

Landon watched as Noel rushed forward, kneeling in front of Pamela. She gripped Pamela's trembling shoulders, her tone gentle yet insistent. "What do you mean they're gone? Who's gone? Tell me what happened."

"T... Tad and Penny," Pamela choked out, her voice breaking on their names.

Landon quickly joined them, his own urgency flaring. He gently moved Noel aside, his hands firmly gripping Pamela's arms. With a steady, commanding tone, he demanded, "What happened?"

Pamela's tear-streaked face tilted up to meet his intense gaze. "They... they went down to the beach with Horticia. They just wanted to play. I didn't think it was dangerous."

Landon's mind raced. He knew Horticia was the housekeeper, a trusted Jamaican woman in her late twenties who worked at several high-end properties within the resort.

"Landon." Noel's soft voice tried to anchor him, her

hand lightly brushing his arm in a silent plea for gentleness.

But there was no time. The situation required immediate action. He shook Pamela slightly, not enough to hurt but enough to bring her focus back. "What happened next?" he barked.

Pamela's sobs deepened. "Horticia came back alone. She said... she said three men came out of the jungle with guns. They grabbed the kids and dragged them away. She tried to stop them, but they hit her. She came running back just before you arrived."

"Where is she?" Landon demanded.

"Here... here, sir," a timid voice answered.

Landon whipped around to see Horticia standing in the doorway, her eyes wide and a small cut above her brow. She was gently dabbing at the wound with a cloth.

Releasing Pamela, Landon strode toward Horticia. He pulled out his phone, already punching in a familiar number. "The kids are missing. Three men from the jungle took them about ten minutes ago," he reported tersely to Sadie on the other end. "I need security footage and surveillance. Now."

"On it," Sadie responded crisply.

Turning back to Horticia, he drew in a calming breath, then let it out slowly. "Tell me everything that happened."

Horticia nodded jerkily, her wide eyes darting around the room. "The children wanted to go to the beach—"

"Didn't they know we were coming?" Mike barked, his voice bouncing off the surrounding tile.

Horticia's gaze shot over to Pamela, and her lips were pressed tightly together.

"Don't look at her," Landon growled. When her gaze shot back to him, he ordered, "Talk to me, and give me everything."

"No. No, they didn't know anyone was coming. Mrs. Fugate only told Roger and me. I was to take the children to the beach for a swim so she could deal with you—"

"Shut up!" Pamela cried, her face morphing into rage. "My children are gone, and you're talking about things you know nothing about!"

"If anything has happened to those kids…" Mike roared, stepping forward and jerking Pamela as his fingers wrapped around her upper arm.

Landon acted swiftly, prying Mike's hand away from Pamela with controlled force. "Don't you dare make this worse," he warned, his voice dangerously low.

"What could be worse than this?" Mike spat. "You're security! Go after them!"

"We need to know who took them, why, and where they are. Charging blindly into the jungle will only screw this up," Landon shot back.

Landon stepped away from them and moved closer to Horticia. He pulled out his phone, hit the button for LSIMT, and said, "This is the housekeeper who was with the kids." Then looking at her, he said, "Keep talking. Everything."

"I don't know. We were down on the beach. The storm is coming, and they wanted to see the waves. Tad went into the water only to his knees. Penny didn't want to get in the water but walked along the beach for a little while, taking pictures with her phone." She shook her head sharply. "No, that's not right. I already had her beach towel out for her. Penny sat on the sand, and… I can't remember!"

"Keep going. You're doing fine. Tad was in the water. Penny was sitting on a towel. Where were you?"

Her eyes widened, and she shook her head. "Surely, you can't think I had anything to do with this!"

Landon stared hard at her, and she could not hold his gaze. Her hands were in front of her, her fingers tightly clamped together. Her hair was pulled back in what had probably been a severe bun, but tendrils had fallen out and were sticking up, indicating that she had indeed run from the beach. Not wanting to have his witness lose her focus and fall into histrionics, he calmly said, "I don't have any idea what happened right now. I just need you to give me the exact facts."

She jerked her head up and down, then said, "I had set up a beach chair to sit in. I had only been seated next to Penny for a few minutes, and Tad was coming out of the water toward us. I looked at the time and knew we should go back to the house soon. I told Penny to put on her shoes. Tad dried his feet and did the same thing. He had just gotten his shoes on when movement to my right caught my eye. I watched as three men, all dressed in black, walked toward us. There were no houses that way, so I didn't know where they'd come from. I thought it was strange that they were in long pants and long-sleeved shirts, but as they got closer, they pulled a scarf up over their lower faces."

Her voice shook, and her hands clasped tighter together. "I saw one pull out a gun. I screamed, but they raced forward. One grabbed me and told me to be quiet. Another one grabbed Penny, and when Tad rushed forward to help, the other one caught him, too."

"Where was Roger?" Pamela interrupted, her eyes wide.

"He was on the deck. He didn't come down to the beach with us. But he heard us screaming and was coming down the steps as I came running up. He ran after them."

"Where is he now?" Pamela screeched.

Landon twisted his head around and saw Jonathan standing at the doorway with their bags, his eyes wide. "Call the police—"

Pamela cried, "No police. They'll make it worse. If the kids have been kidnapped, I need to know what they want!"

Jonathan's face contorted. "I can call, sir, but with the storm coming, the police forces will be working to make sure people are safe. Resources are stretched thin."

Landon shook his head. "Call them anyway just to report it. I want this on the record."

Jonathan nodded and immediately dropped their bags to pull out his phone.

Looking up, Landon spied Noel as she walked over to a bank of windows, staring off to the east. She turned around, her eyes wide. "There's nothing but jungle out there. It's like this house is at the end of civilization, and there's nothing but jungle!"

Speaking into his phone, Landon barked, "What have you got?"

"Working on pulling up satellite now to get the overall image," Todd replied.

"I've gotten into the resort security, and I'm looking at the ones aimed down on the beach. It seems the one on the house they're staying in was turned off."

Whirling around, Landon glared at Pamela. "Why the fuck would you turn the security cameras off at the back of this house?"

Her eyes widened as she shook her head. "I didn't! I didn't!"

Mike wrapped his fingers around Pamela's neck. "I should snap you right now, bitch."

Landon whirled around and brought his arm down on Mike's, forcing his grip away from Pamela. "I told you not to make this worse. We have a better chance of getting the kids back if we know who took them, why, and where they might be located."

"Someone's coming!" Noel cried out, racing toward the sliding glass door that led downward toward the beach.

Landon hustled to her side. Staggering up onto the back porch was a young man with blood running down his face.

"Is that Roger?" Noel threw open the door and started to step out.

Landon gently pulled her back and moved through the door. He recognized Roger from the photographs—

tall, blond surfer looks. In his photograph, he had gleaming white teeth that one of his wealthy female companions had paid for. He now had a cut on his forehead and was staggering from the blow.

Roger weaved on his feet, and Landon wrapped his arm around the other man's waist, taking his weight as they staggered inside the house.

"Roger! Oh my God, Roger!" Pamela cried as she rushed forward and helped him to a kitchen chair. Horticia was right behind with a wet cloth that she pressed to his forehead, her own forehead now with a bandage.

Looking between them, Landon noted their injuries were mirror opposites of each other. "I need you to talk to me. Tell me what happened."

"I was outside... heard Horticia cry out. I ran to the beach and saw the kids being dragged into the jungle. Horticia was bleeding, but I told her to get into the house and let them know. I tried to run after the kids. I got hit and went down."

"See to him," Landon barked to Horticia, then stalked over to the door leading to the patio and stepped outside. Speaking to the Keepers, he said, "This was planned, but I don't know who inside assisted."

"Right," Logan agreed. "They knew the kids would be on the beach right before you all showed up."

"I have a resort security camera on the edge of their property to the west," Sadie reported. "Can't get a visual on the jungle side, but I can see the kids. The boy was at the edge of the water and the girl was putting on her shoes. Horticia packed up their beach towels. She keeps looking to the east... whether she hears something, sees something, or knows something is about to happen, only she can tell."

He felt a hand on his arm and turned to see Noel standing nearby. Her face was pinched tight. With his free arm, he reached down and slid her hand into his. The simple touch was meant to offer comfort, but he found the warmth traveled up his arm. Shaking his head, he looked away from her worried face and continued. "I need everything you can get to me as soon as it comes in. The police will show up, but with the storm approaching, we can't expect much from them."

"Already on it," Todd said. "You'll get what we have."

"I'm sending Cole down. He might not beat the storm, but he'll get to Florida and then to Jamaica as soon as possible," Logan said. "Devil and Frazier will be with him."

"Good. I don't want to waste time running through the jungle on a wild chase that won't get me to the kids. I need to know who on the inside set this up."

He heard Noel's gasp but gripped her hand tighter. He didn't need her to give away anything she was overhearing, so he pulled her a little closer. To anyone on the inside, they would look like two people who were simply standing together overlooking the area toward the beach.

He noticed the beach was hidden from the house by the lush foliage planted along the path leading to the sand. "Who would want to orchestrate a kidnapping?"

Again, Noel's body tightened, but she made no effort to move away. Against his typical protocol, Landon switched the call to speaker. "I have you on speaker now, and Noel Lennox is with me. We're the only ones listening."

She turned her wide-eyed gaze up to him but remained quiet.

"Okay," Todd said. "We know Pamela. She's out for money and probably wouldn't stop at a charade of having someone take the kids just to get more out of Stan—"

"No."

He glanced down to see Noel still staring up at him. She shook her head. "It's not Pamela."

"What makes you say that?"

"She's... distraught. It's real. I don't think... she's not faking that emotion," Noel explained.

"She brought her boyfriend here, and we have no idea what he's up to."

She pressed her lips thinly together and twisted her head to gaze toward the blue waters beyond the tree line. Nodding her head in jerks, she sighed. "Agreed, but I still don't think she perpetrated the kidnapping of her kids, even for show. They would be traumatized."

"You've dealt with moms who have done worse."

She looked back at him, her gaze pulling him in. "I know. I can only tell you what I think of this situation." Lowering her voice, she said, "I just don't think it was Pamela."

"What about the others?" he asked, surprised that the words left his lips.

"I don't know... I don't know enough about them to

form an opinion," she replied. Her face scrunched as though the words hurt to admit.

"Checking out everything we can," Sadie cut in. "I'll send it to you."

"Heading to the beach," he replied before disconnecting. His words were as much for Noel as for the Keepers.

He let go of her hand and said, "Stay here and see what you can find out. I'm heading to the beach before the police come. I want to check the prints in the sand before anyone comes who might destroy the evidence."

"Are you going after them?"

He shook his head. "Not half-cocked. They could be anywhere, and we need the intel to make a plan. The goal is to get the kids back safely and quickly. Not run around aimlessly."

She nodded with her gaze still pinned on him. And even though their bodies were no longer touching, he could still feel her palm resting against his. Clearing his throat, he turned and jogged down toward the beach.

9

Noel walked back into the house. Sucking in a deep breath before letting it out slowly, she calmed her tumultuous thoughts. Then she walked directly to Pamela. The woman was clutching her chest, tears streaming down her cheeks. Pamela wasn't paying attention to Roger, who was still in the kitchen and being attended to by Horticia. Mike paced the floor, his phone pressed to his ear, but she couldn't hear what he said. She assumed he was talking to the Fugates.

Blowing out another cleansing breath, she placed her hand on Pamela's shoulder as she sat beside her. "Pamela, we're going to find Tad and Penny—"

Pamela wailed again, and Noel tried a different tactic. She shook the crying woman's shoulder. "Pamela, I know you're upset, but you must realize how this looks."

Pamela turned her red and swollen eyes to Noel. Her brow furrowed as she shook her head. "What do you mean?"

"You essentially kidnapped your children from their father's home in Montana and brought them to Jamaica."

"I didn't kidnap my own children. It was my weekend to have them, and I asked Stan if we could spend a week on vacation, and he refused, saying they needed to attend school. I'm sick and tired of having to ask my ex-husband for permission to be with my kids."

Noel slowly shook her head. "That's not all you did. You didn't just bring Tad and Penny on a vacation. You sent a message to your husband, telling him that if he wanted the kids to come back, he needed to pay."

Pamela scrunched her mouth to the side, but she remained quiet.

"And Stan said the only way you'd get the money was to sign your visitation rights away. You agreed. That sounds like you decided to sell your kids."

Pamela rocked with her arms tightly wrapped around her waist. "I love my kids. And they're old enough to tell their father they want to spend time with me. I never felt like I was signing my rights away. I agreed that I wouldn't take them without his permission anymore."

"Bullshit!"

Pamela and Noel jumped simultaneously at the sound of Mike's harsh outburst.

"They told me exactly what you said. And you knew we came with the paperwork. You were signing away your visitation with them—no more weekends or weeks. So don't pretend how much you love and care about your kids," he bit out.

"I do love them!" Pamela argued. "I just didn't like having to go through Stan for everything. I'm sick and tired of dealing with his shit."

"Should have thought of that before you banged one too many pool boys—"

"Stop it!" Noel ordered. She wasn't sure Mike would listen or be used to taking orders from a woman. But he closed his mouth and turned to walk to the windows overlooking the beach. Looking back toward Pamela, she said, "You can look at this situation however you want to put yourself in the best light. I can tell you that there was nothing maternal about your actions. You took your kids out of the country even if you say it was for vacation. You took them without permission from their dad, who has physical custody. And then you negotiated a deal with him for them to return to the States. And that deal was that you would receive a large amount of money. I'm telling you right now, Pamela, no judge in the country will believe your story. I guess Mike had it right. I'm calling bullshit, too."

"Okay! Okay!" Pamela cried. "But I never harmed my children. We came here for a vacation, and yes, I wanted money. After being in that family for almost thirteen years, I'm tired of putting up with their bullshit, too. I was pushed around in the divorce and forced to—"

"You were not pushed out of marriage, but you had multiple affairs that were well-documented," Noel pressed.

"Don't kid yourself," Pamela sneered. "Stan was far from a perfect husband."

Noel's patience snapped, her voice sharp and cutting

through the tense air. "You're not getting this! This is not about your marriage. This is not about you and Stan. This is not about whether or not you've spent your alimony and want more. This is about you acting in a way that was not in the children's best interest. And you will be the first person the police look at when trying to figure out what happened to Tad and Penny."

Pamela's lips parted as if to protest, but the weight of Noel's words seemed to finally sink in. The fight drained from her, and a ragged breath escaped her lips. Her eyes shimmered with tears, her shoulders sagging. "I promise," she whispered, her voice trembling. "I had nothing to do with this. I swear, I don't know what happened to them. I just want my kids back."

Noel softened slightly but kept her tone firm. "Then no more excuses, no more lies. If you want to help your children, you need to be honest with me."

Pamela nodded, a tear slipping down her cheek. "Okay... what do you want to know?"

"I want to know why Roger is here. Is he your significant other? Is he your boyfriend? Is he just someone you hang out with? Did he know ahead of time what your plans were? Is this something you planned with him? Did he know you would ask for more money on this trip? Did he know that you planned to shake Stan down for more money and use your kids?"

Pamela's voice hitched. "Roger is my... lover. But also a friend. He gets me... understands what it's like to always want what we deserve. We're not exclusive, but... he's fun." She shrugged. "We like each other."

"Whose idea was it to come to Jamaica?"

Before Pamela could answer, the door creaked open, and Landon stepped back into the room. His presence filled the space, his eyes immediately seeking out Noel's. She stood, turning to face him, her question hanging in the air as she waited for the results of his investigation. His expression was unreadable, but a tension in his posture made her heart pound.

"What did you find?" she asked softly, her gaze locked on his, searching for answers in the depths of his eyes.

He shook his head. "There are prints in the sand that follow what Horticia said. Three larger booted tracks coming from the east. Then all of those except Horticia's footprints go back toward the jungle. I can tell there was a struggle—"

Pamela whimpered, and Noel plopped back onto the sofa next to her.

Landon continued, "The police arrived and are on the beach searching. I talked to the chief. He only had two men he could spare. He agreed that I should work the case and report our findings to them."

Noel glanced outside, hearing the wind pick up. The water in the distance was now choppy whitecaps, and the clouds were a darker gray than when they'd flown in. The rain had not started, but she instinctively knew they wouldn't make their flight back to the States before the storm hit. *The kids are out in this. Oh God, keep them safe.*

"Noel?"

She jumped at Landon calling her name. "Sorry. I was... sorry."

"I asked if any new information had come in from here."

Noel cut her eyes toward Pamela before turning her attention back to Landon. "I was just asking Pamela more questions."

"And?"

"I asked about Roger… if he knew her plans or was in on her plans to come here with the children. Or even if he knew of her plans to fleece Stan."

"I didn't!" Pamela cried. "I was telling you that Roger is my friend. He wanted me to ask for more time down here just so we could enjoy it like we did last time."

"Did he know about your plans?" Noel pressed. She glanced at Landon again, finding his attention riveted on her.

"Yes," Pamela barely whispered.

"Whose idea was it?"

Pamela lifted a trembling hand to her brow, her face contorted in anguish. "I… well… I'm not sure. We talked about wanting to come to Jamaica for a vacation. I hadn't thought about bringing the kids."

Noel looked toward Landon, and he nodded, so she continued to press. "When did your plans change?"

Lifting a hand to her brow, Pamela winced. "Um… I can't… I don't… I want my children back—"

Mike stepped closer, and Noel's gaze shot to him. "You should have thought of that before you tried to sell them to their dad." His voice was as hard as a rock, and his expression was just as unyielding. He was now leaning over the two women sitting on the sofa.

"Back up," Noel ordered, anger flowing through her

veins. "You're not helping to find the children you care so much about."

The tension crackled in the air, thick and suffocating. Tad and Penny were out there somewhere, and every wasted second felt like a blow to Noel's resolve. Just as Mike seemed ready to push further, a furious Landon intervened, yanking him back with a firm grip.

"Move away, man. If we want those kids back and safe, then we've got to know what the fuck we're dealing with. I'm working with my people, and Noel's doing great getting Pamela to talk. If you can't help, go somewhere, sit down, and shut up."

Mike's sneer turned into a grimace. "I love those kids…"

"Then stop interfering," Landon ordered.

Mike turned and walked over to the sliding door, then onto the porch. Noel nodded at Landon, then glanced at Horticia in the kitchen, bandaging Roger's head. Her gaze remained on them momentarily, their mannerisms seeming closer than she would have expected. She jerked suddenly as Landon moved closer. Turning back to Pamela, she kept her voice soft but firm. "If you want your children back, you have to start talking. When did your plans change? Whose idea was it to bring the kids along?"

Pamela's gaze seemed to focus. "I wanted to bring the kids. They live at the ranch and are always doing things there. I live in a condo now, and while there is a pool, a park, and tennis courts, there's not as much for them to do." She scoffed. "At this age, they're so active that when I have them, I can't compete with their life with their dad." Her face started to crumple.

Noel jumped in again. "You asked for a week, then decided to bring them for the weekend. Why? And whose idea was it to threaten Stan that you would keep them here? Which is a really half-baked idea... surely you had to have known that."

"It was mine! Okay? It was my idea!" Noel jumped as Roger walked into the room, his forehead bandaged and blood stains still covering his collar where it had dripped.

"What was the plan?" Landon asked, moving closer to the young man whose face was contorted with either pain, fear, or anger... or a combination of all those emotions.

"She came back from asking Stan if the kids could come for a week and was upset. She was getting the kids for the weekend anyway, so I told her we should just come on and bring the kids with us. They could at least have a weekend here."

"How did a weekend getaway, which the father didn't agree to, turn into an extortion plan to offer giving up visitation rights for money?" Landon continued.

Noel watched Pamela closely. She was more interested in the mom's reaction to Roger's words than in what he had to say. Pamela stared at Roger with confusion, tilting her head to the side.

"When we arrived yesterday, Pamela was happy, and the kids seemed to have a good time. I told her that she ought to let Stan know where the kids were, and... I kinda joked that she could tell him that if he wanted them back, he'd need to up her alimony."

Noel swung her gaze over to see Roger grab the back of his neck, shrug, and look down at his feet. "I don't know… the idea just kind of bloomed from there. We'd been drinking, and she called Stan while the kids were sleeping. It was… it just happened from there."

Pamela's eyes widened, and her lips pressed together. Noel watched Roger who was now staring at Pamela with an almost pleading little-boy expression. Horticia walked into the room, her face splotchy from crying, but her eyes boring straight into the back of Roger's head.

Then Pamela's phone rang, and everyone's gazes jumped to the device vibrating on the coffee table. She looked down and shook her head. "I don't recognize the number."

Noel stood quickly and moved to Landon's side. Looking at him, she whispered, "What's next?"

10

"Answer it and put it on speaker." Landon knew the Keepers were monitoring Pamela's calls, as well as Horticia's, Roger's, and Mike's. He wanted to hear what was being said in real time.

Pamela tapped on the phone to answer the call and immediately hit the speaker button. "Yes? Um... hello?"

"This Pamela Fugate?" the male voice asked.

"Yes. Do you have my—"

"Shut up and listen. We have your children and want money."

She looked up at Landon, and he mouthed, "How much?"

"How much money do you want?" she asked, her voice still shaky.

"Five hundred thousand dollars," he replied.

Pamela's eyes widened, and Noel's hand reached out to land on Landon's arm. The ransom was the exact amount he was carrying. Now, there was no doubt that someone in this room perpetrated the kidnapping... and wasn't very smart.

He mouthed, "Ask them how you know the children are okay."

"Um... how do I know they... my children..." Her voice hitched. "Are okay?"

"Mom?"

Pamela gasped at the sound of Tad's voice. "Tad!"

"Mom, we're okay. Penny's here with me. We—"

"Shut up," the male voice snapped. "They are here and fine... for now."

Pamela's gaze shot up to Landon, and he mouthed, "Ask them how to make the exchange."

"How do we make the exchange?"

"You send money to—"

Landon shook his head.

"No," Pamela cried, her gaze never leaving Landon's face.

"Exchange... at same time," he mouthed.

"We have to make the exchange at the same time. I know I'll be with my kids," she said, her voice stronger.

There was no reply for a moment, and only muffled voices were heard. Finally, the speaker said, "Storm is coming. We will meet you at the intersection by the old mill off the A1. One hour."

Landon shook his head and held up two fingers.

"It will take two hours... um, to get the money."

"Fine. Two hours."

"O... okay," Pamela agreed. She opened her mouth to say something else, but the call disconnected.

Landon immediately turned from the others and

walked outside with his phone pressed to his ear. "What have you got?"

"The call came from an area east of Kellits. The signal came from a group of old houses on that road," Todd reported.

"How long will it take me to get there?"

"About forty minutes," Sadie confirmed. "Sending coordinates to you now."

"I'll go in alone," Landon said, his voice firm, his gaze locked on the screen in front of him. "I'll get the kids and come back here to pick up Mike and Noel."

Logan's voice crackled through the phone, heavy with tension. "Cole won't make it down there in time for backup."

"It won't matter. If the storm has hit, we'll be safe at the resort house. We'll leave as soon as it's safe."

After finalizing a few more details with the Keepers, Landon ended the call but remained engrossed, scrolling through the maps and data Sadie sent him. His focus was so intense that he didn't notice Noel until she was standing right beside him.

"You're not going alone," she said, her voice resolute.

Startled, Landon jerked his head around, his eyes narrowing as he took in her determined expression. "Noel, I can't be responsible for—"

"I'm not asking you to be responsible for me," she interrupted, her tone unwavering. "But I was sent here to ensure the children's well-being. I can't do that sitting here on my ass."

Landon shook his head, frustration lacing his words. "I'm not risking your life—"

"And I'm not letting you go without me," she shot back, her eyes blazing with defiance.

They stared at each other, the tension between them thick. Landon glared, hoping to intimidate her into backing down, but Noel stood her ground.

"Look, Noel," he said tightly. "You'd be in my way. You don't know what I might have to do to get the kids out safely."

She lifted her chin. "If you think you're scaring me, you aren't. I've been inside prisons to talk to parents and pedophiles. I've stood next to child abusers in court, staring them down… wanting to put my fists through their faces, but had to rely on my words and wit to convince the judge or jury they needed to be put away. I might not know how to shoot a gun, but I can at least be close so that when you get the kids away from the kidnappers, I can be there for them."

Her words hit him hard. Landon didn't want her there, didn't want to risk her safety, but he couldn't deny she had a point. If the kids panicked, her calming presence could be invaluable. He took a long, deep breath, feeling the weight of her hand on his arm—a touch that somehow steadied him even as it seared through his skin like a brand.

Finally, he exhaled slowly, nodding. "Christ, I hope this isn't the worst decision I've ever made."

Noel's lips quirked in a small, defiant smile. "If taking me along is the worst thing you've done, I might just be insulted."

He squeezed her fingers gently, the contact

grounding him. "If anything happens to you... that would be the worst."

Her eyes widened slightly, but her resolve didn't waver. She squeezed his arm reassuringly. "Then nothing will happen to me."

"I won't let it," he vowed, his low voice filled with a promise he desperately hoped he could keep. He grabbed his phone, dialing quickly. "Noel's coming with me. I'll update you on our path."

Before Logan could argue, Landon ended the call. He knew the risks, knew that taking a civilian on a mission like this was a gamble he wouldn't normally take. But something about Noel—her strength, her determination—made him relent. "Let's go," he said, his voice steady but his heart pounding with a mix of anticipation and dread.

They turned to head back inside the house when he stopped and looked down at her. "Say nothing about what Mike said. I'll have my people check to see who he had been talking to."

She nodded, then heaved a sigh before nodding again.

"You're fuckin' resilient, you know that?"

She huffed while shaking her head. "I'd better be if I want to make it through this assignment."

"You've got that right. Let's hope the crazy shit is over with."

Once inside, they told the others that they would be making the exchange and bringing the kids back to the resort. "We'll have to wait the storm out here, but we should be safe."

"Pamela, can you show me where I can use the restroom while Landon gets everything ready," Noel asked.

"I'll show you, ma'am," Horticia said. Pamela appeared to be in a stupor, and Noel followed the young Jamaican woman down the hall.

Landon walked to the kitchen table and opened the bag that he had brought with him. Inside was the money.

He pulled on a waterproof jacket, then slipped on the holster that would hold the two weapons he was taking with him. He hoped he wouldn't need them but wasn't sure about anything at this point.

"We're leaving now," Landon said. He had asked the police commissioner to keep a police officer there to watch Pamela, Horticia, Mike, and Roger, but with the worsening weather, he had a feeling that wouldn't happen. Looking around at the four, he was glad Noel was going with him—he didn't trust any of them.

Noel stood at the front door, her jacket on and a determined gleam in her eye. When he lifted a brow, she nodded.

With his hand on her back, they walked outside and over to the SUV Pamela had rented. Once inside and buckled, he looked over at Noel. "Ready?"

"Yeah, I'm ready."

Landon couldn't stop his lips from spreading into a grin. "All right. Let's get the kids."

11

As soon as Landon drove onto the highway and turned to the east, civilization fell away. The farther they traveled, the more the jungle pressed in close on either side, its thick, tangled greenery a stark contrast to the neatly manicured resort grounds. He talked to the Keepers with his ear radio, and Noel stayed quiet in the passenger seat. She could only hear his side, and that was very little as he listened to the intel coming in.

"The buildings they called from are a group of old, abandoned houses. I've gone back to look at the CCTV and can only see the closest camera that's on the main road. I went back over the past day, not just the past hours."

Landon knew it was crucial to know if others were around where the kids had been taken. "What are we facing?"

"There have been no vehicles on that lane other than an older SUV. It came out and headed west about four hours ago and returned about two hours ago."

"Gotta be them. The question is how many are in that house. Just the three who came to the beach or more."

"Working on it, Landon," Dalton assured. "We're combing through the back calls of Roger, Horticia, and Pamela."

"It's not Pamela," Landon said, glancing over at Noel. Her head jerked around, her mouth open slightly. She waited, then nodded encouragingly.

"We're working on who was on the inside," Logan said. "But first, we've got to get you safely in and out with the kids."

The wind had picked up, whipping through the towering palms. Their sturdy trunks stood resilient, but the fronds above danced wildly, thrashing and swaying in the growing storm. The earlier drizzle had turned into a steady rain, droplets pinging sharply against the windshield, blurring the view ahead.

Landon's grip on the wheel tightened as he asked, "How long before the storm hits directly?"

Sadie's voice crackled through the comms. "You've got a reprieve for a bit. While the storm is almost upon you, it has been downgraded to a tropical storm for Jamaica. It's also on track to turn north and skirt by Florida. It'll cause storm surges along the Florida coast, but Cole should be able to get down to you the day after tomorrow at the latest."

Landon nodded, eyes fixed on the road. "We'll be fine. Once we get the kids, we'll head back to the resort and ride it out from there."

"I have the area on satellite," Sadie said. "It's difficult

to see due to the weather and the jungle overgrowth, but there are four buildings. Two appear to have no roof. But there are two, side by side, where they must be. Sending pictures now."

While driving, he handed his tablet to Noel. "Hit the tab at the top. What do you see?"

She did as he asked with no questions, then reported, "It's an aerial view of some buildings that are partially hidden by the trees. Their colors are faded, and two of them look very dark."

"Those are the two missing their roofs."

"Okay." She nodded. "The one closest to the road in front is smaller. I have no idea how big they are."

"That's okay. I'll do reconnaissance once we get there."

"What if there are other people around? Oh God," she moaned. "I didn't even think of that. I was just thinking of three people, and I thought that with your former FBI skills and security company skills, you could just go in guns blazing."

He couldn't help but chuckle. "Believe me, Noel… going in guns blazing is the last thing I want to do."

"Since we know where the call came from, could the police have assisted?"

"Under normal circumstances? Yes. But you saw that only two policemen were spared to come out and do a report on the kidnapping. One of those left, and even though the chief wanted one to stay to keep an eye on our three inside suspects, there's no way to believe that he would do so. Catching a kidnapper would be good for the police here, but with the storm bearing down, they'll have their hands full just trying to keep looters out of the shops."

"Oh, I didn't even think about that." She looked over at him. "We really are on our own, aren't we?"

"I'm afraid so. I don't have time to take you back, but I can drop you off somewhere—"

"No! I'm going in with you."

"You won't be going *in*. I can't worry about Tad and Penny, and getting them out safely while also worrying about you. So you will stay out of sight and with the vehicle. Your part will be to help calm them once I get them out."

Outside the window, they passed a small cluster of buildings—probably shops with apartments above them. The windows were boarded up, and the streets were eerily empty, without a soul in sight. The dense foliage seemed to close in tighter around them as they climbed higher into the mountains. The jungle came alive with the sound of wind and rain. The air was thick with the scent of damp earth and wet leaves, a reminder of the raw power of the storm inching closer.

"It feels like the apocalypse," Noel murmured, her voice barely above a whisper. "Ever since we left the resort, it's like the world has emptied."

Landon exhaled, the sound heavy in the confined space. "I know. It's unsettling." His eyes flicked to the rain-slicked road ahead. "We've got about five more miles of jungle before we reach the intersection where the kidnappers wanted to make the exchange."

"That's not safe, right? That's why you're going in. The element of surprise?"

Landon glanced to the side, spying the anxiety now painting her face. Reaching across the console, he wrapped his hand over hers. She turned her palm up, and their fingers linked together.

"Yes, the element of surprise. They could come with others. They might try to take us as hostages. They might not make the handoff due to the storm. I'm not going to wait to see what happens. We'll have the offensive. We'll call the shots."

"In charge," she murmured.

He wanted to look over at her but the rain had increased, and the dirt and mud road they were now on was difficult to traverse, taking his full concentration. "You okay?"

"Yeah," she rushed to answer. "Well, as okay as I can be in a situation completely out of my control or experience."

"Hey, what happened to the tough woman who was ready to take these guys on?" he lightly teased.

"God, I hope I haven't fucked things up for you by coming," she whispered.

He squeezed her hand. "Just stay in the vehicle and keep your eyes open. I'll do the rest."

Checking his location, he slowed and executed a three-point turn so the vehicle faced out, ready to go as soon as he returned with Tad and Penny.

Landon reached into the bag between the seats, pulling out another weapon with practiced ease. He glanced at Noel, his eyes serious. "I'm guessing you don't have any experience with guns."

She shook her head, her mouth pinched. He swallowed a sigh, though a low grunt of frustration escaped.

"I can do this," she said, her voice steady.

He studied her for a long moment, searching for hesitation or fear. Instead, all he found was unwavering determination. With a small nod, he relented. "Okay."

Handing the weapon to her with deliberate care, he explained, "Here's the safety. Keep it on until you're sure you need to fire. If you're threatened, point and pull the trigger. Aim for the chest—the largest target. It gives you the best chance."

Noel took the gun without flinching, wrapping her fingers around it with surprising confidence. Landon's gaze lingered on her, impressed by her composure.

Satisfied, he dipped his chin again. "Here's the plan. I'm going to slip out, head through the jungle, and scout the house. I have equipment to check inside without being seen. I need to figure out how many kidnappers we're dealing with and locate Tad and Penny. Once I know, I'll neutralize the threat and get the kids out."

Her voice was soft, but her words cut through the tension. "Neutralize the threat. That's another way of saying you're going to kill them."

Landon leaned closer, their faces mere inches apart. "If I can, I'll disable them, wound them. But if it comes down to it, I'll do whatever it takes. No hesitation."

Noel's eyes didn't waver. "I understand. Do what you have to do to keep Tad and Penny safe."

His gaze devoured her, noting every curve of her jaw, the fluttering pulse at the base of her neck, the porcelain shimmer to her skin, and the myriad of emotions passing through her eyes. Blowing out another breath, he reached into his bag again and pulled out a small pouch. Opening the top, he pulled out a chain with a pendant, dangling it in front of her.

Noel's brows lowered together as she first looked at the lighthouse pendant then back to his face. "You keep jewelry in one of your bags?"

He chuckled. "We never know what we'll need. Wear this. There's a tracker inside. If something happens to me, or we get separated, then my people will be able to find you."

Her eyes widened, and unspoken fear poured from her.

"Please, Noel. Wear it."

Her head jerked as she nodded, then moved closer to allow him to fasten it around her neck. As she looked up, their faces were so close that their breaths mingled.

For a moment, Landon forgot the storm raging outside, the mission looming ahead. He found himself caught in the storm of her gaze, a quiet intensity that held him captive. The rain pounded against the windows, the wind howling through the jungle, but inside the vehicle, it felt like they were in their own little world, insulated from the chaos.

Her breathing hitched slightly, her gaze flickering down to his mouth. Without thinking, without weighing the consequences, Landon closed the distance. He tilted his head, capturing her lips in a kiss that was raw and urgent, a hard press of emotion in the face of danger. It wasn't gentle or refined—it was the kind of kiss shared between two people who might not get another chance.

When he pulled back, Noel's eyes slowly fluttered open, her expression dazed yet soft. Landon tensed, expecting her to pull away or maybe even lash out. But instead, her lips curved into a faint smile.

"Come back safely," she whispered.

In the midst of the chaos, deep in the heart of a stormy Jamaican jungle, Landon felt a rare smile tug at his lips. "You can count on it," he replied, his voice low but resolute.

12

TAD

Tad stared at his trembling hands, fists clenched tightly in his lap. The shaking had started the moment those men pointed a gun at him and Penny on the beach, and it hadn't stopped since. His chest tightened with a mix of emotions—surprise, anger, but mostly a bone-deep fear that gnawed at his insides.

Who were they? What did they want? His mind raced with questions, each more terrifying than the last. *Was Horticia hurt after she rushed forward to help? What would Mom do when Horticia told her?* His thoughts shifted to his dad, the solid rock in his life. Dad would know what to do. He always did. If anyone could fix this, it was him. Maybe he was already on his way, rallying help to charge into Jamaica and rescue them. He thought of the trip to Jamaica when Mom said they were going to Florida. *Why did Mom bring us for a weekend when a storm was coming anyway?*

A sharp tug on his arm snapped him back to the present, the man yanking him forward through the dense jungle. Tad stumbled, branches and leaves smacking his face as they pushed deeper into the undergrowth. Every instinct screamed at him to fight, to resist, but his eyes kept darting to Penny. They had her, too. "Leave her alone!" he'd shouted, his voice cracking with desperation.

The men had only laughed, their grips tightening as they dragged Penny along. Tad was only twelve, but working on the ranch with his dad had made him strong for his age. He'd been proud of his growing muscles, the lean strength he'd built helping out after school and on weekends. But now, in the grip of these men, he felt small and powerless. The cold barrel of a gun pointed at Penny reminded him that strength alone wasn't enough to protect her.

The jungle seemed to close in around them, the oppressive heat mingling with the rising storm. Every time Tad tried to glance at Penny, the man holding him yanked his arm harder, forcing him to stumble forward. His heart ached, not knowing if she was okay, but he couldn't risk making things worse for her.

At last, they emerged in a small clearing where an old, battered Jeep waited. Tad's heart sank further when they shoved him and Penny into the back seat. He didn't want to be separated from her, so a sliver of relief slid through him when they stayed together. One of the men squeezed into the seat beside them, forcing Tad to shift closer to Penny. He instinctively moved his body between her and the man, a small barrier but one he hoped would make her feel safer.

Another man climbed into the driver's seat while the

one with the gun twisted around from the front passenger seat, the weapon still aimed at them. Penny whimpered softly beside him, and Tad quickly reached for her hand, squeezing it tight.

The Jeep lurched forward, bouncing along the uneven road. Tad's mind raced again. If it were just him, he might have tried to jump out and run into the jungle, losing himself in the dense foliage until he could find his way back. But he couldn't leave Penny. Not alone, not vulnerable.

Dad's words echoed in his head, a steady reminder of what it meant to be strong—not just in body, but in heart. *Women can take care of themselves, but a good man will always protect them when they can.*

Tad didn't feel like much of a man, but as he held Penny's trembling hand, he swore he'd do whatever it took to keep her safe.

After driving over bumpy, potholed dirt roads, they finally stopped outside a group of abandoned, crumbling buildings. The man with the gun simply ordered, "Get out."

The driver opened Penny's door, and she hesitated. Tad watched the man start to lean forward, and he quickly nudged his sister. "I'll go first." He climbed over her and was immediately hit with the wind whipping around. Turning, he grabbed her cold hands and steadied her as he gently pulled her out of the vehicle. The wind whipped her hair about her tearstained face. He wrapped his arm around her and followed the driver.

"Stay right with me," he whispered. They were

marched into the house, which appeared to be only one room. A door on the far side opened to a small toilet.

"Get upstairs," someone ordered.

Tad reached down and held Penny's hand as they walked together to the bottom of the narrow staircase. The space didn't allow them to walk side by side, but he held her hand as he nudged her to go up first. He tried to keep himself between her and the men. At the top was only one door, and through it, a small, bare room. The window was covered with wood, and the man behind him with the gun laughed.

"Stay here. We'll make a call for money, and we see how much you're worth, yeah?"

The door slammed before Tad could say anything, and he realized that if they called their mother, she wouldn't have the money to pay.

Penny's thoughts must have followed the same line of thinking. "Tad? Mom can't pay," she whispered, her body shaking.

"Mom will call Dad, and he'll take care of everything."

"But how long will it take—"

"Dad can wire the money or something. He'll make sure it'll happen."

Tad glanced around the dimly lit room, the only light filtering through the narrow slats of a wooden shutter. The shadows shifted ominously, but his eyes locked onto the faint glow. He moved toward the window, his heart thudding with a mix of hope and fear. Peering through the tiny gap, he could barely make out the outlines of the jungle beyond. The sky had darkened to a murky gray, signaling the storm's approach.

His breath hitched as he noticed what appeared to be a rooftop adjacent to their makeshift prison. Excitement flared briefly—could this be their way out? He gripped the wooden slats tightly and shook them, but the frame didn't budge. His hope dimmed as his eyes adjusted to the shadows. Several pieces of wood nailed from the outside held the shutters firmly in place. Any attempt to force them open would be loud—too loud.

Tad swallowed hard, his hands trembling as he pushed against the window again. The rattling noise it made was sharp and intrusive in the otherwise silent room. He froze, heart pounding. If the kidnappers heard him trying to escape, they might retaliate—maybe even hurt Penny. His stomach twisted at the thought.

Turning, he saw Penny huddled in the corner, her small frame trembling. Tears streaked down her cheeks as she struggled to wipe them away. The sight of her like that—scared and vulnerable—broke something inside him. Tad clenched his fists, feeling the helplessness claw at his resolve. He wanted to get her out of there, but the fear of making things worse paralyzed him.

Gritting his teeth, he crossed the room and wrapped his arms around her, pulling her close. She leaned into him, her tiny body shaking against his. Tad pressed a kiss to her forehead, his voice soft but firm. "We're gonna get out of this, Penny."

Her wide, tear-filled eyes lifted to his. "How do you

know?" she whispered, her voice quivering with fear. "What makes you so sure?"

Tad drew in a shaky breath, trying to project a confidence he didn't quite feel. He thought back to all the action movies and cop shows he'd watched, hoping he could sound convincing. "We're just leverage to them—a way to get money. They won't hurt us. If they do, it ruins their plans. They'll keep us here until they get what they want, and then they'll let us go."

Penny sniffled, her voice barely audible. "We haven't seen their faces."

"That's a good thing," Tad reassured her, his tone firm. "It means they know we can't identify them. That's why they'll let us go. We're safer this way."

He helped her down to the floor, gently guiding her to sit with her back against the wall. Then he settled beside her, making sure his body was between her and the door. His heart hammered in his chest, the weight of responsibility pressing heavily on his small shoulders. He wasn't naive—he knew he couldn't stop a bullet. But if those men came back, if they tried to hurt Penny, he would do whatever it took to protect her. He would stand between her and danger even if it meant sacrificing everything.

Tad squeezed her hand, his jaw set with determination. "I won't let them hurt you," he whispered, more to himself than to her. "Not while I'm here."

13

Throwing the vehicle door open, Landon jumped out and quickly shut the door to keep the rain from blowing inside. After a last look at Noel, who was staring at him, he turned away from her and jogged to the side of the road, where the leaves hung over the narrow lane and disappeared into the jungle's edge.

The jungle afforded some protection from the heaviest rain and wind. The hurricane was now labeled a tropical storm, skirting by Jamaica, and he already knew he wouldn't want to be in anything more potent. Glad for the bag the Keepers always carried with them, he planned on an extra thank-you to Bert when he arrived back in Montana.

While the former agent always tried to be prepared for contingencies, this simple handoff of money, Pamela's signature, and accompanying the children back to Montana had turned into a clusterfuck. Tapping his radio earpiece, he reported back to LSIMT. "I can see the house in the distance. No lights are on in the two structures without a roof, and no lights are visible in the single-story one. There are lights on the lower level of the two-story building."

As he came to the jungle's edge, he swiped his hand over his face, flinging the water to the side. Visibility was low, but he could easily discern the smaller building to the side and a larger two-story building right behind. "My guess is the kids are upstairs. I'm going to circle the building and use my snake camera. I may not be able to extricate them without deadly force."

"We have already been in touch with the police commissioner and governor-general of Jamaica. We've been permitted to do what needs to be done to retrieve the children safely," Logan acknowledged. "But then we would've done so no matter what they said."

Landon nodded to himself, adrenaline pumping as he crept along the jungle's edge, keeping to the shadows. The smaller structures nearby were empty and dilapidated, their missing roofs allowing the rain to drench the interiors. They were of no use, which only solidified his focus on the larger building ahead.

He moved stealthily, blending with the howling wind and pounding rain. The storm worked in his favor, swallowing the sound of his footsteps as he approached the outer wall of the main building. Pressing his body against the soaked surface, he took a moment to listen, though the storm's roar made it difficult to discern anything inside.

He pulled the small snake camera from his pocket, keeping his head down to alleviate much of the rain hitting him in the face. Once activated, he stretched the thin, bendable wire with a tiny camera at the end and curved it just over the edge of the windowsill. He knew the camera review was being sent back to LSIMT and what he could see on his watch face.

A crude wooden table in the center of the almost empty room was where two men sat in folding chairs, playing cards. They looked young... younger than he'd anticipated. One was barely out of his teens. They wore dark clothing, and dark balaclavas were pushed down around their necks.

No furniture was in the room except a mattress on the floor against the far wall. The single door at the back opened, and a man walked out, buckling his pants. Landon's heart threatened to pound out of his chest for a second at the thought of what that man had been doing. As the man stepped out of the way, Landon observed a small toilet and sink in the tiny bathroom with the door now opened, and he let out a long, slow breath.

"We got fifteen minutes until we gotta go."

The youngest looked up and grinned. "Payday, baby."

The others laughed. "Fucking easy. She set it up so easy."

She? Horticia? Was Noel wrong, and it was Pamela? Landon angled the camera to the other side of the room, where stairs leading to the second floor were visible.

"You gonna go up and get 'em?" the other seated man asked.

"Yeah... wave a gun around and threaten the little shits. They'll be easy."

Gaining the confirmation through his feed that Tad and Penny were upstairs, he knelt beneath the window, his movements deliberate and quiet as he assessed the rest of the structure. No external stairs led to the second floor, but the smaller building abutted the back of the larger one. A boarded-up window on the second story could provide an entry point.

Time was critical. Less than fifteen minutes to extract the kids and get them to safety. He keyed his radio, knowing Sadie would relay his movements to Noel, keeping her updated and ready.

The ground around the house was already muddy, and he slogged his way to a back window of the smaller building, noting a drain pipe running from the flat roof. Climbing onto the windowsill, he was able to reach the downspout. Gripping tightly, he struggled as the rain kept his grip slick. He gritted his teeth, every muscle straining as he shimmied upward. His knee finally found purchase on the roof, and with a final push, he hauled himself up.

Once there, he scrambled to his feet and hurried to the second-story window. The absence of iron bars was a stroke of luck. He could remove the wooden slats without too much trouble. Reaching into his pack, he pulled out a flat metal tool. With practiced efficiency, he slipped it under the edge of the first board, applying pressure until it popped free. The storm muffled the sound, but he knew there was no time to waste.

One by one, the wooden slats came loose, each board discarded silently to the side. When the last piece gave way, Landon pushed the shutters open, the sudden gust of wind and rain spraying his face. He swept his penlight across the dim room, its beam cutting through the shadows.

Moving to the other side, he repeated the action and popped the bottom wooden slat from its fastening. He repeated the action until the wooden shutters could be jerked open.

In the far corner, two figures huddled together. Tad stood protectively in front of Penny, his arms spread wide, shielding her. Landon's heart clenched at the sight, but he didn't let the emotion slow him down.

Slipping inside, he whispered urgently, "Tad. Penny. I'm here to help. Your father sent me."

Tad's eyes widened, flickering between hope and fear. Penny peered out from behind her brother, her small frame trembling.

"Tad," she whimpered, her voice barely audible, "What do we do?"

"I need you both to trust me," he said, pulling out his ID and flashing it quickly. "I'm with Lighthouse Security in Montana. Your dad and grandparents sent me to bring you home. We don't have much time. One of the men downstairs has demanded a ransom. We need to get out of here before they decide to come up."

Tad's gaze locked onto Landon's, searching for the truth in his eyes. Landon held his breath, waiting for the boy's decision. Finally, Tad turned to Penny and wrapped an arm around her.

"I trust him," he said firmly. "Let's go."

Landon exhaled a quiet sigh of relief. The kids hurried toward him, only to recoil slightly as the cold rain lashed through the open window. Landon quickly motioned them forward.

"It's okay. Just stay close to me," he assured, positioning himself to guide them out. Every second counted now, and he wouldn't let anything stop them from getting to safety.

Penny approached first, and Tad helped her over the windowsill and onto the roof, where she knelt, keeping her face down to keep the stinging rain from hitting her face. Tad quickly followed, and Landon led them to the side where the pipe went down.

"Tad, I'm going to lower you as far as I can, and then you can drop. The ground is soft, but I need you at the bottom to help get your sister."

Without hesitation, Tad nodded. "I can do this." With the agility of a monkey, he scrambled down the drainpipe, slipping and sliding until his feet were on the muddy ground.

"Climb on my back like we're going to piggyback." Landon softly ordered as he offered his hand to Penny.

She didn't hesitate, and he squatted while she clambered onto his back, wrapping her arms and legs around him. He wasn't sure if her hasty acquiescence was because she trusted him or if she just wanted to get closer to her brother. Either way, he was glad he didn't waste time convincing her what she needed to do. She was slight in stature, but the descent wouldn't be easy with the elements working against them.

He grabbed the pipe with both hands, gave it a hard shake again to test its steadiness, and then swung himself off the edge of the building so they dangled against the side of the building.

"What the fuck?" an angry voice yelled from the upper window.

"Dammit!" Landon cursed under his breath. The shout came from the upper window, so there was no time for a careful descent now. He let go, dropping them to the muddy ground below. The impact jarred his knees, but he quickly recovered, helping Penny off his back as Tad rushed forward to catch her.

Before Landon could issue any further instructions, a gunshot rang out, echoing through the storm. "Down!" he barked, instinctively reaching for his weapon as he scanned the rooftop.

A heavy thud followed as a body crumpled to the ground, landing mere feet from where they stood. Penny's scream pierced the air, but Landon's focus remained on the fallen man. The older kidnapper lay writhing in the mud, blood seeping from a wound in his chest. His anguished cries mixed with the relentless sound of the storm.

"Shit!" Landon hissed, eyes snapping toward the tree line. There stood Noel, her gun still raised, eyes wide and locked on the man she'd just shot.

Tad and Penny scrambled away, fear evident in their every movement. Landon's voice cut through the chaos, firm and commanding. "Go with her! She's with me!"

Whether it was trust in Landon's authority or sheer instinct, Tad pulled Penny to her feet and guided her toward Noel. His hands gripped her shoulders tightly as they made their way toward the relative safety of the trees.

"Noel!" Landon barked again, his gaze meeting hers. She blinked, snapping out of her daze, the shock in her eyes giving way to grim determination. "Take them!" he ordered. "Get back to the Jeep. I'll cover."

She hesitated, and he barked, "Now!"

Suddenly, she blinked and lowered the gun before whirling and turning toward the kids. "Come on. Stay with me. He'll bring up the rear."

Landon watched them disappear into the jungle, the rain swallowing their retreating forms. Only when he was sure they were safely away did he turn his attention back to the man on the ground. The two younger kidnappers inside were either unaware or too afraid to venture out into the storm after hearing the gunfire.

Kneeling beside the fallen man, Landon took a grim breath. The wound was fatal— he'd seen enough battlefield injuries to know the man wouldn't survive until dawn. And his demise would be prolonged and agonizing. The decision to hasten the man's death was made in an instant, driven by necessity, the cold reality of their situation, and the knowledge that it would show mercy, more than what the man would have shown them.

With a swift, decisive motion, Landon grasped the man's head and twisted sharply. The snap of the spine was quick and merciful. The man's body gave a final shudder before falling still.

Rising to his feet, Landon cast a glance toward the trees where Noel and the kids had vanished. He hated that she'd been forced to shoot, hated even more that she might have had to witness what he'd just done on a mission.

Landon raced to the closest window and peered inside, seeing the two younger kidnappers standing, their gazes filled with surprise as they stared up at the staircase, probably expecting their compadre to come down. He spied another gun lying on the table. Darting to the door, he kicked it in, splintering the wood.

One was reaching for the gun, and Landon fired, dropping the man where he stood. The other threw his hands up into the air, his eyes wide and a wet stain now on the front of his pants. "No, no... I surrender," he cried.

Landon kept his weapon on the young man while he stalked forward and snatched the gun off the table. A glance around gave no evidence of another weapon. "You stay here, and you'll live."

"Yes, yes! I'll stay. I won't leave!"

Backing out the door, Landon ran to the trees on the opposite side where Noel and the kids had disappeared. If he was watched, then the jungle hid which direction they came from. Now, circling the building under the foliage cover, he hastened to where the Jeep was parked.

"Got the kids out of the building," he radioed. "Noel has them. Kidnappers are disarmed. One dead. One wounded. One scared shitless."

"Copy that," Todd said.

"Heading to vehicle. Will make contact when we are on the road. What is the status of the storm?"

"Still a tropical storm, but while it is centered to the north of Jamaica, it has stalled slightly, so heavy rain and sustained winds will be experienced. Hope to get Cole there tomorrow."

Disconnecting the call, Landon swiped at his rain-soaked goggles, pushing through the last of the jungle's thick undergrowth. The muddy lane stretched out before him, slick and treacherous underfoot. His eyes locked onto the Jeep parked farther up the road, the engine running.

Jogging toward it, he felt the weight of the storm pressing down, the rain drumming against his shoulders. As he reached the driver's side, he called out above the noise, "It's me. Move over."

Noel jumped as she whipped her head around. Seeing him, she nodded as a relieved smile eased the furrow in her brow. She clambered over the stick shift, her ass in the air. Landon blinked, stunned that in the middle of a rescue, in the middle of a storm, in the middle of a Jamaican jungle, he was noticing a woman's ass. *Christ...* He shook his head to dislodge the thoughts.

As soon as she was clear, Landon yanked the door open and climbed into the driver's seat. The interior was a welcome relief from the pounding storm. He ripped the goggles off, tossing them onto the dashboard.

Twisting to look at Noel, he softened his sharp gaze momentarily as he took in her appearance. Her wet hair clung to her face, droplets of water trailing down her cheeks. Her eyes, wide and intense, seemed even larger against her pale, rain-slicked skin. For a brief, irrational moment, all he could think about was kissing her again, the memory of their earlier kiss flaring to life. But the sound of movement in the back seat slammed him back to reality.

His attention snapped back to Noel, and the words came out harsher than he intended. "You didn't stay in the vehicle."

Her eyes widened in surprise at his tone, but the flash of relief quickly turned to defiance. She narrowed her gaze, the soft vulnerability replaced by a sharp glare. "And if I hadn't come out, you might be lying in the mud with a bullet in you," she retorted, her voice low but fierce.

Landon clenched his jaw, the truth of her words settling heavily between them. He couldn't deny it. She had saved him.

14

Noel started shaking as soon as Landon left the vehicle, leaving her with a weapon and minimum instructions on how to fire it. He hadn't been gone long when panic overcame her, and she'd slipped from the dry warmth of the Jeep. Staying at the edge of the road where the low, overhanging foliage hid her, she'd headed in the direction he'd taken.

When she spotted the building ahead, her breath caught in her lungs. Landon was on the flat rooftop of the lower structure, moving swiftly. Tad was dropping several feet from the drainpipe to the ground below. Penny climbed onto Landon's back, and he swung over the side of the building. Tad's arms were raised to assist if needed. Noel had started moving toward them when a figure appeared on the roof—a man, his weapon raised.

Her mind blanked with fear, and instincts kicked in. Raising the gun in the direction of the man, she pulled the trigger. The shot rang out louder than she'd expected, and the recoil jarred her arms.

The man's cries were real as he pitched over the side of the building. He clutched his stomach when he hit the ground. She couldn't believe that her gunshot startled him enough to fall off the roof. She was afraid to get closer, but Landon sent the kids to her with the order she was to take them to the Jeep.

Grabbing the kids by the hands, she led them quickly toward the road, the jungle's dense foliage making it hard to navigate. The rain didn't let up, blinding her as it poured down in relentless sheets. "Come on!" she urged, wiping her face, only for the rain to soak her again instantly. They stumbled onto the muddy road, and her heart lifted slightly when the Jeep appeared.

Noel made sure Tad and Penny were close. Tad seemed strong and determined to push through, but Penny struggled, her small frame weakened by fear and exhaustion. Her brother reached over and grabbed Penny's hand, helping her to keep their pace. At the Jeep, Noel threw open the back door, helping Penny inside first. Tad stopped for a moment, swiping at the rain on his face. "Th... thank you for—"

"Get in, honey," she said gently but firmly, giving him a small, encouraging smile.

Once the kids were safely inside, Noel slid into the front passenger seat. She turned to check on them, finding them huddled together, eyes wide with lingering fear. Her heart clenched, and she softened her tone. "Tad, Penny, my name is Noel Lennox. I'm a social worker from Montana."

"Montana?" Tad's voice wavered with a mix of hope and disbelief. "Did our dad send you, too?"

"Yes, in a manner of speaking. But right now, all that matters is that we get you to safety."

"Back to Mom's place?" Penny asked.

Noel nodded, but when she saw the kids shiver, she said, "Let me get the engine started, and I'll turn on the heat." She climbed over the console, and once behind the wheel, she started the engine. Fiddling with the thermostat controls, she felt the air begin to warm. Before she had a chance to talk to the kids further, there was a rap on her window. "Shit!" she squeaked as she whipped around to see Landon standing in the pouring rain. She climbed back into the passenger seat, belatedly realizing she'd practically shoved her ass in his face as she did so. Twisting around, she managed to plop down unceremoniously. Water still dripped from her hair onto her face, and she swiped at her cheeks again.

Despite the chaos, the danger, and the storm still raging outside, there was a brief, shared moment of triumph between them. They had done it. The kids were safe. Even in the bizarre circumstances—soaked to the bone, adrenaline coursing through them—Noel felt the corners of her lips twitch into a small, exhausted smile. They had made it.

Then Landon opened his mouth and ruined the moment when he growled, "You didn't stay in the vehicle."

She blinked in surprise, then anger took hold, mixed

with disbelief. "Seriously? I saved your life, and you're fussing about me not staying here?"

"Mr. Landon?"

His gaze dragged from hers as he twisted around to look at the kids. "Landon is fine."

"Um... are we going to Mom's place now?" Tad asked, his chest heaving.

"Yes. It'll take about thirty minutes... maybe longer due to the weather. But I'll get you there as soon as we can."

It seemed Landon wasn't going to address her lack of following instructions anymore. Letting out a sigh, she sat sideways in the seat so that her body was facing Landon, and she could swing her head to either look out the windshield or to check on the kids in the back.

The narrow Jamaican road was a winding ribbon of asphalt cutting through the dense, rain-soaked jungle. The storm raged relentlessly, rain hammering down in thick sheets, reducing visibility to a few feet ahead. The windshield wipers fought a losing battle, barely able to clear the water before another wave of rain obscured the view again. The headlights illuminated the path ahead, but the jungle seemed to close in around the road, the towering trees and heavy foliage creating an almost claustrophobic tunnel.

Checking the back seat, she was heartened by Tad's and Penny's appearances. They were pale and still shaking with the adrenaline of their experience, but neither were crying nor unable to speak. She wished she could offer them food and water but had neither. As though knowing where her thoughts had gone, Landon said, "Tad? Turn around and open the brown rucksack just behind your seat. There are some protein bars inside."

"When did you pack those?" she asked Landon as Tad and Penny followed his directions and began digging in the back.

"They were already packed in that bag."

Tilting her head, she asked, "How did you know they would be needed?"

He looked at her and lifted a brow. "I packed the guns and didn't know if they would be needed."

Shivering slightly, she pushed down the reminder that she had fired a weapon and scared the man into falling off the roof. "I didn't realize you'd come prepared for *all* contingencies."

"Not all," he admitted. "We have standard equipment we carry. Better to have it and not need it than vice versa."

A protein bar was pushed between her and Landon. "Here," Tad offered.

"Oh, thank you, but you and Penny make sure you have what you need," she said. Her stomach started to growl, and she hoped it wasn't heard over the pounding sounds of the storm outside. They hadn't eaten since her meal on the plane. She had assumed they would have a meal or snack at Pamela's house before they left the island, but that was before everything had blown apart when they arrived.

"Take it," Landon encouraged. "There are plenty." He lifted his gaze to the rearview mirror. "There are some water bottles in the same bag."

Noel ate half of the protein bar, then handed the other half to Landon, glad when he accepted her offering. She looked in the back to see that Penny and Tad each had one but were sharing a bottle of water. She offered a little smile and said, "I know I told you that I was sent by your dad and grandparents. I suppose I should explain that a little bit. I'm a social worker who works with children of all ages."

"I don't understand why they sent you to escort us home from our vacation with Mom," Penny said.

Tad jerked his head around and stared incredulously at her. "Really, Penny?"

Penny looked at him, scrunched her nose, and she sighed heavily. With a voice filled with pain, she asked, "Mom wasn't supposed to bring us here, was she?"

Even though Tad had his arm around his sister, he shook his head. "Duh. Of course, she wasn't. When did she ever do anything she was supposed to?"

"Tad, that's not fair!" Penny looked out of her window and swiped at a tear falling down her cheek. Sighing again, she turned back to him, "You're right. I know you're right. It's just that when we talk about Mom, I sometimes wish you weren't right."

"Me, too, Sis," he agreed, sadness filling his voice.

"I'm really sorry," Noel said. "But I'll be honest with you. Your mom did not have permission to—"

Suddenly, a low rumble reverberated through the air, growing louder and more menacing by the second. The ground seemed to shudder beneath the vehicle. Out of nowhere, a massive wave of mud and debris surged onto the road ahead, a churning mass of earth, rocks, and uprooted trees. The mudslide barreled down the hillside with terrifying speed, sweeping everything in its path.

"Fuck!" Landon cried out as the SUV lurched.

Noel screamed as the road before them seemed to shift and move. Her hand slammed onto the dashboard as Landon stepped on the brakes, bringing them to a skidding stop. He handled the vehicle with expert precision and probably a dose of luck to keep them from sliding too close to the edge of a ravine.

"What is it?" she cried.

"The fucking road has washed out. It looks like a mudslide." She turned to look at him, noting the hard set of his jaw. He put the SUV into reverse and managed to turn around. "We'll have to go a different way."

He tapped into his earpiece. "Mudslide on the main highway. Reversing and going east, up into the mountains. We won't be able to get back to the resort before dark. Let me know what's up here." He was silent, and Noel assumed whoever was on the other end was figuring out where they could go.

"Got it. Send it to me." Another pause. "Good. Yeah. Make the call to the Fugates and to Pamela."

He looked to the side, catching her gaze. "My people are sending info on an alternate route or a place to wait until the storm passes."

He slowed to a stop and studied the images on his phone. "There's a small building not too far from here."

"How far?" she asked. "Can we get there?"

"Only about two more miles. We shouldn't have any problems as long as there are no more mudslides."

Their progress was slow as the rain slashed across the windshield, the road barely visible. The minutes ticked by. Suddenly, a loud crack split through the storm noise, and a tall tree fell across the road. Once again, Landon cursed, hitting the brakes. The SUV careened as it slid toward the edge of the road.

Noel cried out as the ravine loomed closer. The image of them pitching over the side of the mountain flew through her mind before he safely brought the vehicle to a stop again. "Oh God, what now?" Noel cried, dragging her gaze from the rain and wind-whipped visage out the windshield to Landon. His face was hard, his eyes as stormy as the view outside, and his nostrils flared as he appeared to fight to keep his breathing steady. She wondered if he would finally lose control, but he only twisted his head around to peer into the back seat.

"Everyone okay?"

Those two words slashed out but conveyed what they needed to. He was in charge and checking on those he'd vowed to protect.

"Y... yeah," Tad said, his answer coming through his panting.

"Penny?" Landon asked. This time, his voice was softer. Noel felt a pull in her chest at how he took control, handled everything thrown at them, and still managed to care about how his question would sound to a young, frightened almost teenager.

Penny didn't answer, but Noel looked to see her nodding her head.

Landon glanced down at the screen on his watch,

then out the windshield. "It's over there," he said as he inclined his head to the side.

The fear had knocked out all rational thoughts from Noel. "What? What's there?"

"The small shed."

The wind howled around the SUV, shaking it with each fierce gust. Inside, Noel clutched the dashboard, her knuckles white with tension. She cast a glance into the back seat, her heart twisting as she saw the fear etched across Penny's young face. The girl's wide eyes shimmered with unshed tears, her small hands gripping Tad's arm tightly.

Noel turned back to Landon, her voice soft but urgent. "Will it really be safer than staying in the vehicle?"

Landon's gaze flicked to the rearview mirror, taking in the frightened children before meeting Noel's eyes. His jaw tightened, and he spoke in a low, measured tone. "The road's blocked now. We're on a narrow stretch with a steep drop on the north side. If there's another mudslide or washout, we could be pushed right over the edge."

His words hung heavy in the air, punctuated by the relentless pounding of rain against the roof. In the back, Penny whimpered softly, her small frame trembling.

Noel swallowed hard. "Oh shit..." she murmured, the weight of their situation pressing down on her.

Landon made a sound that resembled a chuckle and a scoff. She wanted to be offended, but in truth, either would have been appropriate. Her brain was as scrambled as their trip so far, but Landon seemed to thrive on finding a new way to survive whatever was thrown at them. "Right," she said, hoping she infused the one word with as much courage as she could muster.

"Okay, guys, here's what we're going to do. We need to get out of the vehicle on the driver's side. I'll get the bags out of the back. Then we'll hike about... about the length of a football field to a small barn. At least we can stay as dry as possible, and since the storm winds aren't predicted to get stronger, it will withstand the rain. Any questions?"

Everyone shook their heads, and he continued, "Right. Tad, you're in charge of helping Penny get out, and Noel, you'll carry the brown bag with the protein bars and water."

"I'll carry them," Tad said. "Noel can help Penny."

Noel jerked her gaze from Landon to the back seat, finding Tad's jaw set similarly to what she'd witnessed with Landon. Her heart squeezed, and she smiled. "Okay," she said softly, dipping her chin toward the young man. Shifting her gaze to Penny, she said, "Looks like it'll be you and me together, okay?"

Penny offered a forced smile in return. "Sure. Okay."

Noel was once more impressed with the adaptability of the kids. She turned, her eyes locking onto Landon. This time, her attention was drawn to the subtle shift in his expression. His lips, usually set in a firm, no-nonsense line, were now softened, curving ever so slightly into the hint of a smile. The sight sent a flutter through her chest, and she fought the sudden, overwhelming urge to lean in, to bridge the small gap between them and see if his kiss would ignite the same spark, the same fire as before.

Her heart pounded as her gaze lingered on his mouth, remembering the rough, urgent way his lips had claimed hers earlier. Slowly, she lifted her eyes to meet his, and what she saw there stole her breath. His intense gaze locked onto her, holding her in place as though the storm outside had vanished, leaving only the charged space between them.

At that moment, she dared to hope—hope that he was thinking the same thing, feeling the same pull, the same longing. The tension crackled like electricity, the unspoken question hanging in the air. *Would the next kiss be just as unforgettable?*

15

Landon resisted the urge to fling open his door, instead easing it open with care to avoid jostling the SUV unnecessarily. His boots hit the rain-slicked road with a muted thud, and he took a steadying breath as the storm lashed against him. Rain pelted his face, and the wind howled around him, but it wasn't the storm that had his pulse racing—it was the thought of Noel.

All he'd wanted to do was reach out, cup her face, and kiss her senseless. *What the fuck is wrong with me?* The thought gnawed at him, even as the rain soaked through his clothes. Sure, she was beautiful. That much was undeniable. But this pull, this visceral reaction every time he looked at her, was something else entirely. He prided himself on being in control, especially in situations like this. Yet with Noel, his usual discipline felt like it was hanging by a thread.

She wasn't just a pretty face. From the moment she entered this chaotic mission, she'd shown resilience, adapting to every twist and turn without hesitation. She hadn't flinched when he armed himself or suited up for action. And then, there was the moment when he'd been caught vulnerable—how she'd fired that shot, saving not only him but Penny and Tad too. *Jesus, she hadn't even fired a gun before.*

The sound of the back door next to him opening jerked him out of his thoughts. He turned to see Tad climbing out, his body shaking with the wind but his expression resolute. Landon helped him down, then turned to assist Penny. His hands were steady as he lifted her gently, holding on as her feet landed on the slick road.

Remembering that he told them to get out on his side, he turned around to find Noel's face before him. Noel had clambered over the console, her rain-drenched hair plastered to her face. She paused, balancing on her hands and knees, waiting for him to move aside. Her eyes met his, and for a heartbeat, the storm seemed to quiet.

"Sorry," he mumbled, embarrassed that his thoughts had taken him away from what he needed to be focused on. Offering her a hand, he assisted her down.

"Thank you," she said with a wobbly smile while blinking away the rain hitting her in the face. "My Cinderella chariot was getting wet, but it's even wetter out here." She moved around him and reached out to take Penny by the hand, guiding her toward the back of the vehicle.

He threw open the hatch, pulling out his bag of equipment. With practiced efficiency, he handed Tad another bag—one that carried food but no weapons. The boy took it with a solemn nod.

"Follow me," he ordered before heading up the road. He continually glanced over his shoulder to ensure everyone was all right. Noel guided Penny, with Tad bringing up the rear. He led the way up the muddy road, the relentless wind and rain turning every step into a battle.

Noel walked beside Penny, her arm around the girl's shoulders, offering steady reassurance. Tad trailed them, his face set with quiet determination. The boy's bravery struck Landon. For someone so young, Tad carried himself with a protector's heart. Landon couldn't help but respect the kid—Stan had raised him well.

Penny, despite her small size, pressed on with surprising strength. Landon noted her resolve, deciding she carried more of her grandmother's grit than her mother's flair. The thought gave him hope. They might be battered by the storm, but they'd get through this together.

With everyone falling in line and leaning into the wind, they made their way up the road until he could see the small structure off the side. The intel Sadie had sent made it look like it would be a good choice to wait out the storm. There was a narrow gravel path, and he had to lift the overhanging foliage out of the way. With each frond raised, he'd wait until Penny would pass under, and then Noel would take it from him, keeping it lifted for Tad.

Now, standing outside the small building, he glanced

over his shoulder. "Stand back," he ordered, pulling out his weapon. Knocking and receiving no answer, he shouldered the door open and, with a light in one hand and his gun in the other, swept the interior, finding it empty. It might have been a small home or waystation once, but it appeared to have been abandoned for years. There was no furniture, but at least the hard-packed dirt floor was blessedly dry.

Stepping inside to ensure no animals or varmints were around, he turned and called out, "Come on. It's safe."

Penny entered next, followed by Tad. Noel had stepped to the side before she brought up the rear. Once inside, her gaze swept the room before landing on him, and his heart stuttered as he waited to see what she would say about the rudimentary shelter.

She grinned. "Looks dry, and the wind can't knock us around here."

A release of breath left his lungs, pleased that she continued to adapt to the changes.

"These windows are boarded," Penny whispered.

Landon realized they were like the room where she and Tad had been held, but Noel jumped in before he could say anything. She walked over and stood directly in front of Penny, placing her hands on the girl's shoulders and pulling her in for a hug.

"Yeah, they are, sweetheart. But think of it this way... they aren't here to keep you in... to keep you trapped. They're boarded to keep you dry and safe with us." Noel leaned back and held Penny's gaze. "Right?"

Penny glanced at Tad before looking at Noel again. Then she nodded and let out a relieved breath. "Right."

"Okay, then," Noel said, stepping back and finding Landon. "What should we do to get settled for the evening? I assume it will be tomorrow before the storm stops, and someone can get the road cleared."

He almost informed her that his people would get to them quicker than the Jamaicans could get the road passable. Instead, he nodded and said, "There's a folded waterproof tarp in the bottom of the bag that Tad was carrying. Let's set that up for us to sit on."

Tad immediately knelt and reached inside the bag. He pulled out two pouches, and Landon nodded. "I forgot there were two. That'll give us plenty to sit on without having to be on the floor."

Noel reached out and took one of the tarps from Tad. They unfolded them, then spread them out next to two walls. Tad and Penny sat on one with their backs against the wall. Noel sat on the other one and looked up expectantly at Landon.

Sharing a piece of tarp with her suddenly seemed like an excellent idea… and a bad idea. Good, because he'd be close to her. Bad, because being that close made him think of how sweet her lips were. Determined not to embarrass himself, he placed the weapons bag close and sat with his back against the wall beside her. They were sitting at a right angle with the kids, keeping them close together. Their clothes were soaked, and he hoped they'd be able to stay warm enough.

Noel dug around in the bag that was closest, pulling out another water bottle. "Tad. Penny." Gaining their attention, she asked, "Did you have any water while you were away?"

Both shook their heads, so she handed them another bottle. "Make sure you stay hydrated."

Penny blushed, and Noel leaned closer. "If you need to go, I'll go outside with you."

Penny's lips curved as she nodded. Landon was glad Noel had thought of how a twelve-year-old girl might be embarrassed to ask about needing a bathroom break.

No longer needing his earpiece, Landon typed into his phone, giving their location and plans. He let LSIMT know they would spend the night in the small structure. He also told them that as soon as Cole and the others could get to Jamaica, he would get the kids and Noel west of the mudslide to meet up. The affirmative reply let him know that Logan and the others were in planning mode, and Landon had no doubt they'd be rescued tomorrow.

Looking down at the reply, he saw where Logan had spoken to both Stan and Pamela, each wanting to talk to the kids as soon as they could.

He scrubbed his hand over his face. "Your parents have been told that you're safe, and they want to talk to you. We'll play this however you want to."

"I'll talk to Dad," Tad said without hesitation. He twisted around and looked at his sister sitting next to him. "What about you, Sis?"

Penny rolled her lips inward, pressing them tightly as she looked down at her hands. Finally, heaving a great sigh, her shoulders rounded, and she said, "I'll talk to Dad, too. And I'll talk to Mom."

Landon was typing the request that LSIMT patch him to the ranch, knowing their satellite capabilities could bypass the storm wreaking havoc on cell signals and the internet.

"Wait," Tad said. "Before we talk to our parents, I want to know how this went down."

Landon believed in honesty and full disclosure, but he wasn't sure what to do when dealing with young people and children. Turning, he caught Noel's gaze. "Are you comfortable handling this?"

Nodding, she straightened her back, and an air of determination rolled off her. She angled her body slightly to face the kids more fully. "Your mother didn't have permission from your dad to bring you to Jamaica."

"How did Dad find out so quickly?" Tad asked. "We just got here yesterday, so she must have told him by yesterday afternoon."

"Yes, she did. Your mom called the ranch yesterday evening and talked to your dad. While the actual words spoken between the two of them are not known to me, she did make a demand—"

Tad snorted, his voice tinged with bitterness. "She wanted more money, right? Mom brought us down here so Dad couldn't just come get us, and she wanted more money."

Penny's head swung around, her eyes wide. Her gaze quickly darted to Noel and Landon, seeking confirmation. Landon held her stare for a moment but remained silent, allowing Noel to take the lead with the children.

Noel nodded gently, her expression calm but honest.

"That's true. She wanted your father to renegotiate the alimony agreement."

The four sat silently for a few minutes while the storm raged outside. Landon waited and watched to see how the children would process the harsh reality. Tad's shoulders tightened, his hands balling into fists on his lap. A low growl escaped him, a sound that seemed to rise from deep within his chest. It was obvious that the revelation cut deeply.

Landon shifted his gaze to Penny, and his heart clenched as he saw a tear slide down her cheek. Her small body trembled, her breath hitching as the storm outside seemed to mirror the turmoil within. Tad noticed immediately. He jerked his head toward her, then wrapped his arm around her shoulders and pulled her close, another sign that his protective instinct kicked in.

Noel's voice remained soft but steady as she continued. "I don't know your mother well enough to explain her actions or motivations. But I know she made demands, and your father and grandparents crafted a plan to handle the situation."

"They sent you to come get us," Penny whispered, her voice fragile.

Noel nodded. "Yes. Landon works for a security company. Your father and grandparents wanted to keep this situation out of the public eye, so they opted for a private solution."

Tad's sharp eyes turned to Landon, his voice probing. "Who do you work for?"

"I used to be an FBI agent," Landon replied, his tone

even. "Now I work for Lighthouse Security Investigations Montana."

Noel added, "Your grandfather is friends with a judge in Montana. That judge knew I had experience working on custody cases as a social worker. I got a call from my boss to go to the ranch this morning, and the next thing I knew, I was on a plane to Jamaica to ensure your safety."

"But you had no idea we'd been kidnapped," Penny said, her eyes pinned on Noel.

"That's right. When we came, it was just to bring you back to Montana."

Tad and Penny looked at each other, uncertainty written on their faces. Then Tad asked, "Why did they think we'd need a social worker to check on us if we were just going from our mom to our dad?" Then he looked over at Landon. "And why would they think someone from a private security agency might be needed?"

For the first time, Noel hesitated, looking down at her hands clasped in her lap. Landon knew what needed to be said and understood that Noel was gathering herself before giving the kids the news. Suddenly, wanting to spare her being the one to say the words, he blurted, "Because I brought a down payment to give to your mother."

A small gasp slipped from Noel's lips, Tad's chin jerked back, and Penny's mouth dropped open.

"A down payment?" Tad repeated, his voice cracking.

"Your mother agreed to sign the paperwork giving your dad full custody, and—"

"That sounds like Mom was selling us," Penny murmured, her blue eyes wide. Her hand jerked out, and she grabbed Tad's arm. Giving it a little shake, she said, "Tad? Is that what it sounds like to you, or am I crazy?"

Tad held Landon's gaze for a moment. Landon had no idea what the young man's reaction would be, but he didn't look away. He felt Noel's hand on his arm as though she was also seeking comfort.

"No, Sis, I don't think you're crazy. I think it sounds like Mom was selling us."

Noel sucked in a raspy breath. "That may be putting it in a harsher light than it has to be." Tad opened his mouth, and Landon was sure the boy would refute Noel's statement. But she threw her hand up and shook her head.

"Hear me out. I don't know your mom or her background. I don't know what her motivations were or what her situation is. I have not been privy to the alimony agreement, so I have no idea about her financial agreements. But I can tell you that the woman I met today, whose children had been snatched from the beach, was devastated. She was distraught and begged us to find you."

The kids stared at Noel as though their very reason for existing rested on her words.

"It struck me that perhaps she felt like she needed more money, so taking you all on a vacation and then holding that over your dad's head seemed like a good idea. She never intended harm. She probably assumed she'd still see you. So until you know her motivations for sure, don't assume the worst. Once you have all the facts, you can decide how you want to handle your ongoing relationship with your mom."

Landon thought Noel was painting Pamela in a light she didn't deserve, but he understood the kids needed something to hang on to… something that gave them hope that their mother wasn't as mercenary as she'd acted.

Once again, silence inside the room allowed the wind and rain to create background noise. Landon finally said, "As soon as we arrived, your mom had just found out from Horticia that you were taken. Our jobs changed… well, mine did. Instead of just making the exchange of money and signed paperwork, then ensuring you returned to Montana, my new mission was to rescue the two of you."

"Thank you," Penny whispered. "I can't believe that I didn't say that earlier."

Landon's lips curved slightly, and he inclined his head. "No thanks needed."

"So what now?" Tad asked. "I mean, after the storm passes?"

"We will head out in the morning and walk down the road to where we can be picked up. My coworkers have flown to Florida and will get to Jamaica in the morning. They will have a vehicle to get to us."

"And then?" Penny asked softly.

"Then we will go to your mom's place. We are in touch with your dad and will take our instructions from him. But I assume we will fly back to Montana immediately."

Penny let out a long sigh. "This is so messed up."

Tad tightened his arm around her. "No more messed up than it's always been." He looked at Landon. "I'm ready to talk to Dad."

Landon nodded and began typing on his phone. After a moment, he said, "Mr. Fugate. I have your children here. Tad would like to speak to you."

He handed the phone to the young man and waited as Tad told his dad they were safe and had not been harmed. "Listen, Dad, here's Penny so you can hear her voice, too." He handed the phone to his sister.

"Hey, Dad." She paused, then said, "Yeah, I'm okay. Landon says we should be home tomorrow." After another pause, she smiled. "Yeah, I miss you, too. Love you. Bye."

She returned the phone to Landon, her face contorted into a grimace.

"Are you okay, honey?" Noel asked, leaning forward so her hand rested on Penny's foot.

Penny opened her mouth to speak, but the words seemed to get stuck. She closed it again, her small face drawn with exhaustion and confusion. After a moment, she tried once more, her voice barely a whisper. "I guess I'm just tired."

Tad, sitting close beside her, nodded in agreement. "It's a lot to take in," he murmured, his voice steady but heavy with emotion.

Noel's gaze flicked between them, her eyes warm with understanding. "You're right," she said softly. "How about we let Landon's team tell your mom that you'll see her tomorrow? She already knows you're safe with us."

Both kids nodded, the tension in their small bodies easing just a little. Landon watched a tentative smile pass between Penny and Noel, a fragile but hopeful connection forming amid the chaos.

A thought snuck up on Landon, surprising in its simplicity yet profound in its intensity: he wanted to be on the receiving end of one of Noel's smiles. Not just a polite, passing one, but a real smile that would light up her face and reach her eyes, making him feel like he was the center of her world, if only for a moment.

His chest tightened at the thought, a feeling both foreign and welcome all at once. In the midst of a storm, he found himself craving something soft, something warm. And that something—or someone—was sitting right beside him.

16

Noel recognized the twins' physical fatigue, but she was more concerned with the emotional turmoil radiating from them. "If you want to try to sleep, please do. Get comfortable and just close your eyes."

"I don't think I can." Tad shook his head.

"Me either," Penny agreed.

"Do you want to talk? You can tell us anything, and it will stay just between us," Noel said. "But only if you want to. Only if you think it will help relieve the burden from your shoulders."

They were quiet for a moment, but she witnessed the myriad of emotions racing across their faces.

Finally, Penny said, "Mom always liked nice things. She met Dad when she was a freshman at college, and Dad was a senior." She snorted. "Mom always said she went to college for a MRS. degree. You know… just to find a husband." She shook her head and added, "God, that sounds so ridiculous."

Noel smiled. "While that's an antiquated reason for going to college, I suppose there are still women who have that in their minds."

"Mom's parents both died when we were younger, but they were great. It's not like Mom grew up poor. But their lives were more modest, and she told me that the first time Dad took her to the ranch, she just knew that was the life for her," Penny said. She shrugged, then looked at Tad while chewing on her bottom lip. "This feels like I'm being harsh, doesn't it?"

Tad shook his head. "No, Sis. Mom fell for Dad, and it wasn't a bad thing just because he came from more money. Until that became what meant more to her than anything. And then things at home weren't much fun anymore."

Noel continued to lean forward, listening carefully while keeping her gaze on them. She'd never counseled in the middle of a violent storm while sitting on a dirt floor in an old shed, but she'd always taken life as it came. And this was no different. "Did you feel more at ease or worse when your parents divorced?"

"Easier," Tad and Penny said at the same time, the word rushing from both before they chuckled ruefully.

Noel's chin jerked down as she blinked, then smiled. "Wow, that was definitive."

"I don't think Mom realized what was involved in running a ranch. She thought Dad should have a job where he wore a suit every day and hobnobbed with the governor or some such shit."

"Tad... language," Penny rebuked.

"Seriously? You think Dad and Grandpa don't curse?"

Penny's brow furrowed. "Well, not in front of me."

"After today, don't you think it's a little late for telling me not to say shit?"

"Okay, guys, I know your emotions are all over the place," Noel acknowledged. "Let's focus on those emotions right now."

Penny pressed her lips together but nodded.

"All I know is that Mom spent more time hounding Dad when he was trying to do his job… running the ranch. I heard them argue about me spending time on the ranch doing many of the jobs that ranch hands do. Dad said it was the way for me to appreciate all that went into having a successful ranch. Mom said it was demeaning to have her son shoveling horse shit."

Penny slowly nodded as her gaze met Noel's. "Yeah… she wanted me to go shopping or to weekend events, but I wanted to ride my horse. By the time we were ten, Dad was done fighting with her. We never heard the details, but she moved out, and we were told they were divorcing. Then we had to go to her condo to visit, so that changed some of our weekends."

"Only if she wasn't with one of her boyfriends."

Penny's shoulders slumped, and Noel felt for the young woman. "It's hard to accept when we realize our parents aren't perfect. Or perhaps they aren't acting in the way we wish they would."

Penny nodded. "I knew Roger was her boyfriend before this trip. He'd been over at her house, but I didn't know she was taking him with us until we got to the airport. He gives me the creeps."

Tad's head swung around as Landon barked out, "Why?"

Noel glared at Landon, then back to Penny. "Any special reason he gave you the creeps?"

"Just the way he looked at me on the plane. Not when Mom was around, but sometimes I'd look over, and he always stared at me. Then when we got here, he said we needed to spend as much time on the beach as possible since a storm was coming and we'd have limited beach time."

"This whole trip was stupid," Tad grumbled. "As soon as we got here, Horticia kept talking about the storm that was coming. Mom just grinned and said it might keep us here a couple of extra days. I told her I had a math test coming up, but she ignored me. Then Mom got mad at Roger and pouted in her room."

"When did Roger and Horticia get so close? I could see them outside my window when they were down in the garden after Mom stayed in her room," Penny asked Tad, twisting around to look at his face.

"Mom said she'd come down here before. Something about a man she knows who had invited her. What's weird is that I know she brought Roger here at least once because he mentioned it. Since Horticia works for some of the guests here, I guess she'd met Roger before."

"Horticia and Roger were awfully chummy yesterday." Penny huffed as her eyes narrowed. "I think he's a gigolo."

Noel's eyes bugged out as Tad snorted.

"Mom probably makes Roger jealous with talk of the other man, and then he makes her jealous with Horticia." Tad shrugged, then grimaced as he looked at Noel. "Mom doesn't make good choices."

Noel sighed and nodded. She had an intuition that Pamela's boy toy was banging the housekeeper. But then it seemed that Pamela was involved with the man who'd invited her to the island before.

"How chummy were Roger and Horticia?" Landon's low, steady voice broke through Noel's swirling thoughts.

She turned toward him, finding his sharp gaze fixed on the kids, his eyes narrowing slightly as he processed the information. His intensity was palpable, a constant undercurrent she had come to recognize.

"Um… after we got here yesterday, I saw them talking. I was looking out at the back gardens from my bedroom, and they were behind some of the bushes. They were talking at first, but then it looked like they were arguing. I couldn't hear what they were saying, though. After a while, they stepped out of my sight. Horticia came back into the house, but I saw Roger down on the beach later. I didn't want to go down there if he was around," Penny said.

Noel had no idea what was going through Landon's mind, but she turned to look at him. He held her gaze, but she couldn't read his thoughts. He sent a silent message with a quick shake of his head. She turned her attention back to the kids, sensing the need to shift the conversation.

"Is there anything else on your mind that you want to talk about tonight?" she asked gently.

Tad shook his head. "Not for me. I guess I'll figure out what to say to Mom when we see her tomorrow. But honestly, now that I know she brought us here without telling Dad and then tried to get more money from him... it makes it hard to know what to say to her."

His shoulders slumped, the weight of betrayal pressing down on him. At that moment, the determined young man was replaced by a heartbroken boy, and Noel's chest tightened with empathy. Before she could respond, Penny straightened, her hand reaching out to cover Tad's in a gesture of comfort.

"It'll be okay, Tad," she whispered, her small voice steady but filled with quiet resolve. "You know Mom's always been a little... flighty. I think she loves us in her own way, but it's not a healthy kind of love."

Noel's breath caught, the air rushing from her lungs. She had been bracing herself to console them, but now, here was Penny, taking on that role with a maturity beyond her years. "It's been a rough couple of days," Noel said softly, her voice thick with emotion. "Why don't you both try to get some rest?"

Tad nodded, his movements sluggish. "I'm not sure I can sleep," he admitted, though a yawn betrayed him.

As they settled down onto the tarp, their breathing soon deepened, the exhaustion of the past few days pulling them into sleep. Noel watched them for a moment, her heart aching for the burden these two young souls carried.

She leaned back, the storm's howling winds and

relentless rain filling the silence. Landon sat beside her, his focus glued to his phone, his fingers tapping furiously as he updated his team. The glow from the screen illuminated his face, casting shadows that emphasized the hard lines of his jaw and the determined set of his mouth.

Noel sighed, dropping her chin to her chest and rubbing her tired eyes. The whirlwind of the past twenty-four hours weighed heavily on her mind. What was supposed to be a straightforward trip had spiraled into chaos—an attempted extortion, a storm, a kidnapping, and a desperate rescue. *And I shot at a man.* The thought echoed in her head, the gravity of it still surreal. She couldn't imagine how it would feel if she'd actually hit him.

She'd been in the presence of law enforcement many times in her job, but none seemed to carry themselves with the edge of danger she felt pouring from Landon. Not danger to her or the children... but danger to anyone who might try to harm them. He'd charged ahead as soon as they'd neared the place where the kids were kept. His movements were sure and resolute. And even though he'd told her to stay in the vehicle, just being in his presence made her want to rush headlong into the unknown to ensure the kids were safe. *Who am I kidding? I wanted to make sure he was safe, too.* It had been a reckless act, yet, she hadn't hesitated. Not after the kiss they'd shared. She had never kissed someone on a case. Or kissed someone after just meeting them. Or kissed someone with such intensity. But just like in a movie, the kiss had felt right. The right time with the right man. She glanced to the side as though drawn to him.

His phone landed in his lap, and his gaze landed on her. "You okay?" he asked.

His voice was soft, making sure the kids were still asleep. She nodded. "Yes. Just a lot on my mind."

"Want to talk about it?"

A bubble of laughter burst forth, and she quickly slapped her hand over her mouth to muffle the sound. Seeing his brows draw together in a silent question, she whispered, "You're doing what I did to the kids earlier."

He smiled and nodded. "Yeah, but it helped them get their feelings out. Maybe it'll help you."

She had to admit his reasoning was sound. She leaned back and rested her head against the rough wooden wall. "I was trying to make sense of this day, but I'm not sure that any of it makes sense." She inhaled deeply, then slowly let the air free from her lungs. "I told you before that one of the things I like about my job is that everything is different. Some days more mundane than others, but even in my toughest cases, I've never had a day like today."

She rolled her head to the side and found his gaze on her. It was something she'd come to learn about Landon—when he listened, he gave his full attention. A warmth bloomed inside her chest, and she realized that the trait was rarer than most people would think. She had come to know we live in a society where people's attention spans have gone from about twenty minutes to about twenty seconds with all the distractions of cell phones and tablets. When world news was at our fingertips, the ability to truly listen to another human as they sometimes bumbled and fumbled through tangled emotions became lost. Counselors and social workers were trained to listen, and she supposed that investigators were, too.

She was suddenly very curious about him. "Is your day usually like this?"

A little smile played at the corners of his lips. "Like yours, my days vary. Sometimes, I'm the one in the office helping one of the other Keepers in the field." He shrugged. "Today, it was my day to lean on the others to help guide us through this."

"You may have leaned on them, but it was you running through the jungle to rescue those kids."

A chuckle rumbled from his chest. "If I recall correctly, I wasn't the only one who raced through the jungle to get to them."

She exhaled heavily while shaking her head. "I honestly can't tell you what I was thinking. I just knew I wanted to have eyes on you and them, not sit in the vehicle and just wait to see if someone was coming back for me."

"Well, you saved us, for sure."

"I think the saving was yours," she admitted. "I just happened to scare the man on the roof. I had no idea he'd fall off after hearing the gunshot." As soon as the words left her mouth, she noticed Landon staring at her, confusion flashing through his eyes before his face became blank again. She had to admit he was one of the most complex people she'd ever met. She also had to admit that she wanted to peel away the layers and find out more about him. He had not only piqued her curiosity but called to something deep and elemental inside her. Something heretofore untouched.

"What do you think about Pamela and what the kids told us?" she asked.

"Probably not much different from you. While I wouldn't want to say this to the kids, I'd have to agree that while I think she loves her children very much, she's driven by a selfish motivation. The Fugates are wealthy, no doubt about it. In many ways, their land is rich, even though I'd have to say they're not hurting for money in the bank or investments. Everything I turned up on them and then meeting them this morning, they struck me as hard-working people who appreciate what they've been given but didn't mind the effort it took to keep it going. Everything I knew about Pamela going into this was that she was considered money selfish. I think her actions today showed that she does love her children, but her actions placed them in a situation of being in danger."

Noel nodded. "We'll see how things go tomorrow, but at the moment, my recommendation will be that she has supervised visits with the kids, regardless of how the alimony situation gets settled. She's proven she can't be trusted."

Landon nodded. "I think that's the right decision." He chuckled and shook his head. "I realize you don't need my approval—"

"I might not need it, but it's nice to hear your thoughts were running along the same as mine." Rolling her head to the side, she added, "Something else came up that I wanted to ask you about."

He didn't say anything, but his attention stayed riveted on her. She glanced over to see that the children had not moved and then looked back at him. "It had to do with Penny's observation about Roger and Horticia. I felt your intensity change. Why was that? What do you think was happening?"

17

Landon had been sending messages to LSIMT, wanting them to investigate Horticia and Roger. From what the kids indicated, the two had met before yesterday and might have had an arrangement by the time Pamela devised this trip.

His gaze drifted to Noel, her profile illuminated by the dim glow of the flashlight perched nearby. She had been a revelation from the start—smart, resilient, fiercely protective of the kids. During every step of this chaotic mission, she had repeatedly proven herself. She wasn't just along for the ride but a vital part of this operation. He'd realized that, in truth, those qualities made her very similar to him.

And the kiss? Hell, he'd spent hours trying to push it from his mind, but it lingered, gnawing at him, refusing to be ignored. It wasn't just about attraction—though, God knew, he felt that in spades—it was about the way she had fit against him, the way her lips had sparked something deep and undeniable. And now, sitting so close their legs touched, her hand occasionally on his arm, he couldn't help but hope she'd want to kiss him again.

His fingers stilled as he finished his message. He looked over, drawn to her like a moth to a flame. Her head was down, but he could feel her attention on him, her presence grounding him in a way he hadn't expected. Her hair, still damp, had dried into soft curls framing her face, the earlier storm leaving its mark in the most enchanting way. She shivered slightly, her wet clothes clinging to her frame, and he hated seeing her cold.

When she finally spoke, her voice low and filled with concern, she pulled him from his thoughts. "What do you think was happening?"

He met her gaze, the vulnerability in her eyes pulling him closer. "When I surveilled the building where the kids were held, I overheard one of the men say something about it being payday. Another responded, 'Fucking easy. She set it up so easy.'"

Noel gasped. "She? Oh my God, do you think it was Pamela?" Before he had a chance to reply, Noel shook her head. "No, their mom had nothing to do with it. It must've been Horticia. Either on her own or with Roger."

"That's my guess, too."

"But won't he disappear? Now that they know the kids are safe?"

"I know the police have a lot to do, but with the storm passing farther away from the island and not hitting us directly, I assume their resources wouldn't be stretched so thin. My boss has already been in touch with the governor-general and the police commissioner. They've got Pamela's house under surveillance."

Eyes wide, Noel gasped again. "They suspect her?"

He shifted, turning fully toward her, their knees pressing together. The touch was subtle but searing, grounding him in the moment. He reached out, covering her hand with his. "I know this sounds harsh, but she set the wheels in motion that led to all this. She'll have to face that, at least until we get back tomorrow."

Noel let out a long, weary breath. "I hate it when kids are hurt by the people they should trust the most. Roger was after money, sure, but to go this far? To kidnap and terrify those kids? It's beyond despicable. Fucking worthless shits."

Her blunt words, so at odds with her gentle demeanor, caught him off guard. A bark of laughter escaped him, startling in its suddenness. He quickly stifled it, glancing at the kids to ensure they were still sleeping. His gaze flicked back to her, amusement lighting his eyes. "You're this pint-sized ray of sunshine, but damn, you've got a mouth on you. It's hilarious and unexpected."

A grin spread across her face, her eyes twinkling with a mix of pride and mischief. "Good to know I can still surprise you."

"Oh, you're a surprise, all right."

Their gazes held for a long moment. They were close—not close enough for him to taste her lips again, but close enough that he thought about it. And wondered why the hell he was thinking about it.

"Why did you leave the FBI?"

He blinked, her question coming out of the blue. "What?"

She hefted her shoulders in a little shrug. "I just wondered. I've worked with agents before. Not a lot, but in a couple of cases. Mostly when a parent took a child and crossed state lines." She shook her head and added, "Anyway, I just wondered. Why you left?"

He opened his mouth to give a pat answer, then shut his mouth as he stared at her. Her attention was riveted to him. He could feel her interest wasn't idle curiosity but something real. Something almost tangible. His tongue dragged over his bottom lip. Her gaze dropped to his mouth before shooting back to his eyes. Forcing his mind to her questions, he replied, "I got tired of the bureaucracy."

Her lips curved slightly. "Imagine that... the Bureau having too much bureaucracy."

He chuckled again, and this time, her smile widened until she pressed her fingers against her lips to hold in the sound.

"Smart-ass," he accused.

As their mirth waned, she said, "Sorry, I made a joke. I really do want to know."

He nodded and settled back to get more comfortable while making sure his leg still touched hers, wanting the physical connection. No... he needed the physical connection. Gathering his thoughts, he said, "I told you that my dad was a police officer. I didn't mention that he'd served in the Marines before that. I remember my dad wearing his uniform every day, and I thought he had the best job in the world."

"You wanted to be like him?"

"Oh, yeah. Absolutely hero-worshipped my dad." He smiled at the memories. "I was Recon for a tour but knew the military wasn't where my career lay. The bottom line was my commander was an asshole who ended up putting all of us in danger before he was reassigned. He was not booted out like he should have been but just reassigned so he could be an asshole to someone else. Anyway, I was recruited by the FBI, and I thought I'd found the right place for me. I was still following in my dad's footsteps but in a different way. I was trained as an investigator and became an agent. While the cases I worked and closed successfully kept me going, the politics, red tape, and posturing of those above made the field agents' jobs almost impossible at times."

"You started to doubt yourself, didn't you?"

Her words startled him. His gaze searched her eyes but found no recrimination in their depths. He nodded slowly. "I wondered if the problem was me. I left the Marines. I wanted to leave the Bureau. I never considered myself a quitter, but... fuck, yeah... I doubted myself."

"What did you do?"

"I was assigned to a California area, and I met Carson Dyer, the founder of Lighthouse Security Investigations West Coast." Seeing her head cock to the side, he explained, "The original is in Maine. The West Coast was the second branch."

"That's right. You mentioned that on the plane. It's such an interesting concept."

"The original one in Maine was near a lighthouse on the coast. It had significant meaning to the man who started the company. The employees are known as Keepers after the old lighthouse keepers."

"I was fascinated with lighthouses when I was young. My family would always visit them when we were traveling. I saw some in North Carolina and New England one summer." She pressed her lips together. "But... I get Maine. And I get California. But Montana? That's brilliant to think of light towers. Are there many in Montana?"

He grinned and nodded. "Not as many as there used to be, but it's the only state still with standing light towers on some mountains."

Her eyes widened, and even in the dim light, he could swear they twinkled. "Light towers guided the planes over dangerous peaks, and the lighthouses guided ships around dangerous shores."

"Same principle."

"Are you also known as a Keeper?"

"Yeah."

She leaned a little closer, her voice soft. "I like that, Landon. You seemed all hard and intense when we first met. Now you seem more... real."

Their gazes remained locked on each other, and the desire to lean closer to erase the distance was strong. But with the kids sleeping so near, he sucked in a deep breath through his nose and leaned back. She blinked and then shifted back, as well.

Clearing her throat, she asked, "So, um… you were talking about your job…"

"Right. Yes. Well, I finally was able to use the skills the Keepers used. They investigated without the red tape and restrictions that were placed on me. They often solve cases and then turn over the evidence to the police, the Bureau, or the CIA. They didn't care about the glory. They just wanted to keep people safe. After several years, I knew I wanted to do that."

"So you joined?" As soon as she asked the question, she shook her head. "But that was California? How did you get to Montana?"

"I felt the need to start over. When I learned that the LSI Montana was just beginning, I met the man who would become my boss. I was offered the chance to get in on the ground up and be part of the beginning. It was an offer I couldn't refuse."

Her gaze dropped to his mouth. "And from the smile on your face, I take it that it was the right career move."

His chest moved up and down as he chuckled. "Hell yeah. I finally found where I fit. Best boss and the best people to work with. And the cases are ones I can sink my teeth into. Some are more boring than others. But all are different, allowing me to learn, grow, and do what I was born to do." As she cocked her head to the side again, he said, "Protect."

Her face lit and he was struck with the full force of her smile. Everything about her was beautiful—pale complexion with a smattering of freckles across her nose, and her eyes appeared large as her now dry hair waved about her shoulders.

"And your family?"

He jumped slightly, dragging his focus back to the topic. "My parents moved from Pennsylvania to South Carolina when Dad retired. My brother lives in California. He's got a degree in some tech field. We're not real close since he's almost eight years younger than me. But he's got a good job, and we see each other for the holidays."

They settled into a comfortable silence, one that wrapped around Landon like a worn, familiar blanket. It had been a long time since he'd felt this kind of ease with a woman. His years with the Bureau had left little room for personal connections. Dating within the agency was a complication he'd avoided, knowing the messy entanglements that could follow. Outside the job, his relationships had been fleeting, often limited to short-lived encounters during the tourist season in Montana—no strings, no expectations. Just a nice dinner, some conversation, and a mutual physical release that ended with no lingering attachments.

But Noel was different.

He glanced over at her, taking in the way she leaned back, her eyes gently closed, her features softened in the dim light. She had been a surprise from the start—insightful, dedicated, and fiercely caring. She wasn't afraid to step into danger, even when it meant chasing him in a storm with nothing but sheer will and a gun she'd barely handled. *Impulsive, sure.* But he couldn't deny her bravery, her determination.

And she was beautiful. Not just in the way her features were arranged, but in the way she moved, the way she cared for the kids, the way she stood her ground. Something about her got under his skin in a way he hadn't expected, hadn't wanted, but now couldn't shake.

He'd requested her background from LSIMT the moment he knew she'd be joining the mission. He'd learned the essentials—born and raised in Billings, a younger sister named Joy, parents still alive and evidently enthusiastic about family holidays. It made him realize how little he knew her beyond the dossier facts and how much more he wanted to know.

The thought of her surrounded by family, laughter, and love painted a picture so different from his own solitary life. His family was loving, but they didn't see each other often. She didn't stir, and her breathing was even, though he could tell she wasn't asleep. A serenity about her drew him in, and without thinking, he spoke softly. "Are you asleep?"

Her eyes fluttered open, locking onto his. A soft smile curved her lips. "No, just resting. I'm tired, but I don't think I can sleep right now." She tilted her head slightly, her gaze steady. "Did you need something?"

Landon hesitated for a moment, his fingers twitching with the urge to reach out. "I was just wondering about you. I've done all the talking but realize I don't know much about you."

Her eyes lit up, a spark of warmth that seemed to glow from within. His chest tightened at the sight, a strange mix of anticipation and something deeper, something he wasn't ready to name. But as she held his gaze, he felt an unspoken understanding pass between them.

"I'm an open book," she said softly, her smile widening. And at that moment, Landon knew he wanted nothing more than to read every chapter of her story.

"Compared to your life, mine is very simple, Landon. I suppose we have a lot in common. My family is very close. My parents are still living together, which is becoming rarer in this day and age. You have a younger brother, and I have a younger sister." She laughed, then clapped her hand over her mouth and glanced toward Tad and Penny. Turning her attention back to Landon, she continued to whisper. "My sister is three years younger, and her name is Joy. My parents met in college at a Christmas dance. They began to date, and two years later, my dad asked her to marry him on Christmas Eve. They were married a year later."

"Christmas Day?" he asked.

She shook her head. "No, but they did get married on Christmas Eve."

A smile stayed on her face as she continued. "My dad is the kind of man who not only went out to cut down a Christmas tree for us but would go to the local tree farm and pay for ten other trees to be given to families who couldn't afford them. The tree farmer always worked with various churches and social services to find out who might need help."

She smiled at the memory. "My mom had been an office assistant in a medical group. When the doctor retired, she learned about an opening at our local

Department of Social Services. She worked for them for fifteen years before retiring. My parents didn't just talk about helping others—they lived that kind of life. We weren't wealthy, but we had money. I never had to worry about clothes, food, or housing. But my parents ensured that my sister and I understood that many people didn't have those basic necessities. When I was in high school, I started a community service project where anyone in the school who wanted to adopt a family for the holidays could do so. Their names were kept private, but the wishes of the kids, their ages, and sizes were given out, and we helped seventy-three children have the most amazing Christmases."

"That's amazing," he said. "I'm incredibly impressed, Noel."

She shook her head and waved her hand dismissively. "I just had the idea, and Mom helped me develop the plans. But it was all the people in the school who worked together to make that happen."

He thought back to the women the Keepers in California had ended up with—all wonderful, accomplished women with big hearts. He hadn't met anyone like that until now. The more he learned about Noel, the more he wanted to know.

"So you carried that kind of concern into your career."

Nodding, she said, "My mom had the opportunity to work for several social workers, and one summer after my freshman year of college, I did an internship with them. From that moment on, I felt like everything I'd been planning for my whole life came to a pinpoint, and it helped me discover that was my calling. And working with children just came naturally for me."

"It's a difficult job," he said. "And one that I can imagine takes a toll on you."

"The first time I was called to the hospital to work with a child who'd been abused," Noel said, her voice soft yet steady, "I walked in, smiled at the little girl, and then immediately turned around and walked back into the hall. I started crying. I couldn't help it. The weight of it all just hit me."

Landon's eyes never left her, sensing the vulnerability in her words.

"There was this kind nurse," Noel continued, her gaze distant as if she were back there. "She saw me falling apart and gently guided me to the break room. She didn't say much at first, just let me cry. Then she told me something I've never forgotten. She said, 'If you ever get to the point where you don't cry when you see an abused child, that's when it's time to quit.' Her words... they saved me that day. I was questioning everything, wondering if I was even cut out for this."

"Jesus, Noel," Landon whispered, the raw emotion in her story slicing through him.

"I washed my face, pulled myself together, and walked back into that room." Her voice wavered slightly, but her determination shone through. "I smiled and talked to a little three-year-old girl who had two black eyes, a broken arm, and a head injury. She was so small, so scared. The only comfort was knowing she was medicated enough to dull the pain. And at that moment, I made a promise to myself—I was going to do everything in my power to take down the monster who did that to her."

Landon studied her, his chest tightening. The petite woman before him radiated a quiet strength, one that had been forged in experiences most people couldn't fathom. She might appear delicate at first glance, but her resolve and fierce compassion made her a force to be reckoned with. And damn, if that wasn't the most enticing combination he'd ever encountered.

He clenched his fists, struggling against the overwhelming urge to pull her into his arms, to feel the warmth of her body against his and kiss away the shadows in her eyes. His gaze flicked to the sleeping kids, their peaceful faces a reminder of why they couldn't afford any distractions right now. *But if we were alone...*

His eyes found hers again, and for a moment, the world narrowed to just the two of them. The storm outside, the chaos they'd endured—it all faded. All that mattered was the woman beside him, her courage and vulnerability drawing him in like a siren's call.

18

Noel blinked her eyes open, her senses slowly coming to life. Something had woken her, though she couldn't immediately pinpoint what. The unfamiliar weight beneath her head wasn't her usual pillow, and the air around her was eerily still. She strained to listen but was met with... nothing. *Nothing?*

Then the realization hit her like a wave. The storm had passed. The once relentless wind and rain were gone, leaving an almost suffocating silence in their wake.

A slight movement behind her tugged at her attention. Her mind processed the sensations slowly—a warm body pressed against her back, an arm wrapped snugly around her waist, and a leg tangled with hers. *Tad and Penny were on the other tarp...*

Her breath caught as clarity struck, and her eyes snapped wide open. There was only one possible explanation. *Landon.*

Before she could react, the arm around her waist

tightened briefly, a possessive yet gentle squeeze, before loosening. "Morning," said a sleep-rough, distinctly male voice, warm and low against her ear.

The deep timbre sent a shiver down her spine as he shifted, pulling away. The loss of his warmth left her feeling oddly bereft as well as chilled.

"G... good morning," she managed, her voice unsteady as she pushed herself up to sit. She glanced down, taking in their tangled sleeping arrangement. She had spent the night wrapped in Landon's arms, the man who had swooped in like a hero to rescue the kids and, quite possibly, her heart.

And waking up in his arms felt good. Really good. The kind of good that made her wish they'd slept in the same position in other circumstances. *Such as a big bed after a night of hot, sweaty sex.* She closed her eyes at the thought, not wanting to look at him in case his X-ray vision could see the images racing through her mind.

Her heart pounded, and she could only hope he didn't notice the heat creeping up her neck. This mission was complicated enough without adding her traitorous desires into the mix.

Tad stirred, groaning as he sat up and looked down at Penny, still curled on her side, although her eyes were now open.

The two kids looked adorably rumpled, and if she didn't know better, she could almost imagine they hadn't been through the kidnapping yesterday. Tad scrubbed his hand over his head, making his hair stand up.

But as Penny sat up, her sleep-eased expression

morphed into fear. "Is the storm over? Can we go home today? I want to go home!" Her voice rose with each word, panic on her face.

"Hey, hey, hey," Noel comforted, pushing to a stand before crouching in front of Penny. "You're fine, honey. We're all fine. We've got a gourmet meal of more protein bars and water. We slept in this five-star accommodations—"

Penny giggled, a sweet, melodic sound that cut through the tension lingering in the air. Tad snorted, his expression softening, and Noel felt a wave of relief wash over her. She considered that a win. "Let's get moving. How about you and I visit the ladies' room, otherwise known as a tree with lots of leaves around?"

Penny giggled again before her eyes turned to Tad. "You okay?"

"Sure, Sis. You go on with Noel."

Noel glanced toward Landon, seeking his silent approval before stepping outside. His intense gaze was locked onto her, and her heart skipped a beat, her breath catching in her throat. Blinking rapidly, she murmured, "Is it safe for us to go out?"

Nodding, Landon said, "Let me take a look first." His gaze dragged from her over to Tad. "Stay here and keep an eye on them while I check out there, and then we can go out after them."

She swung her head around in time to see Tad's look of pride. Landon had given him a sense of responsibility, a role to play amid the chaos. It wasn't about gender or strength—it was about giving Tad something solid to cling to in a world that had spiraled out of control.

Landon stood, stretching his arms high above his head. The motion was fluid, unhurried, and Noel couldn't help but notice the way his muscles shifted beneath his shirt. She swallowed hard, her gaze trailing after him as he strode toward the door, the memory of his warmth still vivid against her skin. And the memory of their kiss yesterday. Fast, hard, and full of unspoken promise. It had left her reeling, her heart pounding in a way she hadn't felt in years.

He came back in and nodded. "It's good for you to head outside. It's wet, and the ground is slippery, so don't go too far."

Nodding, she scrambled up and offered a hand to Penny. "Let's go powder our noses, shall we?" she asked in an overly exaggerated haughty tone.

Penny laughed, and the two walked outside. They walked down the path a little way. She wasn't surprised the area was soaked from the storm, but it certainly made it harder to find a place to squat.

"Boys have it easy," Penny grumbled.

Noel chuckled in her agreement. She shoved a tissue from her purse into Penny's hand. "Okay, a spot behind that tree is about as dry as you'll get. I'll go on this side of the path." They separated, and a moment later, after their bladders were relieved, they met on the path again. Penny's color had returned, and so had her shy smile.

"Feel better?" Noel asked.

"Yes, and thank you, Noel."

Noel wrapped her arm around the young girl's shoulders. "How are you doing this morning?"

Penny looked up at her and pressed her lips

together. "It seems like a bad dream. I mean... all of this." She sighed. "Mom is doing her typical selfish stuff, always trying to get one over on Dad. Then those men —" She sucked in a shallow breath.

"Hey, sweetheart," Noel said, turning to face Penny, then bending slightly so she was directly in front of her. "We are not going to pretend that yesterday didn't happen. We're going to talk about it. Face it. We'll get you home with your dad and grandparents and make sure you have a good counselor to talk about it. And keep in mind that you and your brother are survivors."

She shrugged. "I didn't do anything..."

"That's not true. When I arrived, you were on Landon's back as he scaled down the wall like Spider-Man."

Penny chuckled, and her eyes lit. "It was kind of crazy, wasn't it?"

"Honey, it was beyond crazy. But you did what he asked. You didn't fall apart. You followed directions. You helped save yourself, even if that was just helping the person sent to save you."

Penny held her gaze. "You're good at this."

Cocking her head, Noel waited.

"You know... good at making me feel better."

Smiling, Noel brushed her hand over Penny's hair and cupped her cheek. "Thank you, sweetheart. Just keep remembering that you're safe." She moved closer to the door. "Now, let's go have that gourmet breakfast."

As soon as they entered, she found Landon's gaze on her again. Even more intense than before. Tad walked past her to go outside, and as Landon followed, he stopped next to her. Bending, he whispered, "You are good at this. I'm glad you forced yourself on me."

She blinked as she stared up at him. "Forced myself on you?" She suddenly wondered what she had done in the middle of the night when they were curled around each other.

His lips curved in a slow grin. "Yeah. Forced yourself to accompany me on this part of the trip."

"Oh. Oh... yeah... right." Her face heated, and her eyes narrowed as his grin widened. Playfully slapping him on the arm, she said, "Go on. Get out of here."

He dipped his chin, then turned and followed Tad out the door. She let out a long, slow breath, gave a moment for her cheeks to cool, then slapped on a smile and turned around. Penny was staring at her but didn't say anything, for which Noel was glad. If the young girl had wondered what was happening, Noel would have had no idea how to explain it when she didn't understand it herself.

She found the stash of protein bars and handed one to Penny and another bottle of water. "You'll need to share the water with Tad when he returns." Penny nodded and leaned against the side wall as Noel picked up the tarps and began to fold them.

Near the back, she heard voices. She hadn't planned on listening, but her ears perked up.

"I was scared," Tad said.

"Nothing wrong with that," Landon replied. "I would have thought something was wrong with you if you hadn't been scared."

There were a few seconds of silence before Tad

admitted, "I was afraid of what they might do to Penny. I didn't know what to do, but I knew I had to stay between them and her. But I keep thinking, what if—"

"Don't," Landon ordered. "Don't torture yourself with *what-ifs*. Just think of what you said—you knew you had to stay between them and her. You put yourself out there to protect your sister. At your age? That's fucking huge, Tad. That means that at only twelve, you've learned about being a man besides just enjoying being a kid. You've got the heart of a protector. You hold on to that. You nourish and nurture that part of you."

"You think so?"

"I know so."

"Thanks, Landon. Coming from you, that means a lot."

Noel barely breathed as she leaned closer to the back wall. No more sounds were heard until footsteps neared the door, and she jerked around to find Penny still staring at her. She had a feeling they had both witnessed Tad's fears and insecurities as well as Landon's words of praise. Her chest swelled with an emotion she couldn't define, but as Landon walked through the door, she had to force her legs to stay in place so she wouldn't run and throw herself at him.

Tad moved over to take the water from Penny's outstretched hand while Landon stopped and stared at Noel. She knew a goofy smile must be on her face as his gaze wandered over her, and his lips twitched. "Here," she said, handing protein bars to Tad and Landon. Then before she embarrassed herself more, she bent to fold the last tarp, shoving it into the pack.

Landon knelt next to her and placed his hand over hers. "I've got it," he said, his voice still growly, but now the sound oozed through her like melted chocolate—gooey and delicious.

Clearing her throat, she asked, "So, what's the plan?"

"Storm is passed. We need to walk down the road and past the mudslide. My people have just flown in and will get a vehicle up here to meet us."

"And then?" Penny asked.

Landon stood, offered his hand to assist Noel, and turned to face Penny. "Then we'll go back to your mom's place. You need food, a shower, and a chance to get your things."

"Oh my goodness," Noel said, her eyes wide. "We forgot to tell you that your dad sent Mike Westerly to come with us. He's a familiar face to make you feel better."

"Big Mike is here?" the kids shouted with broad smiles on their faces.

"Yes. He's with your mom, and you'll see him soon. Then we'll fly back to Montana."

Tad and Penny nodded, the news seeming to give them energy. As Landon swung his pack over his shoulders, Tad leaned down to grab the lighter bag. They filed out of the small shack, and Noel glanced back. Hard dirt floor. Cinder block and wood walls. Rudimentary and crude. Yet the small building would stay in her memory as a shelter. A respite. And a place where she got to know more about the man who'd captured her attention.

19

The golden light of the post-storm day stretched across the sky as the four of them made their way down the mountain. The asphalt road was slick with patches of lingering puddles. The sun's warmth began drying the foliage, but where the jungle canopy was thick, the road remained damp, casting a subtle gleam underfoot. Landon took the lead, his steps measured and steady, ensuring the pace was comfortable for everyone. Tad followed closely, his youthful energy tempered by the events of the past days. Penny and Noel walked just behind, their soft conversation blending with the sounds of the waking jungle.

Tad's voice broke the peaceful quiet. "So how do you get to do what you do? Are there like… classes you can take or something?"

Landon glanced over his shoulder, catching the boy's curious gaze. He chuckled, shaking his head slightly. "It's not exactly about taking a class. It's more about… finding yourself."

Tad frowned, his brow furrowed in confusion. "Huh?"

Landon paused, considering how best to explain. He was used to answering questions from adults, not from a boy still discovering his place in the world. His thoughts drifted back to Noel, her gentle yet probing questions the day before about his journey from the Bureau to his current role.

"I was in the military first," Landon said, his voice steady. "After I got out, I joined the FBI."

"The FBI?" Tad's eyes lit up, his face a mix of awe and excitement. "You were an FBI agent?"

Landon chuckled at Tad's enthusiasm, a flash of amusement brightening his features. "Yeah, but it's not as glamorous as it sounds."

"And you left?" Tad's voice was filled with disbelief, as though leaving something as cool as the FBI was unthinkable.

"I had the chance to join a private security and investigative firm. I found that I liked it more—it gave me different challenges, a different kind of freedom. So, when they opened a new office in Montana, I made the move."

"Whoa... that sounds really cool," Tad admitted, his admiration clear. "I've never really thought about doing anything except working on the ranch, like my dad and grandpa."

Landon's gaze softened. "There's nothing wrong with that, Tad. Your family has taught you the value of hard work, dedication, and strong morals. Those are the kind of things that can take you far, no matter what path you choose."

Tad nodded slowly, digesting Landon's words. They continued walking, the early morning light filtering through the trees and casting alternating sunspots and shadows across the road. Birds, silent yesterday, now chirped loudly. Penny's and Noel's soft laughter floated on the breeze, and for now, the world felt safe.

Landon couldn't help but glance back, his eyes catching Noel's. She offered him a small smile, and his chest tightened. She had a way of grounding him, even when the world around them felt like it was spinning out of control. *Maybe finding yourself isn't just about the work you do... perhaps it's also about the people who walk beside you.*

"What about you, Penny?" Noel asked. "What would you like to do?"

"I've thought about the ranch, too. I could help Tad run it. But I really like to write."

Noel's brows lifted. "Fiction? Stories?"

Penny blushed but nodded. "I like to write stories about the ranch."

Tad twisted around and grinned. "Her stories are great. They're better than a lot of things I read from the library."

"Maybe you could be a rancher-writer-horse rider-author," Noel said. "The sky is the limit, sweetheart!"

Landon glanced back and witnessed Penny's broad smile, Tad's grin, and how Noel's face lit with excitement. And his chest twinged at the sight.

He kept his watch vigilant but neither saw nor heard

anything remotely suspicious or dangerous. With the downed trees behind them where they'd left the vehicle and the mudslide still ahead, they didn't come across any other people for the first hour they walked.

His phone vibrated, and he grinned when he saw Devil's name. "Hey, man. You make it to Jamaica?"

"We're here. Sadie sent your location. Looks like you're on the old mountain pass road."

"We're not to the mudslide yet, and I have no way to tell if there's more than one place the road is impassable."

"Let us worry about that. According to what we can find out, that's the only one that has the road closed, and some locals are already trying to dig out enough to get at least one lane passable. Frazier and I came in with Cole. The charter that couldn't wait for you isn't here, but Cole's got a Gulfstream, so we've got plenty of room for heading back. Although if Pamela plans on coming, too, she might have to fly on the wing."

Landon barked out a laugh. "Don't think that'll be a problem. It'll just be us, Noel, the kids, and Mike Westerly."

"We didn't stop at the resort. We got a vehicle and started up the road as soon as we landed."

"It'll be good to see you."

"I'll let you know where we'll meet."

Disconnecting, he looked at the interested faces of the others. "One of my people. They've made it to Jamaica and are in a vehicle on their way up the mountain. Hopefully, we'll meet up with them soon."

They continued their steady pace, the quiet of the morning broken only by the rustling leaves and the occasional call of a distant bird. After a while, Penny's soft voice rose above the ambient sounds. "It's pretty here, isn't it?"

Landon glanced over his shoulder, catching sight of Noel's gentle smile as she looked over at the young girl.

"When we first arrived at the resort, I thought it was beautiful," Penny continued. "All the flower gardens, the perfectly trimmed trees and shrubs, the mowed lawns, and those beaches with the little thatched huts for shade. Even the servers bringing snacks to the beach seemed... nice." She wrinkled her nose, her tone shifting. "But it's all for show, isn't it?"

Tad tilted his head, curiosity piqued. "What do you mean?"

"It's like our ranch," Penny explained, her voice gaining confidence. "Daddy always says it's a working ranch. It's beautiful, sure—big barns, open paddocks, and wide fields. But it's real. I remember Mom once said she wished it was more... glamorous. She'd been to one of those vacation ranches and liked how they brought wine to the guests while they rode horses. She didn't get why Dad wouldn't turn our place into something like that."

She snorted, shaking her head as if the memory was ridiculous. "Dad said he wasn't about to have tourists sipping wine while his hands were out there busting their butts doing real work."

Tad nodded, his gaze sweeping the dense jungle

surrounding them. "I get it now. There's nothing wrong with those fancy places, but this... this is the real Jamaican jungle, isn't it?"

Penny's face lit up with understanding. "Exactly. It feels so real out here. The trees are tall and wild, and you can hear the birds calling from deep in the forest. I'm not happy about what happened... but now that we're safe, it's kind of amazing to see this part of the island."

"I've just got to say that I think you two are the neatest kids I've met in a long time," Noel said, smiling. "Totally and completely resilient." Then she looked at Tad. "I'm going to tell you the same thing I told your sister this morning. What you went through is traumatic, and we're going to make sure that you have a counselor to talk to about it. And I am always available. But you should be so proud of how you are handling everything. There's no shame in being upset, but I think it's amazing how resilient you are."

Landon nodded in agreement, his deep voice steady. "I second that." He reached out and clapped Tad on the shoulder, his touch firm but reassuring. "Your dad and grandparents are going to be so proud of you both."

His phone vibrated again, and he looked down at the message, then his head shot up. "Look ahead," he called out. Before them, the road was blockaded with mud and rocks, but they could discern a group of people with shovels and tractors with loaders moving the debris from the outer lane.

"Oh, my goodness!" Noel cried out. "There are so many people working to clear the road!"

"It's a main road through the area," Landon said. "People depend on it being passable." As his footsteps moved through the mud, he reached over to take Penny's hand, proud to see Tad do the same with Noel. They made their way past some of the people working, waving as they called out their thanks and greetings.

A small boy was running back and forth, pushing his shovel along the rough asphalt, helping to clear the path. Penny stopped and reached inside her pocket, offering the last protein bar. The little boy ducked his head and then smiled as he took it. A woman to the side hurried over and held out a basket with fruit. "Please, take some."

Penny looked at Landon, and he nodded his permission. Penny took a mango and then offered one to Noel. Thanking the woman who now had moved to stand near her young son, they continued past the work area.

Landon looked ahead and grinned, tossing his hand into the air. Ahead of them, among the line of cars and buses, was a large SUV, and standing outside were Devil and Frazier.

"Those are your friends?" Noel asked, her eyes wide.

Landon swung his head around, a strange gut-punch of jealousy hitting him. "Yeah," he said, eyeing her carefully.

Her attention was riveted on him. "Well, thank God they're as reliable as you. I had no idea they'd get to us so quickly." Shoulder bumping him, she smiled, her gaze not wavering from his face.

He shook his head and grinned in return. *No pretenses with her. She's as real as they come.* He had no idea how he could be so sure after only knowing her a day, but there was no doubt.

As soon as they neared, he was engulfed in man-hugs and back slaps, first with Devil and then Frazier. Turning, he made the introductions. "Gentlemen, I'd like you to meet Ms. Noel Lennox. And this is Tad and Penny Fugate." Waving his hand in the Keepers' direction, he continued, "These are two of my coworkers, Jim Devlin and Frazier Dolby."

Handshakes ensued with a smiling Noel, an awestruck Tad, and a blushing Penny. Chuckling, he looked over at his friends. "You are a sight for sore eyes."

Devil glanced at the others, then settled his gaze back on Landon. "All okay?"

He lifted his chin. "Ready to get back home to Montana, but yeah… all okay."

"All right, then," Frazier said, waving his hand toward the large SUV. "Let's hit the road. I'm sure you all are hungry, tired, and ready for food and a hot shower."

Agreeing, the group moved past the row of other vehicles lining the road. Throwing open the doors, Frazier stood to the side and said, "Tad, can you and your sister squish in the back seat?"

"Sure, no problem." Tad climbed in and slid to the far side.

Frazier stepped back, and Landon knew his friend had considered Penny's ordeal, not wanting to overwhelm the much smaller girl. Stepping up, Landon offered his hand to Penny, pleased when she accepted his assistance into the SUV. She clambered into the back seat with Tad, taking the middle of the bench seat. Frazier started to offer Noel his hand, but Landon moved closer. "I've got her."

Frazier grinned widely, then climbed into the front passenger seat. Devil had walked to the other side and settled behind the steering wheel. Landon took the remaining space on the back seat and patted his lap. Noel rolled her eyes but sat on his lap.

They hit a pothole as Devil turned the SUV around to head back down the mountain, and Noel laughed. She turned, and her face was so close to Landon that their noses were almost touching.

"You're going to severely regret having me sit on your lap if we keep hitting potholes," she said with a smile.

His arms tightened around her, and he shook his head. "I'll be fine." He turned his head so that it looked like he was staring out the window when he was moving his mouth closer to her ear. He whispered, "There's nowhere else I'd rather you be than where you are right now." To punctuate his words, he gave her a little squeeze. Leaning back, he watched her eyes widen, and he could've sworn they twinkled.

"Oh, my gosh," Penny said. "Look at this."

It was the first chance that Landon, Noel, and the kids could see the evidence left from the storm. Some trees were blown over. Wooden structures had lost their roof. And some of the lower streets were still draining water. The Jamaicans were out and about with shovels and brooms, sweeping, and cleaning.

"They're smiling," Penny said with a touch of wonder.

"This was just the outer edges of a hurricane—really only a tropical storm for these people. They've lived through many and know how much worse it could've been."

Both kids' heads swung back and forth to look out the windows, taking it all in.

Landon was impressed—for twelve years old, they were smart and intuitive. It seems they had much more of their father than their mother.

As they neared the resort, Tad asked, "What's the plan?"

"We're going to your mom's place, where you will see her, also Mike. I know you're hungry and would love to take a shower and have clean clothes. I know you want to return to Montana, but there's no rush. You'll have a chance to talk to your dad, and once you're ready, packed up, have eaten, and said goodbye to your mom, then we head to the airport."

Looking toward the front, Landon asked, "Is Cole with the plane?"

Devil nodded. "Yeah, he stayed at the airport. He wanted to ensure the plane was safe, even though it was in the hangar. He'll be ready whenever we are."

It was strange, the feeling that moved through Landon. At the end of each mission, he was always glad when it was over. But now, with his arms around Noel's waist as her ass was settled in his lap, thoughts of her lips and the way she felt remained firmly in his mind. And the idea that they would say goodbye and never see each other again struck him.

Deciding not to worry about that now, he determined he'd make sure he'd see her again.

20

The SUV pulled into the resort house driveway and barely stopped when the front door opened. Mike rushed out, followed quickly by Pamela, both shoving each other out of the way. It was easy for Noel to see that the two of them could barely stand to be in each other's company, both vying for the kids' attention simultaneously.

Pamela pushed by the older man and screamed as she raced down the walk. "My babies! My babies!"

Tad opened his door and alighted. Pamela tried to grab him, but he turned and helped Penny down. Pamela continued to scream their names as her arms encircled them both. Frazier opened the back passenger door and lifted a brow at Landon. If she wondered why Frazier didn't offer his hand to her, it was apparent when Landon grunted, "I've got her."

Frazier grinned. "Figured you did."

A smile curved her lips. She never thought the

caveman approach was sexy but was about to change her opinion. Once she was out of the vehicle, all thoughts of the sexy Landon were set aside as she rounded the vehicle to stand with the kids. Mike hugged Tad and Penny while Pamela had blessedly stopped screaming as she stood to the side.

"Big Mike! I can't believe you're here!" Tad's smile grew wider as he looked up at the familiar ranch manager.

"Your dad sent me to make sure you two had someone you knew to travel with you on the way home. But we never counted on anything happening." He teared up. "Damn, I'm glad to see you. Your dad and grandparents will be overjoyed."

"They've got their mother here!" Pamela bit out.

Seeing Penny's pale face and dark circles underneath her eyes, Noel stepped forward. "The kids need a shower, clean clothes, and a good meal."

"Yes, yes," Pamela agreed, nodding emphatically. She looked toward a wide-eyed Horticia, standing at the entrance with Roger beside her. "Don't just stand there! Get some food!"

Horticia nodded in haste before darting back inside, quickly followed by Roger. The fact that they had almost identical bandages on their foreheads struck Noel, something she hadn't taken the time to notice when they'd first learned the kids had been taken. She glanced over at Landon, who stood with Devil and Frazier. The three men's gazes were locked on the front where Horticia and Roger had stood, then bent their heads together as they talked. Pressing her lips tight, she returned her attention to Tad and Penny. "Let's get inside."

Horticia had sandwiches quickly made, along with an assortment of chips, salad, and a veggie tray. It struck Noel that the housekeeper must have known when they'd arrive, considering the food was already prepared. She encouraged the kids to go first, and then followed, not ashamed to admit she was hungry. Glancing over her shoulder, she made eye contact with Landon and smiled, knowing he would eat after the others were served. Tad and Penny sat at the table, while the adults moved around the open rooms. Noel stood at the counter, wanting to keep an eye on them while not hovering. After a few minutes, Roger sat at the table beside Tad.

"How're you doin', man?" Roger asked.

Tad turned to him, confusion in his eyes. "Um... good."

"Must have been scary, getting taken like that."

Tad's brows snapped together, and he glanced at Penny before turning his attention back to his lunch and mumbling, "Yeah."

Noel set her sandwich down on her plate, ready to blast Roger for his insensitivity. As she started to push away from the counter, she caught Landon's gaze on her and the hasty but distinct shake of his head. She didn't know why he wanted her to stay where she was, but she trusted him even though it felt wrong. Pressing her lips together, she remained in place but turned her attention back to the kitchen table.

"So, uh... did you talk to them or anything? Like

have a conversation... or, um... hear them talking?" Roger pressed while glancing furtively around.

Noel noted Landon was facing Frazier, but she had no doubt his attention was focused. Casting her gaze, she noted Mike was near the glass door leading to the patio, and Horticia was at the opposite end of the counter, her hand rearranging the food on the platters while her eyes were on Roger. And Pamela was near the family room, looking at her phone.

The scene before her felt surreal, but Noel kept her mouth shut and monitored the kids. Penny was eating, but her slumped posture indicated the fatigue that Noel was sure the young girl would succumb to once she was fed and clean. But Roger appeared determined to ferret out more information.

Tad's lips pinched as he finally glared at Roger. "No. They talked to themselves, but hardly anything was said to us. And why are you asking anyway? You've never shown interest in me or Penny before."

Penny now gazed at the two of them, her eyes wide. "What's going on?"

"Roger just keeps wanting to talk about what happened when we were gone," Tad bit out.

Roger leaned back, and his hands lifted. "Hey, man, don't get attitude. I'm just checkin' on you—"

"Tad's right," Penny said, her eyes narrowing. "You're just here because Mom brings you."

Noel was no longer willing to wait before wading in, but suddenly Pamela walked over, obviously finished with her texting.

"Oh, my babies, don't be upset. You're home with me now," Pamela said, her eyes still teary.

Penny pushed away from the table and moved over to the counter to stand beside Noel. "I'm fine where I am," Penny replied, her tone soft but with conviction.

"With her? But I'm your mom. I'm who you should come to—"

"Really, Mom? You're going to play that?" Tad bit out, now swinging his glare from Roger to Pamela.

Noel watched as his facial muscles tightened. No evidence of the little boy remained, as his actions were now fully replaced by those of an angry young man.

"Tad!" Pamela cried. "Don't be like that! Roger, what did you say to them?"

"Me?" Roger growled, his face now red. He shoved his chair back, the legs scraping over the tiled floor. He stomped down the hall, and Noel noticed Horticia slipped quietly after him.

Noel wondered if Pamela had noticed the two disappearing, but her attention was focused on Tad.

It appeared Tad had reached his limit. "We *know*, Mom. We know why you brought us here. We know what you were doing with Dad. We know you were selling your rights away. We know!"

"Stop," Pamela shouted, her gaze darting around the room, finally landing on a tearful Penny. "You're upsetting your sister!"

"No, Mom," Penny jumped in. "Tad's just telling the truth."

Pamela threw her arm out at Noel and narrowed her eyes. "What have you been telling *my* kids?"

"Stop it, Pamela," Mike roared, his face red and mottled. "You and I know the truth. Stan shared it all with me. How you thought you could keep it from Tad and Penny, I have no idea."

Noel stepped between Mike and Pamela while placing her hand on Tad's shoulder and reaching for Penny with her other hand. "Penny, show me where your room is. Tad, you, too. I can help pack while you shower, and then we'll leave."

At her instructions, the kids moved in unison toward the stairs. Pamela opened her mouth, but Noel got there first. Leaning in, she added power to her words. "Your children have been traumatized. You don't get to call the shots. This isn't about you." She looked up at Mike. "It's not about you, either."

He clamped his mouth tightly shut but nodded before walking over to where Landon, Frazier, and Devil stood. As her gaze moved to Landon, he winked, and her lips twitched. She dipped her head before following the kids up the staircase.

Once upstairs, she followed Tad into his room, pulling Penny along with her. Once inside, she turned to face them. "Guys, I know this is an emotional homecoming. My advice is to step back from your mom's drama. Whatever is going to happen isn't going to happen right now. Landon will report to your dad, and when we get back to Montana, you can talk to your dad about your feelings concerning the custody. But right now, you need to take care of yourselves."

"Mike never liked Mom," Penny said, her voice low.

"You can't worry about that now," Noel advised. Once she'd gained nods from both kids, she looked around. "I see you have your own bathroom, Tad. Do you have one, too, Penny?"

"Yes. And there's lots of hot water," Penny enthused, offering the first smile on her face since they'd arrived back at the resort. "You can use my bathroom and take one, too."

"I'll offer mine to Landon as soon as we're finished so you both can shower," Tad offered.

Noel blinked at the thought of her and Landon taking a shower… of course, her mind was filled with the image of them showering together—

"Noel?"

"What?" she blurted, then blushed, seeing Penny's gaze on her. "Sorry, I was just… never mind. Um… you two get cleaned up." She followed Penny into the bedroom across the hall. It was filled with cream furniture, turquoise bed linens, and cream curtains blowing from the open balcony door. As Penny showered, Noel busied herself with placing the girl's suitcase on the bed.

Hearing voices from outside, she moved to the balcony. Peering down, she observed Landon speaking to Mike.

"I want to know who the fuck had those kids kidnapped," Mike growled.

"My people are monitoring the situation and reporting back to Stan," Landon replied. "What you need to focus on is to stop arguing with Pamela. You said that your purpose on this trip was to provide a familiar face for the kids to trust when we showed up to take them back to Montana. That plan went to shit when they were kidnapped, and they now trust me and Noel. But they still have that connection with you. What they don't need now is you getting in their mom's face."

"I know, I know," Mike moaned, his fists landing on his hips as he shook his head slowly back and forth. "She just makes me so goddamned pissed. She thinks the kids don't know what's going on. But they've known for years that their mother was a mercenary bitch—"

"That," Landon bit out, his forefinger waving toward Mike's face. "That right there needs to stop. You can feel how you feel, but don't let that out to the kids after all they've been through."

"Did she sign the paperwork and take the money?"

Landon sighed. "What do you think? With everything that's happened to Tad and Penny, she's playing with their sympathy. And your arguing with her isn't helping. So, no, she just informed me that she's not signing her rights over. She thought she could do it secretly, and the kids wouldn't know. She also assumed she'd still see them when she returned to the States and was willing to sign anything to get the money. Now? She's not going for it until she talks to Stan again."

"She wants more money," Mike growled.

"You're probably right. But let me handle this, and then I will turn it over to be dealt with between Stan and Pamela and their attorneys." With that, Landon walked back inside the house, and Noel heard the door close.

She started to walk back into Penny's room, but her attention was snagged on Mike when he moved down the path a little ways and pulled out his phone. Curiosity had her listening to his side of the conversation.

"The kids are back and safe. Yeah, they seem to be as good as possible after their ordeal. I'll take care of things here right before we leave." After a long pause, Mike said, "I waited until the kids got back so that I could stick to our original plan. I'll contact you as soon as it's done and we get on the plane to come home. It'll be good to get back to Montana."

After another pause, he said, "Yeah, it'll also be good to take care of this once and for all. No more wondering what the hell might come up next."

With that, Mike stood for a few minutes, staring at the beach. Finally, he turned and took a step toward the house when his body jerked, and a gasp escaped his lips. His hand shot to his chest, his face contorting in pain. The color drained from his skin, leaving it an eerie gray. With a strangled cry, he dropped to his knees, and his body pitched forward, collapsing onto the wet ground.

"Mike!" Noel screamed, her voice slicing through the air. Without thinking, she bolted out of the room, her heart pounding in her chest. Halfway down the stairs, she collided with Landon, who was racing up, his expression hardening at her panicked face.

"It's Mike!" she gasped, clutching at his shoulders. "I saw him on the patio... he clutched his chest and collapsed!"

Landon grabbed her hand, pulling her along as they

rushed toward the sliding glass door. The officer watching the house came from the front, followed closely by Devil and Frazier. Landon threw the door open and sprinted toward Mike, who lay motionless on the path leading to the beach.

Noel was right behind him and watched as they rolled Mike over. His chest heaved with shallow breaths, his face pale and slick with sweat. She loosened his shirt buttons, and Mike reached up and tried to grab her arm. His mouth worked, but no sound came forth.

"Mike, Mike," Noel said, leaning down closely. "We're getting help. We're calling for an ambulance."

He gasped, his hand reaching for hers again. Landon's hands pressed firmly into Mike's chest, his focus unwavering as he began compression-only CPR. Noel looked at Landon, fear filling her, then up to Devil, who was on the phone.

"Ambulance is on the way. There's a doctor at the resort, and he's coming."

Mike worked his mouth, his eyes on her. She leaned down, turning her head so that her ear was close to his mouth.

"Ca...Ill..." he rasped, the word barely audible.

Jerking her gaze back to him, she asked, "I know you're ill. We're getting help." With all the noise around them, she looked up as Penny and Tad arrived downstairs, being held back by Frazier. Penny was sobbing, and Tad's face was filled with anguish. She wanted to rush to them, to hold them, but Mike's faint whisper pulled her attention back.

His lips moved again. This time, Noel pressed her ear close, straining to hear. His breath was weak, but the words chilled her to the bone. She blinked as she looked at his face again, but now his eyes were closed, and his lips stayed parted. It only took another minute before an ambulance arrived, alongside a car with a doctor inside.

Landon continued CPR until the rescue workers could load Mike onto a stretcher. As soon as the doors were shut and they drove away, Landon assisted Noel in standing. She didn't move as cold seeped through her body. He wrapped his arms around her, pulling her close.

Landon's breathing was steady, and she basked in his embrace, wanting to burrow deeper until she was no longer shaking. Finally, looking up, she swiped at the tears in her eyes.

"Noel," he began, but she shook her head.

Seeing his brows lower, she glanced around before lifting on her toes. "Landon, I don't want anyone else to hear this, but Mike whispered something to me."

His eyes darkened. "What the hell did he say?"

Hesitating, she just stared wide-eyed up at him. She then looked around but didn't see anyone close enough to hear what she needed to say. Nonetheless, she lifted on her toes with his hands still around her and whispered, "He said... he came to kill her."

Landon's body jerked, and his arms tightened around her. "What the fuck? Kill who?"

Shaking her head, she said, "I thought he just came to be with the kids. But he said, 'I came to kill Pamela, but tell him I didn't get a chance.'" She held Landon's gaze, still shaking her head. "That's all he said."

"Christ, this is turning into a—"

"Clusterfuck," Noel supplied.

"Yeah," Landon breathed as his arms stayed locked, pulling her close.

21

Landon wrapped his arm around Noel, his touch protective as he guided her into the house. Around them, worried faces were frozen as the red lights of the ambulance vanished down the drive.

Leaning close to her ear, Landon said in a low, urgent whisper, "Don't say anything to anyone about Mike speaking to you."

Her gaze shot to his face, her eyes wide. "I... um... okay."

He started to turn, his focus shifting back to the others, but her hands clung to the fabric of his shirt. "Landon," she whispered, her voice trembling with unspoken questions.

Landon paused, his full attention snapping back to her. To anyone watching, it might seem like a comforting embrace, but within the cocoon of his arms, the world fell away. His gaze locked on hers, steady and unwavering.

"He was talking on the phone just before he

collapsed. I thought it was to the Fugates, but I don't know."

"What did he say?"

"Just that the kids were safe, and he would stick to the original plan. He said it would be good to get back to Montana."

Landon's gaze never left hers. "Anything else?"

Her brow furrowed, and she blew out a shaky breath. "Um... oh, he said that it would be good to take care of it once and for all." She tightened her grip on him. "What did it mean?"

His jaw tightened. "I have no idea, sweetheart." The endearment had slipped out, something he never did. Landon wasn't in the habit of calling any woman sweetheart, babe, darlin', honey, or anything other than their name or title. But seeing the fear on her pale face, the word sweetheart fell from his lips. If she was offended, she didn't react, but then he wondered if she'd noticed. "I don't want Pamela or the kids to know what he said. I'll talk to my people to trace his calls. He had his phone in his pocket."

"Okay," she said, sucking in a deep breath. She straightened, and he could see the instant she steeled her spine. Patting his arm, she said, "I'll see to the kids."

Nodding, he watched with pride as she moved around him and walked directly to Tad and Penny. Pamela stood to the side, probably too shocked to begin her dramatics, and Noel took advantage, pulling the kids gently into the house. He followed their progression, seeing the trio headed up the stairs.

His eyes tracked their progress until they were out

of sight. The tension in his chest eased only slightly as he turned back to Devil and Frazier. Pamela had retreated into the house, but he shifted his stance, ensuring their conversation remained private.

Devil groaned. "This should have been the easiest mission, and has turned into nothing but a fuckin'—"

"Tell me about it," Landon agreed. "But there's more." He watched as the other two Keepers' eyes flared with interest. "When waiting for the ambulance, Mike managed to speak to Noel. He told her that he was here to kill Pamela—"

"You have got to be fucking kidding me," Frazier bit out.

"He also said to 'tell him I didn't get a chance.'"

"Him? Who him?" Devil asked. "Does he mean somebody sent him here to fucking kill Pamela?"

"Your guess is as good as mine. I want to see what he's got in his overnight bag."

"Did he bring a bag with him when he came?"

Landon nodded. "I'm going to find what room he stayed in last night. That's got to be where his bag is."

"He sure as hell needed a way to kill her that wasn't going to be messy or loud," Devil said, his eyes narrowing as he thought of the possibilities.

"I wonder if he planned on doing something when you, Noel, and the kids were leaving. Something he could do that wouldn't immediately be traced back to him," Frazier pondered aloud. "Couldn't be loud or messy."

"And who sent him? Stan Fugate? Or Stan's father?" Devil asked.

"Had to be someone who had complete trust in Mike, knowing he was loyal to the family," Landon said.

"I'll call it in and tell Todd to check his phone records. There's got to be a trace," Frazier offered.

Landon nodded before he requested, "Make sure Pamela stays away while I go search."

Frazier clapped him on the back. "You got it."

With no one around, he bounded up the staircase and heard Noel comforting Tad and Penny in Penny's room. Glancing across the hall, he spied a pair of Tad's jeans lying across the bed and assumed that was his room. At the end of the hall was the apparent owner's bedroom with Pamela's clothing strewn about and an empty vodka bottle on the nightstand.

No other bedrooms were upstairs, so Landon headed downstairs. A hall bisected the living room and dining room, going by the kitchen and leading toward the back of the house. Horticia was standing in the kitchen, so he asked, "Where did Mike sleep last night?"

"He stayed in the downstairs guest room, sir. Uh… Roger's room is the first one on the left, and Mike was at the end of the hall."

"Is Roger still in his room?"

Horticia's eyes widened. "Uh… I'm uncertain, sir."

Dipping his chin, he glanced over his shoulder and caught Devil's eye. Without saying a word, he indicated that the other Keeper should stop Horticia from leaving the kitchen.

Devil moved forward and smiled at her. "Ma'am? I think we can all use a cup of tea if you don't mind."

Horticia's eyes were wide, and her hands shook

before she clasped them tightly. Nodding, she moved over to the teakettle.

Landon slipped down the hall, went to the farthest room, and opened the door. Shutting it behind him, he looked around at the guest room. The bed was made, and a small overnight bag sat on the covers. Next to the bag was Mike's jacket. Glancing around, he saw no other personal items belonging to the man. He stepped into the en suite bathroom, but it was also void of anything personal. "It looks like he was all packed up and ready to go," Landon murmured.

He moved over to the bed and unzipped the bag. Not wanting to stick his hand into the unknown, especially if there was a weapon, he pulled a penlight from his back pocket and peered into the bag.

Two pairs of boxer briefs, socks, khaki pants, and a denim shirt were inside, along with a toiletry kit. Upon examination, he found nothing untoward, even after unscrewing and sniffing the shampoo and toothpaste. It wasn't until he sniffed the small travel bottle of generic aftershave that his eyes widened. He didn't know how to identify poison by scent, but he'd bet his left nut that whatever was in the bottle wasn't aftershave unless a musty odor was what Mike wanted to smell like.

It wouldn't have been hard for Mike to slip something into Pamela's drink after the rest of them had gotten into the vehicle to head to the airport. By the time she drank and then died, the kids would be off the island and on their way to Montana. Once there, the family would have been able to control the narrative of how their mom died.

He returned the bottle to the toiletry kit and settled it into the overnight flight bag. Zipping it, he grabbed the bag and the jacket and carried them out of the bedroom. Instead of returning to the kitchen, he moved through the laundry room and hustled around the house while making a quick call to Frazier. "Meet me at the SUV."

He stowed the bag and explained what he'd found. "I want the vehicle locked at all times."

Frazier agreed and checked the doors once the key fob was clicked. "By the way, Todd checked Mike's phone records. His phone wasn't used close to the time he had his heart attack."

Landon let out a muffled curse. "Burner. He must have had a fuckin' burner."

"Think it's in the garden or patio?"

"I'll check. Has Cole been notified?"

Frazier nodded. "He's on standby."

Landon looked around. "Where the fuck is Roger? He wasn't with us when Mike was taken away."

"Shit, man, I don't know," Frazier groaned.

"Goddammit!" Landon cursed, walking back into the house to look for the burner phone Mike may have been using. Noel and the kids were still upstairs. Pamela stood on the path leading to the beach, chatting with a silver-haired man who appeared enamored with her. Landon slipped to the patio and searched the garden surrounding the area closest to where Mike had fallen. It wasn't hard to find a mobile phone lying just under a palm plant. It also wasn't difficult to determine it was a burner. He pocketed the phone, then walked inside.

Devil walked to Landon. "What's up?"

"Where is Roger?"

Devil jerked. "I thought he was in his room."

"He's not." Landon grabbed his phone. "Sadie, can you check the cameras now that they are working? Tell me if you see Roger leaving the area."

"Give me a second." After a pause, she said, "He left by the back door when the rest of you were on the patio dealing with Mike. He was alone and disappeared into the jungle with a case in his hand."

Landon scrubbed his hand over his face, wondering if the mission fuckups were ever going to end. "Okay, see if you can discover when and where he was picked up. I'll contact the police commissioner, and they can search for him. Get Todd to check any correspondence between Roger and Horticia. They've been chummy yet noticeably scarce since the kids came back. And I have the burner."

"Give it to me, and I'll at least send what information I can to Todd," Devil said.

"Think they arranged the kidnapping?" Sadie asked.

"The kidnappers asked for half a million, the exact amount that I had for Pamela. It was an inside job. I want to know all about him. We've got Horticia here. I'll have the police lean on her."

Disconnecting, Landon then called the police commissioner. After giving him the information on Roger and Horticia, the chief agreed that they would search for Roger. Walking back to the kitchen, he watched as Horticia appeared to fade into the background, but the officer who'd been assigned to the house stayed right with her.

Landon's phone vibrated. When he looked at the caller ID, his brow knit as he answered. "This is Landon Sommers." He dropped his chin to his chest as he listened to the news. It just kept getting worse and worse. Thanking the caller, he looked up at Frazier, then at Devil, who walked over. "That was the hospital. The police commissioner gave them my number when Mike was taken in as the person to notify. He didn't make it."

"Goddamn," Devil cursed, shaking his head.

For a long moment, the three stood in silence. Finally, Landon said, "I'm going in to talk to the kids and Noel. We may need to stay the night. No way do I want to upset Penny and Tad any more by pulling them away when they're this upset."

"Do you want me to call the Fugates?" Frazier asked.

Landon nodded. "Tell them only what happened and who they can contact at the hospital. I had already talked to Stan to let him know that Pamela had changed her decision to sign any new paperwork. I'm now leaving that between them and their attorney. Our assignment is to get the kids home safely. Devil, talk to Logan and let him know what's happening. Then get ahold of Cole." He scrubbed his hand over his face. "Jesus, what a mess."

With Devil and Frazier heading off to take care of calls, Landon walked back into the house. The atmosphere was heavy, charged with unspoken tension. In the family room, Pamela sat rigidly on the sofa, a cup of tea cradled in her hands. Her lips were drawn into a tight line, her eyes narrowing as she met his gaze.

"I suppose you think I should be upset, right?" she bit out, her voice sharp.

Landon's expression remained unreadable, but his tone was firm. "Pamela, you always seem to believe the world revolves around you. Let me assure you, I don't care how you feel about this situation. What I do care about is talking to Tad and Penny about a man they've trusted their entire lives."

He didn't wait for her response, his patience already worn thin. He turned on his heel and headed up the stairs, each step heavier than the last. He hated the burden of the news he had to deliver.

Stepping through Penny's door, he observed Tad and Penny sitting on the edge of the bed. Noel sat on the thick-cushioned window seat directly before them. Penny was no longer crying, but her pale face and red, swollen eyes gave way to shock. Tad's fallen expression gave him the appearance of someone with the weight of grief on his shoulders, and he swiped at his nose and eyes. Landon ached for them but steeled himself, knowing he was going to make things worse.

Noel watched him carefully as he made his way into the room. He wished he could convey everything to her in a glance to help prepare her for what was to come. Though they had only known each other briefly, she seemed to grasp the weight of what he was about to say. Her shoulders slumped slightly, bracing herself for the inevitable.

Hesitating wasn't in Landon's nature, but now, faced

with the enormity of this moment, he faltered. Noel extended her hand toward him in an unspoken offer of solidarity. He took it gratefully, her touch grounding him. Sitting beside her on the bench, he turned to the children.

"Tad, Penny... there's no way I can say this easily or try to sugarcoat what I need to tell you. You witnessed Mike having a heart attack earlier, and I'm so sorry that I couldn't protect you from that. I need to let you know I just received a phone call from the hospital. Mike did not survive the heart attack. I'm sorry, kids. He died on the way to the hospital."

Noel's grip on his hand tightened, her fingers digging into his. The intensity of her hold mirrored the helplessness coursing through both of them.

Penny's wail sounded out, her anguish spilling over, and she began to sob again. Loosening her grip on his fingers, Noel moved to sit between the kids. She wound one arm around Penny, and the other reached for Tad.

Landon lost track of time as he sat quietly, allowing the children to deal with the initial grief. He let his thoughts wander to Mike. He was a familiar face they had grown up with—a friend, a mentor, and a surrogate family member. And now, someone who had admitted he'd come to commit murder.

He sighed, pushing those thoughts aside as Noel took Penny's weight. Tad leaned to the side and rested his head on Noel's shoulder.

Landon's mind wandered to the women he had known in the military and the FBI—strong, capable, and fierce. They could take down opponents twice their size, shoot with deadly precision, and handle high-stress situations with ease. Yet looking at Noel, he realized that strength came in many forms.

Here was a woman who had chosen a path of compassion and care. She bore the weight of others' grief, offering them a safe space to fall apart. She listened, she understood, and she validated their pain, giving them a chance to heal.

And at that moment, Landon knew—he wanted to be the one she could lean on. The one who would carry her burdens when it was her turn to break. He wanted to be the person who gave her the strength she so selflessly offered to others.

22

Hours later, Noel walked down the stairs quietly, fatigue pulling at her. The past two days had been exhausting. *God, was it actually only about forty hours ago that my boss called me to tell me about coming here for Tad and Penny?* She had experienced bizarre cases and had exhausting workdays, but she'd never experienced all that had been packed into these hours.

As she reached the bottom of the stairs, she was met by Landon. She offered him what she thought was a smile, but as his gaze dropped to her mouth, she felt it was more of a grimace than a genuine smile.

His eyes lifted, and he jerked his chin upward. "How are they?"

"They're both finally asleep. Penny was exhausted, and after eating and taking a hot bath, she quickly fell asleep. I hope that she doesn't wake up until the morning."

"And Tad?"

"Pretty much the same. The trauma, the drama, and then the grief finally knocked him out."

She stood on the bottom step, bringing her height closer to his face. His hands reached out and gently rested on her waist. In a movement so natural to her, she lifted her hands to his forearms and slid them upward to his shoulders, her fingers curling around the back of his neck. It was an intimate gesture, one easily found between friends or lovers. They certainly weren't lovers, but after what they'd been through, she hoped they were friends.

Staring into his stormy gray eyes, the idea of them being lovers moved through her in a way that caused her fingers to grip a little tighter. She wondered if he picked up on the same feeling when his fingers dug in tighter to her waist.

She dragged her gaze beyond his shoulder to see who else was near. Not seeing or hearing anyone, she asked, "Where is everybody?"

"Cole has a room near the airport. He doesn't want to have any problem with the plane for tomorrow."

She nodded. "Where are Frazier and Devil sleeping?"

"A two-bedroom guesthouse over the garage has a small kitchen and a large bathroom. Devil and Frazier will sleep there and be ready to leave first thing in the morning. Plus, that keeps them close by in case we need them. No one has seen Roger since he left, but the police are watching for him at the airports."

She snorted and shook her head. "And Pamela?"

Landon grinned. "While you were upstairs with the

kids, Pamela finally went into her room with the vodka. She's halfway to being stinking drunk by now."

"I get the feeling a lot happened while I was upstairs with the kids for the past couple of hours." After the kids had eaten, Pamela had tried to cozy up to them, but she couldn't keep her mouth shut without making snide comments about Mike. The kids, still deep in the fresh throes of grief, were not in the mood to listen to their mom. Noel had encouraged them to walk outside with her for the fresh air and a little exercise. And even though it was early evening when they came back in, she encouraged the kids to try to get some sleep.

She sat with each of them and encouraged them to think of their good memories of Mike. They had questions about how his body would get back to the States, and she answered them honestly. They both video-chatted with their dad and grandparents, and while she didn't hover, she stayed close in case they needed her. By the time all that was over, the kids had finally fallen into their beds, sleep coming quickly.

"I'm not sure what it says about me," she said, still hanging on to his shoulders. "But I honestly couldn't care less if Pamela continues to drink through the night and isn't even around for goodbye in the morning."

Landon grinned and leaned in closer. "I think it says that you're tired of her bullshit, you've done everything in your power to help the kids, and you're ready to go home."

Her lips curved, and she also leaned closer. "I think you're right."

He slid his hands from the sides of her waist to her

back. "What about you, Noel? You've spent the day taking care of others. What do you need?"

She sucked in a quick breath, her eyes never leaving his. After two days of being surrounded by people, they were suddenly alone. And as tired as she was, she had no desire to squander the opportunity to spend more time with Landon. Especially alone time. With his body so close. And his hands on her. And their lips—

She erased the scant distance, her lips landing on his. The kiss was light. Just a whisper, giving him plenty of opportunity to pull back if kissing wasn't on his agenda of things he wanted to do.

But he didn't move away. Instead, his tongue licked over her bottom lip, and she opened eagerly for him. He didn't waste a second as he plunged his tongue into her mouth. Her fingers clutched the back of his head as his velvet tongue swept over hers.

As a child, when Noel ate icing off a cupcake, she would say that the sugary sweetness made her mouth tingle, and her sister, Joy, would always laugh. Now, as his tongue danced over the roof of her mouth, the movement gave her the same tingles. Only this time, they shot straight to her core.

Angling her head to gain better access, she quickly realized he had taken charge of the kiss and used the new angle to draw her closer. His tongue now explored as it tangled with hers. Her knees felt weak, and she was glad his hands offered support.

As though he could anticipate her every need, his arms banded tighter around her waist, taking her weight while giving her his strength.

Just when she wanted the kiss to keep going, he began nibbling at her lips, offering sweet little kisses before leaning back. The kicking mewl she heard came from her own lungs. For the moment they'd kissed, she needed him more than her next breath. And now that he'd lifted his mouth away from hers, she thought breathing was overrated.

He smiled, and his handsome face morphed into what she'd come to think of as drop-dead gorgeous territory.

"You asked me what I needed," she said with a return smile. "I think you've already got the right idea."

"I have a lot of good ideas for you and me," he admitted, angling his head to kiss the corner of her mouth. "But if you want to keep doing nothing more than just this, that's fine with me."

Her hands tightened on him again, and she leaned forward, giving all her weight to him. "This is great, but I'd like to hear your other ideas. It's good to give a girl some choices, you know."

He kissed the other corner of her mouth and mumbled, "It is?"

"Oh yeah. Especially after a day like today, a girl needs to know what her options are to relax and forget."

He leaned back, and their gazes held, and she could've sworn time stood still. There were no sounds in the house other than her heart pounding in her chest, which she felt sure he could hear.

"Roger's room is empty, and so was the one Mike used. Believe it or not, Horticia had already cleaned the bathrooms and hung fresh towels. That was, of course, before she was hauled off to be questioned by the police."

A giggle slipped out, and Noel shook her head. "At least she was a good housekeeper, even if she was a kidnapping instigator."

Landon grinned, then continued. "I stripped the beds and put clean sheets on. I set your bag in one of the rooms and mine in the other. And if all we've done is get to know each other and share these kisses, I'm good with that, Noel. But if you want more, just let me know because I'm really interested in spending time with you. I just don't want to wake up in the morning and see regret in your eyes."

"The only way that would happen is if we woke up in separate bedrooms." She winced and shook her head. "I realize that was presumptuous. A lot of people only want sex and then not share a bed. And that's okay, too, if—"

"I can't think of a better way to spend the night than with you, doing whatever you want and then curling around you all night. So if you'd regret not waking up to me in the morning, just know I would, too."

Her heart felt lighter than it had all day, and her smile widened. "Then I guess I'll let you choose," she said.

"Choose?"

"Yeah. Which room we stay in."

His arms tightened, and she gave a little hop. Her legs wrapped around his waist, and with one hand under her ass and the other banded around her back, he turned and started down the hall.

She was impressed that he was able to carry her down the hall and into the bedroom, and managed to do it with his mouth sealed over hers.

Everything about Landon had captured her since the moment she'd met him, but right now, in his arms, she gave over to the notion that he was the most impressive man she'd ever been with. *And we've only kissed!* She couldn't wait to find out what else he could do with his impressive mouth and body.

She had no idea which bedroom they were in, but as she loosened her feet from around his waist, and he continued to hold on until her feet were steady on the floor, she glanced around.

"This is the room that Mike would have slept in last night. I figured it might be cleaner than Roger's room since I'm fairly certain he's *entertained* Horticia when Pamela wasn't in the house."

She wrinkled her nose. "Probably a good choice. She might not have cleaned their cooties from the room."

He chuckled just before his hands cupped her face, and his fingers danced along the edge of her hairline. She closed her eyes as the slight pressure massaged her temples.

"I finally got you to eat. Would you like a shower?"

Her eyes opened as a smile played about her lips. "Is that your polite way of saying I stink?"

He barked out laughter and shook his head. "You made sure the kids had a chance to get clean and relaxed, but neither of us has done that. I just thought maybe you'd like to take a shower."

"Thank you." She nodded. "Since you haven't showered either, would you like to share?"

"Well, it would save on water, wouldn't it?"

"Oh, absolutely," she said, still nodding. "I'm all about conservation."

"Me too. Whatever I can do to save the planet."

Unable to contain her laughter, she dropped her forehead to his chest and giggled, feeling her shoulders shake with the mirth. It felt good to have that release of pent-up emotions.

When she lifted her head, he slowly dragged his fingers down her arms and then, linking hands with her, guided her into the bathroom.

She looked around, and her eyes widened. "Oh wow. This is bigger than I thought it would be."

The bathroom was well appointed, with a single sink but a wide granite countertop. The toilet was hidden in a small closet, and the shower was huge. "For a guest room, this is really nice. But then the whole resort is impressive."

When she turned her head back to stare at Landon, she found his gaze pinned on her.

He bent and kissed her lightly, then turned toward the shower and flipped on the water.

Noel stepped back, and her hands moved to the bottom of her shirt. Without hesitation, she pulled it up over her head and dropped it to the side. His gaze now landed on her satin bra, and she watched his eyes grow stormy. She unbuckled her pants and shoved them down, kicking them to the side after toeing off her shoes.

Standing proudly in front of him in just her underwear, she stepped closer and grabbed the bottom of his shirt. "You're not shy, are you?"

"Not at all," he said with a smile. He quickly jerked his shirt over his head, and it soon joined hers on the floor.

"Good, because I hate the idea of all this gorgeousness hidden from view." And what a view it was—long, lean muscles, not overly bulked, but ropey and strong.

"I might not be an exhibitionist, but I have no problem with you viewing whatever you want to."

With that, she laughed as her hands moved to his belt. Once again, he took over and soon shucked his pants and boxers after he ditched his boots and socks. She allowed her gaze to roam from head to toe, finding every inch of him as though sculpted from marble.

He stepped under the water as she finished stripping. Then wrapping her fingers around his, she followed him. She groaned as the spray from the side pounded her tired muscles, and the rainwater faucet above soothed and warmed her.

She placed her hands on his waist, shifted them so the water hit his back, and then dropped slowly to her knees. His erection bobbed in front of her, and she dragged her tongue from base to tip, keeping her eyes on his face. She watched his eyes roll back in his head, and a deep groan left his lips. She loved seeing this very controlled man as he handed the control to her.

Now, she slid her mouth over the tip and then down the shaft. She sucked and licked, both hands caressing his balls and gripping his shaft firmly. His hands were on her head, his fingers massaging her scalp, occasionally gripping her hair. The slight sting only drove her to take him harder and faster.

"I'm going to come," he warned, bending slightly to place his hands on her biceps as though to pull her up.

She continued, and with a few more thrusts, he threw his head back and roared his release. Water was dripping down her face, but she kept her eyes on him as she sucked him dry.

When his chin dropped to his chest, and his eyes bore straight into hers, his hands now cupped her cheeks. He assisted her up, pulling her close. Their naked bodies were pressed tightly together, and with her ear against his chest, his heartbeat was strong.

"Christ, babe," he murmured. "Damn, Noel. I never expected you to do that."

She smiled as she leaned back and held his gaze. Before she could think of anything to say in response, he licked her lips, then pressed her back against the tile.

This kiss was wild, with noses bumping, lips melding, and occasional teeth scraping. She had wondered if the blow job would exhaust him, but it seemed to have given him new energy, for which she was glad. She wanted to keep experiencing this man. She wasn't ready to walk away without having shared and tasted everything he had to offer.

23

Landon had never intended for him and Noel to end up where they were, but to say he was thrilled would be the understatement of the century.

He had watched her jump into the assignment and go above and beyond to care for, counsel, and hell... even shoot a man for them. He knew she thought she had only shot toward the man without hitting him, but Landon was willing for her to keep that assumption. The last thing he wanted was for her to feel guilt about a man who would have killed all of them with no compunction.

She'd offered a shoulder for the kids to cry on, a listening ear, and a heart with the capacity to carry other people's burdens. She was also not a pushover. She was an enigma that had surprised him, and he wanted to know more.

While she'd been upstairs helping the children to pack when their own mother had taken to a bed with a bottle of vodka, he'd talked to the other Keepers before they headed to the garage condo, then made sure the two guest rooms downstairs were ready for him and Noel.

He'd waited at the bottom of the stairs, and when she came down, he could see the dark shadows underneath her eyes, the bits of mud that still clung to the bottom of her pants, and the slump of her shoulders that told him she was exhausted. And all he wanted to do was hold her, give her someone to lean on, and take care of her.

The kiss yesterday had been an impulse he rarely gave in to, catching him by surprise. Her kissing him this evening had been just as much of a surprise but not unwanted.

The feel of her body pressed against him, the trust she offered him, and the taste of her lips combined to make him know he wanted more. But he would've never pushed.

But the kiss seemed to have sparked something ready and willing inside her.

It had been a while since he'd experienced a blow job, but watching her drop to her knees in the shower was unexpected. As soon as her lips wrapped around his cock, all thoughts of going slow flew out of his head. He had the presence of mind to warn her that he was about to come, but she didn't stop, and watching that gorgeous woman as she sucked him off nearly took him to his knees.

Now, he wanted to return the favor. First, he was determined to care for her how he'd intended when he met her at the bottom of the stairs. He reached around behind her and grabbed the shampoo. "Turn around."

She acquiesced, and he lathered her hair, massaging her scalp and running his fingers through the tresses. She dropped her head back and moaned, the sound shooting straight through him.

Turning so that the water would rinse her hair, he grabbed the bottle of conditioner. Following the same motions, he was soon finished with her hair. He grabbed the shampoo again and quickly did his own, giving a shake to send the water droplets flying.

She surprised him when she snagged the body wash first, but he held his hands out and she squirted a generous amount in his palm. Their hands slid over each other's bodies, cleansing and stimulating all at the same time.

As his hands moved over her breasts, she sucked in a quick breath and dropped her head back. Her hands hesitated for a second, but then she quickly continued to smooth them over his body.

He explored every inch of her luscious curves, and he gave her full access to do the same. He was glad for the continuously heated water as they completely forgot their conservation ideals.

He thought of lifting and taking her in the shower but wanted their first time to be in a bed. She deserved a soft mattress instead of hard tiles cradling her back. Flipping off the water, he led her out of the shower and dried every inch, starting with her head. He quickly toweled off as she ran a comb through her hair. She squirted lotion onto her hands and lightly moisturized her face and body.

He'd never considered something as mundane as a shower or watching a woman get ready for bed as sexy. But with Noel, every movement she made called to his instincts to take her, care for her, and be part of her world.

She turned to him and smiled. "You've been watching me rather closely."

"I find you fascinating," he said, not bothering with a flippant answer but giving her the truth. "Fascinating, and someone I want to know better."

She stepped forward and placed her palms on his chest, peering up at him. Both naked, he felt her nipples against his skin as his erection nudged against her soft belly. "How much better do you want to know me?" she asked, her lips curving upward.

"I want to know everything. But only taking whatever you want to give me willingly."

She dragged her fingers down over his abs, and just when he thought they would wrap around his cock, she diverted to the side and linked fingers with him. She turned and walked out of the bathroom, and he willingly followed.

She flipped off the light, leaving the small lamp next to the bed on. Grabbing the covers, she pulled them down, then turned, sat on the edge of the bed, and scooted back. "I want you to know me better, too."

He stood for a moment and stared at this beautiful naked woman offering herself to him and realized what a gift he'd been given. He crawled forward until his shoulders nudged her legs open. He could smell the soft scent of the body wash, but it was her arousal that held him captive. Bending, he sniffed at the trim curls at the apex of her thighs. With her legs splayed open, he dove in and feasted on her folds.

He licked and tongued, tasting and memorizing. He inserted a finger in her channel as his tongue circled the bundle of nerves before sucking. Her body bowed off the bed.

She writhed underneath him, her fingers clutching the sheets. He looked up, finding her eyes on him, and just like when she'd stared at him in the shower, he was captured by the intensity of her gaze. His free hand roamed upward over her belly to her breasts. He massaged both, tugging lightly on her nipples.

They moved in tandem, and he felt her tense just before she cried out his name. As her orgasm rocked her, he licked her essence. Then slowly, he crawled up her body, kissing the soft skin along the way. His mouth moved between her breasts, teasing and tormenting each distended nipple. Holding his weight off her with his forearms, he suddenly realized he was bare. Kissing her deeply, he thrust his tongue inside her mouth so she could taste the combination of them together.

Murmuring, "I'll be right back," he hastened to the side and slid off the bed, feeling like an untried teenager who couldn't get his shit together.

Grabbing his pants from the floor of the bathroom, he snagged his wallet and opened it, finding the two condoms he always kept for *just in case*. He was careful to keep new ones, never wanting them to expire, especially since his *just in cases* weren't frequent.

Back to the bedroom, he found that she'd rolled to her side, with her head propped in her palm and a wide grin on her face.

"I'm glad you remembered," she said. "To be honest, I'd completely forgotten about a condom. I guess you can tell this isn't something I do often."

He rolled the condom over his cock and slowly shook his head. "I may have come prepared, but it's a rare occurrence for me, too."

As he crawled onto the bed, she rolled to her back and opened her legs, allowing him to nestle his hips against hers. Her arms wrapped around him as the tip of his erection found her sex.

"Are you sure?" he asked, peering closely into her eyes.

"Yes, I'm sure. I want you. I want this now. And I want you for as long as we can last."

Plunging into her warm channel, he allowed her words to wash over him. He couldn't have said it any better. He wanted this now and to spend more time with her when the sex was over.

From that second on, all rational thought left as he reveled in the warm, tight, slick channel that gripped his cock, sending his senses into overdrive. He wanted to close his eyes and drift along the building excitement. But more, he wanted to see the beautiful woman underneath him.

Her hips moved up, and she matched his rhythm, thrust for thrust until all they could hear was their breathing and the sounds of their bodies crashing together.

Her fingers had dragged along his scalp but now gripped his shoulders tightly. Her eyes were closed, and she threw her head back. "I want to see you. Open your eyes," he gently ordered.

Her eyes flew open, and he felt her body as she hurtled through her orgasm.

That was all he was waiting for because the tingling strengthened, and his release jolted through him. He continued to thrust until he was spent. He finally withdrew and, leaning up on his knees, took care of the condom. Looking down, he watched as her complexion was now cream and pink, and she had the lazy smile of a well-sated woman.

He kissed her lightly, stealing her breath, before he whispered, "I'll be right back."

He took care of the condom in the bathroom and washed his hands. When he walked into the bedroom, she'd pulled the covers partially over her body, but it was obvious she was still naked. "Fucking perfect."

She chuckled. "I was just thinking the same thing about you."

Turning off the lamp, he slid underneath the covers, wrapped his arms around her, and pulled her deep into his embrace. He had no idea what the next day would bring or what would happen after they parted ways in Montana. But he knew he wanted to see her again and prayed that she would feel the same in the morning light.

Soon, her breathing grew deep, and he knew she'd found sleep. Closing his eyes, he quickly joined her.

Landon woke the following morning and stretched, a smile on his face. A warm body lay next to him.

"You know, we woke up a lot like this yesterday," Noel said.

He chuckled, then rolled and wrapped his arms around her, pulling her tight. "Yes, but today, we're a hell of a lot more comfortable."

Her laughter rang out as she nodded. "I can't argue with that." Their gazes held and then they leaned forward simultaneously, their lips meeting.

He would have taken the kiss much deeper, knowing exactly where he'd like it to go, but they woke in the wee hours of the morning and used his second condom.

Noel pulled back and sighed. "I know, I know. I just can't help but wish we had a box of condoms."

"You've got that right," he replied with a groan.

Laughing together, they climbed from the bed. "I'll shower and then go check on the kids."

"I would suggest we shower together, but—"

She placed her finger over his lips. "We'll never get off this island if we have another shower like last night."

He groaned, pulling her closer, loving how her body fit so perfectly with his. "You're right. You shower first."

"Afterward, I'll go check on the kids and see what I can find for breakfast. We have to forage for ourselves."

"Yeah. Even if Horticia was let go after questioning, I doubt she'd come back here." He kissed her quickly, then watched her sweet ass strut into the bathroom, willing his cock to calm the fuck down. When she was finished, she dressed and started packing her overnight bag while he headed into the bathroom. "When I'm done, I'll find out when we can leave."

She smiled and started to turn away, but he reached out and snagged her hand. Gently pulling her closer, he leaned down to kiss her smiling lips.

When he finished his shower, he packed his bag and walked to the front door, placing his next to hers. He could hear her voice coming from upstairs. Pulling out his phone, he called Devil. "Do we have a departure ETA?"

"Frazier talked with Cole and said he can file a flight plan when you're ready. He'll wait until we get there, but we won't have much of a wait before we can get into the air."

"Anything new from Logan?"

"I talked to him late last night," Devil said. "They had spent their time working on the connection between Roger, Pamela, and Horticia, uncovering the kidnapping plot. The information was sent to the Jamaican police commissioner. The police want to have all the facts before they arrest her. Sadie and Todd just started yesterday evening, taking a look at who might have sent Mike to kill Pamela."

Landon dragged his tongue over his bottom lip as thoughts flooded his mind. "Any idea what he plans on doing with that information?"

"He didn't say, but if I had to guess, it's just to make sure no one is also after you all or the kids."

It was the kind of information that would sometimes give Landon pause. When he was with special operations, he just took orders—never worrying about the results. However, in the years spent in the Bureau, he constantly looked to uncover clues leading to arrests and prosecution. That wasn't always his job as a Keeper, but he found it sometimes challenging to let go of that mindset.

"Noel is checking on the kids, making sure they'll be ready to go soon. Once we leave here, I know we all want to get to the airport, get on the plane, and get the fuck out of here. I haven't seen Pamela this morning—"

"She left in the middle of the night. Picked up by whom I assume is her new sugar daddy. They returned to his house in this resort in a golf cart."

"She doesn't waste any time."

"You got that right," Devil said before disconnecting.

His thoughts wandered to Noel as he disconnected, and a soft smile crept onto his face. Their night together lingered in his mind, and he couldn't shake the warmth he felt. He had no idea what would happen between them once they were back in Montana, but he was ready to give it a chance. Whatever it took, he wanted to see if something real could be found with her.

A slight sound made him turn, and there she was, slipping quietly into the kitchen. Noel moved toward him, her steps light and sure. Without a word, she wrapped her arms around his waist, leaning into him.

Her warmth spread through him as he instinctively pulled her closer.

"The kids are getting ready and packing up. I told them to bring down their suitcases and check their rooms to make sure nothing gets left behind," she said softly, her voice warm in his ear. She leaned back, her eyes sparkling with a hint of mischief. "Didn't see Pamela in her room. Guess she wasn't as drunk as we thought."

"Don't worry about her," he replied, brushing a strand of hair from her cheek. "She spent the night with Roger's replacement. Looks like this one's got money."

Noel's brows lifted in mild surprise, but then she just shook her head with a small laugh, her gaze drifting over his shoulder toward the patio doors. She seemed lost in thought for a moment, the light in her eyes softening.

"Would you mind if I took a quick walk down the beach?" she asked, her voice barely above a whisper. "I just want to fill my lungs with that salty air and feel the sand under my toes one last time. This might be my only trip to Jamaica, and I'd like to see the beach up close at least once."

He smiled, brushing a tender kiss across her lips, tasting her sweetness in that fleeting moment. Then he nodded, jerking his head toward the door. "Don't be long."

She made her way down the path, her fingers grazing the leaves and flowers on either side, her hair catching the golden morning light. As she reached the sand, she paused, letting the breeze tug at her clothes, her gaze cast out to the endless stretch of sea and sky.

He dragged his gaze away from her and moved to the refrigerator. Opening the door, he was glad to find eggs and bacon. Glancing toward the counter, he discovered there was also bread. *Perfect... we can fucking eat before we leave.* He soon had the bread toasted, the bacon sizzling, and the eggs scrambled.

Devil and Frazier entered the kitchen after dumping their bags by the front door. He quickly started breakfast, and then the sound of Penny screaming, "Landon!" He tossed the plate to the counter and whirled around just in time to see Penny racing down the stairs. He darted to her with Devil and Frazier on his heels.

Her eyes were wide with fright as she lifted her finger toward the back patio. "It's Noel! There's a man on the beach, and he's got a gun pointed at her!"

24

Noel wandered along the path that led through palm trees, flowering shrubs, and thick foliage. It wasn't a long walk to get to the sandy beach. Growing up in Montana, she rarely took any trips to the beach. And she'd never seen anything like this. When she finally stepped onto the sand, her breath caught—it was so brilliantly white, nearly dazzling in the early morning light. She squinted and laughed softly to herself, thinking she should have brought sunglasses.

Her gaze drifted out over the endless blue stretching before her. She tried to recall the shades of blue from her high school art classes—cerulean, azure, maybe cobalt? But none of those words seemed adequate to describe the color of the water here, vibrant yet somehow calming, shimmering under the golden sunlight. The rhythm of the waves entranced her.

What was meant to be a quick stroll became something else entirely as she slipped off her sandals and darted toward the surf, her laughter ringing out as the warm water lapped against her feet, a welcome surprise.

If only she could stay here longer, basking in the beauty and tranquility. "I'd never be able to afford a place like this on my salary," she murmured with a smile, but even a few stolen moments felt like a gift. She continued to kick up the water playfully, savoring the way it sparkled around her ankles.

Eventually, she turned back toward the house, the reality of the day tugging at her. It was time to return Penny and Tad to their Montana home. And she needed to get back to hers. Her thoughts drifted to Landon, her heartbeat quickening at his name. What would Montana feel like now, with the memories of their time together lingering in her mind? Would he even want to see her again, or had last night been just a fleeting connection? The thought made her heart ache slightly. Two days with him and the idea of never seeing him again felt unbearable.

Unable to determine what she and Landon would be, if anything, once they landed in the States, she turned her thoughts to Penny and Tad. She didn't know what custody arrangements awaited them once they returned, but from what she'd seen, Pamela needed close monitoring. Supervised visits seemed like the best option, allowing Penny and Tad to decide their relationship with their mother when they came of age.

A sudden, sharp voice broke through her thoughts. "You!"

Noel gasped, her hand flying to her chest as she spun around. She'd been so lost in her musings she hadn't noticed someone else approaching. Standing barely twenty feet from her was a young man, Jamaican by appearance, his expression somewhere between fear and desperation. He looked so young, hardly more than a teenager, his clothes disheveled and his hair a tangled mess as though he'd been anxiously running his fingers through it.

She wasn't sure what he wanted. *Money?* Surely, he could see she had no purse with her. *Shit... not even my phone!*

"You!" he shouted again, his voice edged with something darker this time, something closer to rage than fear.

Her gaze darted toward the house, a surge of instinctive panic filling her. Could she outrun him? She took a small step backward, but he mirrored her move, edging closer. Just as she prepared to sprint, he raised his arm, and her eyes fell on the object in his hand. A strangled gasp escaped her lips as she registered the gun, its barrel glinting in the morning light, pointed directly at her.

"Wh… what…" Noel's breath caught, her heart pounding wildly as she raised her hands in surrender, her feet glued to the gritty sand beneath her. She had no idea who this man was or why he had such rage in his eyes.

"You killed my cousin."

Her mouth fell open. Of all the things she expected this man to say, that would never have made the list. *Oh God... he's crazy and has the wrong person!* She shook her head back and forth, saying, "No, I didn't," she stammered, her voice trembling as she shook her head furiously. "I haven't killed anyone. You've got it all wrong."

His grip on the gun tightened, and a shudder ran through his hand. "I saw you," he said, his voice a sharp, unsteady shout. "You shot him."

"No! No, you're wrong," she pleaded, fighting to keep her voice steady, her hands raised in a calming gesture despite her panic. "I swear, I didn't kill anyone!"

He didn't seem to hear her. His gaze was wild, filled with hurt and fury, his hand gripping the gun like a lifeline. "I saw you kill my cousin. He was on the roof, and when I heard the shot, I ran to the window. You were standing at the edge of the trees with a gun. He fell right after. It was you!"

Understanding finally dawned in her fear-filled mind. "No, no! I didn't shoot him. I don't know how to shoot," she said, her words tumbling out. "I… I fired the gun, but I didn't hit him. I aimed, but I just fired. He fell because he was frightened. He may have died when he hit the ground. I don't know."

She tried to think of what she'd seen, but with the storm raging and her attention on Landon and the kids, she had no idea what happened. Her mind strained to remember anything useful, but the memory of that night was blurred with the chaos, the storm, and her worry over Landon and the kids. "It was raining. It was stormy. You didn't see everything," she cried, desperately hoping he would lower the weapon.

"You think I don't know?" he yelled, stepping closer. "I saw him after the man left. I ran out and saw my cousin dead on the ground. He was shot!"

Noel's heart hammered in her chest, her pulse roaring in her ears. She could see the anguish behind his anger, but his grip on reality was slipping. She'd been in dangerous situations before, but never like this, never this alone. She had no way to reach Landon, and no one was here to stop this man's anger from spiraling further out of control.

A flash of hopelessness washed over her as she took in the empty, windswept beach. The waves crashed behind her. She might die here, under a bright Jamaican sky, without ever getting a chance to live the life she'd longed for.

Suddenly, a shout came from behind. "No, no, Jevaun! You can't do this!"

Noel didn't move out of fear, but Horticia sprinted to her side with her arms raised toward the boy.

"She killed our cousin, Horticia!" he shouted in return.

"No, no, she's good. Please, Jevaun, this has to stop!"

"Tarone is dead, and she killed him!"

"He was doing wrong. We were all doing wrong! We should never have agreed to do this thing."

The air dragged in and out of Noel's lungs as she watched the young man struggle. The gun was still pointed at her, and she wasn't sure if Horticia's words penetrated his need for revenge.

A crack rang out, echoing over the water. The young man's scream followed as he dropped to his knees, clutching his arm as the gun tumbled from his hand into the sand. Horticia screamed and raced to the boy, falling onto the sand beside him.

Noel's breath snagged in her throat, and instinctively, she stumbled backward. The instinct to flee overpowered any impulse to help, and her only thought was to get away. She stumbled, not heeding where Horticia was. Her legs felt like lead as she tried to run, the sand dragging at her feet, turning each step into a battle. Her balance teetered as her legs gave way beneath her.

She expected to fling headfirst into the sand, but strong arms wrapped around her and pulled her upright, cradling her in a tight embrace against a solid chest.

"Fuck, baby, fuck! Jesus, baby, fuck!"

She didn't need to turn around to see who held her, recognizing Landon's voice. Relief flooded her, making her legs give out, but he was there, scooping her up into his arms and holding her close, carrying her as if she weighed nothing.

Her head spun as he carried her back toward the house, the world around them blurring. She barely noticed Devil and Frazier rushing past, sprinting toward the wounded man on the sand. Lightheaded and gasping, Noel struggled to catch her breath, but her lungs wouldn't cooperate, as if they'd forgotten how to expand. "C... c... can't b... brea..."

She was lowered to the patio, and she fell back, his hands cradling the back of her head to keep it from hitting the ground. He loomed over her and, through her spotty vision, could see the look of concern.

"Noel, baby, breathe with me."

Dots danced before her eyes, the edges of her vision fading. Then suddenly, his face sharpened into focus—those deep-set, stormy eyes framed by slashes of dark, thick brows. His hair was slightly damp, tousled from his morning shower. His intense gaze cut through the fog, grounding her in the moment. *I want to see that face forever*, she thought distantly, the panic ebbing.

"Breathe with me. In. Out. In. Out." His hand was pressed between her breasts, gently pushing against her chest in rhythm with his words.

She focused on his mouth and watched as he breathed in slowly, held it, and breathed out, struggling to match his rhythm.

The fear began to loosen its grip, and the spots in her vision faded, allowing her to truly see him again. She wanted to reach up, trace the line of his jaw, press her face into the warmth of his neck, and let him take away every last trace of the nightmare she'd just endured.

Behind him, just over his shoulder, she caught sight of Tad and Penny, huddled together, their faces drawn and tear-streaked, their eyes fixed on her in fear. The sight of their worry jolted her, stirring something protective within her. She didn't want to be the source of their distress. Slowly, she reached up, placing a trembling hand on Landon's arm as his hands braced on either side of her shoulders, steady and grounding.

But his hand pressed lightly against her shoulder, holding her down gently. "No, stay down, Noel," he said, his voice soft but firm. "I don't want you getting up too quickly." His eyes searched her face, his thumb brushing gently across her cheek as if reassuring himself that she was safe with him. He twisted his head and said, "Can you get her some juice?"

Tad whirled around and raced into the house, returning a moment later with a glass of orange juice.

Noel struggled to sit up, but Landon supported her, and Penny knelt at her side, holding the juice for her. She sipped and then said, "Honestly, I'm fine. The dizziness is gone."

Noel looked over, following Tad's gaze to the commotion on the beach. The distant sound of an ambulance siren grew louder, and she squeezed her eyes shut, a sigh slipping from her lips. "The Jamaican police must think we're cursed," she murmured. Opening her eyes, she turned to Landon, her voice a desperate whisper. "Landon, please... can we go? Can we just leave all of this behind?"

He held her hand tightly, his eyes softening. "I promise, Noel. We're heading to the airport as soon as we finish up here."

"I don't understand what happened," she said. "He kept saying I killed his cousin. He said that I shot his cousin, but I tried to tell him that I just shot in the direction of the roof. I told him that I didn't hit anything. I just scared the man, and he fell off the roof."

"Noel, you *did* hit him," Tad said.

She looked up, stunned, confusion swirling in her gaze. Landon's head whipped toward Tad, giving a silent shake of his head, his jaw tightening. Tad's face paled, his eyes widening as he stammered, "Oh, uh... maybe... I mean, I don't really know..."

Her heart raced, and she tightened her grip on

Landon's hand. "Landon!" she cried, desperation coloring her voice. "Don't shush him! Tell me what really happened! I couldn't have hit him… I don't even know how to shoot!"

Landon's shoulders slumped as the air rushed from his lungs. Shaking his head, he ran his hand over his face. "Noel, we can talk about this later—"

"No! I want to talk about this now!"

"Look, honey, Devil and Frazier are telling the police about what happened this morning. They are arresting Horticia. Devil is the one who got a shot off to hit the man's arm. I knew he had the best aim and was in the best position. The police are going to ask for your statement, too. I don't want to discuss what happened in the jungle. Let's get this over with and get to the plane."

Landon helped her to her feet, but she clung to his arms, her fingers digging in as she searched his face. "Just tell me. Did I kill that man on the roof?"

His gaze softened, his hand moving to cup her cheek, his thumb brushing gently against her skin. "No, Noel. You didn't kill him."

But something in his voice held back, and she couldn't help but wait, searching his face for the truth.

He sighed again and said, "Somehow, you managed to hit him in the upper chest with your shot. He fell to the ground, but I sent you and the kids away. He was still alive, so *you* didn't kill him. He was injured badly from the fall, and I knew he wouldn't survive. That's all I'm going to say right now. You did not kill him. Keep your answers to the police to the exact truth as you know it. Don't embellish. Don't add extra comments."

Her mouth opened to respond, but just then, the police inspector arrived, and Landon's arm wrapped around her, holding her close as she answered the inspector's questions. Her voice was steady despite the whirlwind of emotions within her.

"No, I've never seen the young man before," she said calmly. "No, I don't know why he thought I killed his cousin. No, I don't know who his cousin is."

Landon's answers were similarly brief, and the inspector soon closed his notebook, his expression softening. "I believe we're done here, Mr. Sommers and Ms. Lennox. I understand you're ready to leave?"

Devil and Frazier walked up to the patio after ensuring the EMTs had loaded the young man into the ambulance.

Landon nodded. "We're already packed and ready to head to the airport as soon as you're finished with us."

"We can consider that time to be now. I wish you well, but I know your stay in our country has not been peaceful. If I can extend an invitation to visit Jamaica in a less adventurous time, I will do so."

He nodded, then walked away, and Noel watched as everyone around her seemed to hustle into the house. Devil and Frazier followed Penny and Tad, telling them to check their rooms. The idea of breakfast had been abandoned.

Noel allowed Landon to lead her. She felt sluggish, once more like her feet were slogging through quicksand.

The scene inside the villa felt surreal. Everyone bustled around, grabbing last-minute items, checking bags, and clearing rooms. Even the idea of breakfast had been abandoned. Her exhaustion weighed on her, slowing her movements, and her feet felt as if they were sinking into quicksand with every step.

The front door opened, and there was Pamela, sweeping into the foyer with a flourish, a silver-haired gentleman at her side—her sugar daddy who, for once, might be more age-appropriate. Pamela hurried over to embrace Tad and Penny, introducing Henry and promising to see them in Montana soon. The kids nodded awkwardly, stepping back from her grand declarations, embarrassment evident on their faces.

Landon pulled Pamela to the side. "You always manage to be just outside all the shit that swirls around you!"

Pamela's joyous demeanor fled as her eyes narrowed into a glare. "What are you talking about?"

Henry stepped forward, taking a stand just to the side of her. "How dare you talk to her this way. I'll have you know that I'm—"

"Don't give a fuck, man," Landon growled before turning his attention back to Pamela. "Your boy toy was banging your housekeeper, and the two of them decided you shouldn't get all the money."

Pamela blinked as her mouth opened and closed several times like a fish out of water. "What?"

"Seems they cooked up the idea to pay someone to snatch the kids off the beach. Horticia called her cousins to take them and hold them until you paid. And they were too stupid to ask for a different amount than what you had coming, which led us to know it was an inside job."

Her face reddened as her gaze darted from Landon's hard-set expression to her children and then to the side to see Henry's brow furrowed in concern. And she couldn't have missed Henry taking a slight step back.

Her loud protestations came—"I had no idea! How dare he try to extort the money from me! This wasn't my fault!"

Landon sneered, apparently done with her. "Horticia is in jail along with her compadres. Roger has left but the police will keep looking for him. And if he contacts you, the FBI will be very interested and will probably consider you an accomplice—"

"I didn't know!" she continued as she looked at Tad and Penny. "Babies, I would never do anything to hurt you."

The kids remained quiet as Henry shushed Pamela, then wrapped his arm around her to usher her back. Landon turned to walk back to Noel, disgust written on his face.

Noel watched it all, numb to the scene around her. She felt like a ghost in her own life, hovering on the edges, detached from the chaos. In the back of her mind, she knew she should check on the kids and make sure they were holding up, but her thoughts were scattered, and her focus slipped.

"Noel?" Landon's voice cut through the haze, his eyes filled with concern as he turned her gently to face him.

The world slowed as he lifted a hand to cup her

cheek, his thumb brushing softly across her skin. "Sweetheart, talk to me. What's going on in that head of yours?"

She took a shuddering breath, the weight of everything pressing down on her. "I don't know," she whispered, her voice fragile. "I shot someone, Landon... I can't even process that. I don't know what to think." Her eyes closed as his arms wrapped around her, pulling her close, the solid beat of his heart steadying her.

"Take me home," she begged, her cheek pressed against his chest. "I just... I just need to go home. Away from all this."

25

"I just need to get away from all of this."

Those words echoed relentlessly in Landon's mind, circling like a recording on replay. Over and over, he heard them but wasn't sure of her meaning. *Get away from the island? Get away from the assignment? Get away from discovering she'd actually shot a man? Get away from me?* The last question had his gut in a knot. Glancing over at her, he was afraid to ask.

She had moved through the motions of leaving the resort with numb efficiency, her expressions a mask as they made their way to the airport. The plane Cole was flying was not nearly as plush as the charted flight they took to Jamaica. The seats were side by side with no tables. There was also no attendant, but there was a bathroom and a stocked refrigerator with food and drinks for self-serve.

Now, on the plane, she'd finally settled with the kids, color slowly returning to her cheeks as she encouraged them to eat. Despite everything, a soft smile played on her lips as she leaned close, giving them her undivided attention. But to him, there was a distance in her gaze, a subtle emptiness that unnerved him.

"She's pretty amazing." Devil's rumbling voice broke Landon's reverie. He looked over to see his friend seated across from him, his dark eyes softened in unexpected reflection.

Landon nodded, his voice rough. "Yes, she is."

"Things seemed to be intense between the two of you," Devil commented, the edge of his mouth twitching with amusement.

Landon managed a short laugh, glancing over. The large man with a dark beard could change between the devil and a teddy bear with just a glance. "Are you here to offer me relationship advice?"

Now, it was Devil's time to snort. "Do you need it?" Then his grin faded slightly. "If you do, I'm not sure I'm the right person to offer any."

Landon remembered overhearing another Keeper mentioning that Devil had once had someone serious in his life, but Devil fucked it up. But then, as Landon glanced over toward Noel, he wondered if he had also fucked things up.

"She seems okay now," Devil said.

It was strange for Landon to realize how well he seemed to know Noel after only meeting her a few days ago. Her voice was warm as she spoke with the kids. She smiled at them, nodding as they talked, and he knew she was counseling them about everything that had happened, including their complicated and ever-changing relationship with their mom. She spoke about their mom, both instructively and with great empathy. But he could also see the rigid way she held her body as though slightly disconnected and not quite there. Her spine was stiff, and her smile was warm, but it didn't reach her eyes. Tension lines bracketed her mouth.

"She wasn't prepared for this," Landon muttered, his voice low. "I shouldn't have let her go with me to get the kids. None of this was what she signed up for. She's strong, sure, but she's not used to... this." He glanced over at Devil. "You and I, we're used to assignments that go FUBAR. But Noel? She might've dealt with intense moments in her job, but nothing like what happened during that storm. Or what she faced on the beach today."

Devil raised an eyebrow, thoughtful. "Noel's resilient. She's trained to manage tough emotions and keep moving forward. She'll get through this."

Landon's brow furrowed, his voice barely a whisper. "I just can't get her last words out of my head."

Devil's dark brows snapped together. "What did she say?"

"She said she just wanted to get home and forget about everything."

Devil's expression continued to convey confusion. "I hate to break it to you, bro, but that sounds pretty normal."

Landon held Devil's gaze and asked, "But what does she mean? The whole trip, or does she mean me?"

"Don't get pissed, but I take it the two of you... um... got together?"

"Yeah, you could say that. We didn't have time to talk

about anything in the future when we got back to Montana, but we both said we wanted to see how far this thing between us could go."

Devil nodded, and he slightly lifted his hands. "Well, there you go. She doesn't want to forget you. She just wants to forget all the shit that happened on the trip."

"I can't be sure of that." Landon scowled, the knot in his chest tightening.

"Well, you sure as fuck aren't gonna know by just sitting here grumbling to me."

He wanted to tell Devil to fuck off but knew his friend was right. Landon was used to asking questions for information. He was used to finding out things. He was used to interrogations, watching body language, and listening to what was both said and unsaid. But glancing over at Noel, he felt lost. And he hated that feeling.

After a while, Penny yawned, and Noel stood to help lean her chair back. Tad did the same, and soon, both kids were asleep. Noel took blankets from the overhead bin and draped one over each of them. Devil stood and walked toward the back.

Noel glanced over, then moved to Landon.

"How are you?" he asked, reaching out to take her hand.

She offered a little smile. "Good. I'm good."

Still holding her hand, he guided her to the seat that Devil had just abandoned. She quickly sat, and he took heart that she wasn't avoiding him.

"How are the kids?"

Noel's gaze shot over to where Tad and Penny were

now sleeping. "I've said it before—kids are very resilient, and that certainly goes for those two. I'm going to suggest to Stan that they get counseling for a lot of reasons. Obviously, the kidnapping was traumatic, and certainly what happened today was, too. But I think they're trying to bury their hurt over their mom's actions."

Landon nodded. "I can understand. I've never gone through anything like that because I've always had my parents' love and their actions to back up that emotion."

"Same here." She sighed. "And you put it very well. I think Pamela loves her children in her own way, but her actions don't back up the emotion she should carry. In talking with them, I think Tad gave up on his mom earlier… even before this trip. Penny was hoping that her mom was just unused to small children. As Penny became older, she hoped they might have more in common. She is struggling with the realization that Pamela just isn't maternal."

Landon nodded again but remained silent, trying to think what to say. After two days of him and Noel talking so easily, he was utterly stymied about what topic he could bring up that would keep them conversing. He glanced over, watching as she appeared fascinated with something out the plane window. *Jesus, she's not even looking at me.*

He hated the way their morning had ended. *If we could've just lain in bed a little longer. If we could have fixed breakfast together without worrying about anyone else in the house. If we had had a chance to talk about what we hoped might happen when we got home.* He grimaced and scrubbed his hand over his face. Here they were, worlds apart in the same space.

"It looks like we can have good weather going back," Noel said.

"Um... yeah. Looks like it'll be nice."

"Maybe it'll be nice in Montana too," she murmured, her gaze fixed on some distant point outside.

"That'd be good," he replied, inwardly cringing at the hollow words that hung between them. This was what we'd become? Talking about the damn weather?

"Do you know what you'll recommend to the courts?" he asked, desperately trying to think of something they could discuss. It seemed like the only interesting thing he could come up with right now was about Tad and Penny. But considering the kids were the actual assignment, they should have been first and foremost on his mind anyway. *Fuck, what the hell was happening to me?*

Noel glanced his way, her expression shifting slightly. "I'll recommend supervised visits. No unsupervised time with Pamela, and certainly no overnights. If Stan decides to fight for full custody, I'll support him in that."

He nodded and mumbled, "Good." Another heavy silence settled over them, each mile they covered on this flight feeling like another wedge driving them apart. He glanced at his watch. *This is going to be a long, fucking flight.* Yet, it seemed as though time was slipping away.

Landon sensed someone beside him and turned, only to see Devil towering in the aisle, his expression caught somewhere between exasperation and determination.

With a dramatic sigh, Devil glanced first at him, then at Noel, and announced, "I can't stand this anymore."

Landon's brow knit in confusion, and his gaze met Noel's equally puzzled expression before they looked back at Devil.

"Uh… I'm sorry, what?" Noel stammered, her voice laced with bafflement.

"The fucking pair of you," Devil declared, his large hands settling onto his hips like a displeased parent.

For a fleeting second, Landon wished for turbulence to witness the colossal Devil flop down onto his backside. But instead, he kept his tone calm as he said, "Look, Devil, this isn't really your—"

"Don't even think about finishing that sentence, Landon," Devil interrupted, shooting him a stern look. "First of all, you're a friend and a Keeper, which means I'm forced to care. And second"—he pivoted to Noel, his tone softening—"you're a fierce, amazing woman. You deserve someone who knows it. And third—" His gaze swung back and forth between them like an umpire caught between home plate and first base. "If I have to listen to one more minute of your awkward, painful small talk on the rest of this flight to Montana, I'll lose my fucking mind. I can't find my earbuds, so I'm stuck listening to the two of you."

Noel's mouth dropped open, and her eyes widened. "I… I…"

"Shut it, sister," Devil chided, raising a brow.

Landon couldn't decide whether to laugh or stand

and shove his fist into Devil's face. "Devil, this isn't the time or the place. And, if you ever tell Noel to be quiet again, you and I will have problems, friends or not."

Devil's face lit up with a self-satisfied grin as if Landon had just confirmed everything he suspected. "Yep, that's what I thought," he said, with a wink that seemed to promise more meddling yet to come.

Landon and Noel exchanged another look, both wide-eyed and speechless, their mouths slightly parted in shock. Before they could gather their wits, Devil leaned in with a knowing smirk, cutting off any protest.

"If you didn't have feelings for her, you wouldn't have threatened me. Oh sure, if you thought I was disrespecting a woman, you might have said something, but you wouldn't have been quite so vehement."

"Devil," Noel said softly, drawing his attention down to her. "You're acting as though Landon has done something wrong. He's been nothing but wonderful this whole trip. Kind and supportive. Fabulous with the kids." She looked up at Landon with a fond smile. "And so amazing with me."

Devil's lips curled upward into a grin. "Yep, that's what I thought, too. Seems to me like Landon has been a lot more than just kind."

He lowered himself to their level, bracing his forearms on the aisle armrest with a thoughtful sigh. "Listen, I get it. Missions make everything intense. Landon's been through this, and Noel, as a social worker, you've seen your share of high-stakes situations. Emotions can get heightened. But that doesn't mean two people hook up just because of intense circumstances."

Noel gasped, and Landon clenched his jaw, feeling the heat rise in his face. "Goddammit, Devil. We didn't hook up. That's not what this was, and you have got to shut the fuck up." If they hadn't been in an airplane flying over the southern part of the United States, he might have considered shoving his so-called friend out of the emergency exit.

Devil shrugged, unfazed. "That's what I mean. You guys didn't hook up. Look, there's some kind of connection between the two of you, and whether or not it leads to anything is private. Believe it or not, I can understand private. But you two gotta talk about it. I realize this morning scared the shit out of you, Noel."

Landon's gaze jumped over to see her eyes widen and her face pale. Before he could say anything, it was apparent Devil wasn't finished.

"You feel guilty, shocked, and have a large dose of what-the-fuck-happened running through you. Am I right?"

She nodded, her gaze holding on Landon before moving back to Devil.

"Think of it this way, sweetheart. What if you hadn't fired the gun? Taken that shot? Would you rather have had Landon shot? Or the kids—"

"No!" she bit out, her eyes still wide. "No, not at all!"

"Then here's what you gotta think about. Just like any case you have where you have to make a difficult choice, you choose to do the right thing. Whether you never fired a gun or not, taking that shot was the right thing. The fact that you ended up hitting the fucker saved lives. It's fucking amazing. Wish I'd seen it, and as it is, I'll be telling that story for years."

Landon rolled his eyes but could see where his friend was going with his speech, so he remained quiet.

"Noel, honey," Devil continued. "The only bad guys in this whole scenario were the actual bad guys. Once you accept that, you let go of the guilt."

Noel stared momentarily, then Landon watched as her expression softened, and she nodded. Her small hand reached out and laid on Devil's much larger one. "You're right. Thank you. It was all shocking, and I haven't had time to process it, but you're right."

"Well, good. Glad we sorted that out," Devil said. "And because of all the shit that's been swirling around, two people who I happen to like have now started to doubt what might be going on between them. We got some hours before we land. I suggest the two of you stop talking about the fucking weather or the kids and have a fucking conversation about what the two of you would like to do once we land and get all the fucking assignment business taken care of."

Landon looked at Noel, seeing her lips twitch upward. She stared at him, and as her gaze dropped to his mouth, he knew she was also witnessing his smile.

Her gaze moved to Devil. "You curse more than I do," she said with a chuckle.

"Damn straight." He grinned. "Well, it looks like my business here is done." Devil rapped his knuckles against the armrest, then pushed himself to a stand.

Landon was surprised the seat didn't buckle with

Devil's considerable weight pushing on it. With a wink and a swagger, his fellow Keeper walked to the back of the plane and settled into one of the seats.

26

Noel let out a soft sigh, her lips curling into a smile as she shook her head. "He's... well..."

"Crazy?" Landon supplied, his brows arching playfully.

She chuckled, feeling her cheeks warm. "I was going to say intense. But also... honest. And he's got this strange way of being caring. It's a little... scary, but in a good way."

Landon shrugged, hands open as if to say *it is what it is*. "He's a good friend."

She nodded her agreement, then blew out a long breath as nerves skittered along her spine. "So, um... I guess we should talk."

"Yeah." Landon's voice softened, his gaze holding hers. "But first... I'm sorry it took someone like Devil to make you realize you shouldn't feel guilty about what happened when we were rescuing the kids. I should've told you myself, and been there for you after."

Noel looked down, her fingers tracing an invisible

pattern on her pants. "I don't know if that would have made a difference," Noel admitted. "At the time, everything was so surreal. I was incredibly naive to insist on going with you to get the kids, but I'm glad I did. I got to see you in action... the way you handled everything. I was able to spend more time with you and ensure the kids were okay. And I now know I actually fired a gun toward someone and, by sheer dumb luck, managed to hit them—something I still can't entirely process. But when I take into consideration what Devil said, I'm glad it was the bad guy who got shot."

Landon leaned closer, his gaze steady, unwavering. "As straightforward as it sounds, Noel, he was the monster who took those kids. As you got them safely back to the vehicle, I took care of him and one of the other men inside, who pulled a weapon on me. I wasn't going to tell you this, but you need to know. In these situations, I have to make life-and-death decisions, and I have to make them in an instant. I'm always going to choose life for myself and for those I'm sworn to protect."

"Thank you," she whispered, feeling the weight of his words settle over her like a warm blanket. Her gratitude was simple, perhaps even understated, but she hoped he felt the depth of it. Slowly, she turned her palm up in silent invitation. Her stomach tightened, a blend of anticipation and nerves twisting within her.

He didn't hesitate to reach over. His hand met hers, and their fingers laced together. She was stunned by the intimacy of how something so small could feel so monumental. Her heart thudded, and she drew a steadying breath, readying herself.

Inhaling another cleansing breath, she plunged ahead. "I feel like we should talk about last night. But... honestly? I'm terrified." She let out a breathy laugh, shaking her head. "That sounds ridiculous, doesn't it? I fired a gun and faced down people who wanted to hurt us, yet I'm afraid to talk about—"

She paused, her eyes flicking to the kids sleeping nearby, ensuring they were undisturbed. When her gaze met Landon's again, her voice softened. "About the... intimacy. Waking up with you. It doesn't have to mean everything, but... for me, it meant something. And if... if it didn't for you, that's okay. I just needed to say it."

Landon's grip on her hand tightened ever so slightly, his expression serious, almost vulnerable. "I hate that we didn't get a chance to talk this morning. But I need you to know something, Noel... it's been a long time since I've spent the night with anyone. I'm not someone who just... plays around. When I meet someone for..." He hesitated, then winced.

"Just sex?" she supplied, wanting to put him at ease.

He chuckled and nodded. "Yes, when I do meet someone just for sex, there is no cuddling or sharing a bed for sleep. So what we did last night meant something to me, too."

A breath escaped her, long and trembling as if she'd been holding the air in without realizing it. The weight of wondering what he felt had settled over her like a storm cloud, and now, with his words, it began to lift. She glanced down at their entwined fingers, feeling the warmth of his hand that had held hers so tenderly, the same hand that had held her close in the quiet moments of the night, had traced over her skin with a tenderness she hadn't expected—yet had also defended her, fiercely, even lethally. The realization stole her breath, igniting something deeper. His touch made her crave more, want more.

Gathering her courage, she looked up and met his gaze head-on. "We have to decide whether it means anything before we return to Montana." Her words tumbled out quickly, the vulnerability almost overwhelming. "I'm not asking for a commitment," she rushed to clarify, "I know it sounds... well, intense, given we've only known each other for a few days. But do you... want to see me again?"

His fingers twitched. She held his gaze, watching for any hint of what he truly felt, needing to see it in his eyes as much as hear it.

"Yes, Noel," he said, his voice soft but confident. "I want to see you again. There might be a few logistic challenges—since you live in Helena," he added with a grin, "but a three-hour drive? We can make that work."

"I actually live north of there, and I've also looked," she admitted, her cheeks warming. "It takes about two hours to get to you in Cut Bank. I don't have to drive into Helena every day. I have a wide territory, which is from Helena to Great Falls. My apartment is about halfway between."

His facial muscles relaxed, and his lips curved. "Two hours. That makes it even better. And since my house is south of Cut Bank, we can probably knock that down even more."

She leaned forward, smiling as he did the same. "If we keep talking, we'll get it to where we have no commute to see each other."

He barked out laughter. "That'd be fine with me." He reached with his free hand to grab his phone. "Can I have your address?"

She reluctantly let go of his hand to dig in her purse, then eagerly traded phone numbers, email, and physical addresses.

For the remainder of the flight, the conversation flowed effortlessly. She loved sitting in a seat next to him, close enough to feel the warmth of his arm around her, and to lean into him as the exhaustion from the whirlwind of this morning's events began to settle heavily on her. The idea of resting her head on his shoulder and drifting off, surrounded by his quiet strength, was tempting.

She was captivated by the subtle expressions on his face as he spoke of his family, his life back home, and his loyalty to his team. His dark brows framed his deep-set eyes, which shifted in color from a mysterious stormy gray to a soft blue-gray as if reflecting the depth of his emotions. The flight to Jamaica was enjoyable but filled with the unknown and being with someone she wasn't accustomed to. Now, after only a few days—albeit action-packed and emotionally draining—he was no longer a stranger.

Her gaze would casually drop, wandering over his body. Having felt his strength last night, she knew exactly what lay beneath his clothes—a sculpted, powerful physique that still had her pulse racing. She couldn't deny it; the thought of being close to him again, of feeling his skin against hers, stirred an ache of anticipation.

Tad, Penny, and Devil woke by the time they had a meal, and she was thrilled to see that the kids appeared more at ease after their rest and food. Now as they continued to the small airport near the ranch, she let out a long exhalation.

"What are you thinking?" Landon asked.

Her gaze jerked from looking out the window back to him, and she smiled. "Everything seems so surreal. It was just a few days ago that you and I met. And now, we're in a… um, new friendship… beginning of something." She covered her face with her hands. "God, I sound so juvenile!"

He barked out laughter and nodded. "I'm not sure I can describe this any better than that."

She smiled, nodding. "And everything else feels surreal, too."

"Like what?"

"A few days ago, I was excited about flying to Jamaica. Knowing we would be there briefly, I hoped to appreciate its beauty and at least see the beach. Now, when I think back, I realize that the past few days have been wild. Crazy. Unpredictable. Unexpected. So out of the norm, it's tough for me to wrap my mind around it."

He nodded again. "Again, you've hit the nail on the head. I'm not sure I could describe it any better. Whatever you're feeling, I think that's normal."

Laughing, she said, "I have normal feelings about very abnormal events."

"Exactly," he said with a grin. "You're handling it better than you think."

"What about you? While this assignment didn't turn out how you thought it would, is this normal for you? And I know you can't talk about specifics, but I just wondered about the feelings."

"As I told you, one of the things I like about my job is that every assignment is different. Some very mundane. Some are intellectually interesting, like when I go to a place and analyze what type of security system might work best. Sometimes, I'm tasked to accompany someone who needs extra security, and it may be to a boring conference or just for travel, and nothing unexpected happens. Yes, a few things go FUBAR."

She captured her bottom lip with her top teeth as she tried to remember what the letters stood for.

He must have recognized her confusion because he said, "Fucked up beyond all recognition."

Now, laughter bubbled from her. "Oh my God! I think that describes how I feel about this trip perfectly!"

As they taxied along the runway, she added, "Except about meeting you. That may have been unexpected, but it was not fucked up."

His grin widened. "Same here, Noel."

As soon as they walked down the stairs from the plane, they were met by an SUV. Stan leaped from behind the wheel to rush toward them, radiating nervous energy.

"Dad!" Penny and Tad shouted in unison, their voices brimming with joy.

Stan opened his arms wide, pulling both kids into a fierce hug, holding them so close that Noel wondered if they could even breathe. The deep lines etched on his face seemed softened, a testament to the anxiety he'd carried these past days. Her heart swelled, knowing she had played a part in reuniting them. This was the moment she'd hoped for.

Then unexpectedly, Devil walked over to her, a rare softness in his usually guarded expression. "This is where we part ways for now, Noel," he said. With that, he hugged her, his arms wrapping around her with surprising warmth, lifting her right off the ground.

"Hey, enough of that!" Landon's voice cut in. He was half joking, but his tone showed a hint of possessiveness.

Devil just laughed as he set her feet on the ground. He whispered, "I like you for my boy here. It takes a strong person to be with a Keeper. I think you're perfect for the job." He leaned back and held her gaze. "And I think he's perfect for you."

"Are you playing matchmaker, Devil?" she asked with a smile.

"If I can't do it for myself, I might as well do it for others," he replied with a smirk. He bent to press a soft kiss to the top of her head before saying his goodbyes to Tad and Penny, who clung to him in heartfelt hugs.

Cole and Frazier were more reserved in their goodbyes. A round of handshakes and claps on the back later, they bid farewell to Landon and strolled into the small terminal.

Stan pulled Landon into a hug before moving over to do the same with Noel. She felt the rancher rarely showed such emotion, but a business handshake wouldn't do. She could tell he was a man who didn't wear his heart on his sleeve, but today, the usual formalities were replaced by an overwhelming gratitude.

"Thank you," he murmured, his voice thick. "Thank you, thank you." As he stepped back, she noticed the glistening in his eyes, and her own throat tightened as she swallowed down a lump of emotion.

With their bags loaded, Tad hopped into the passenger seat while she, Penny, and Landon slipped into the back. Landon reached over, his hand finding hers, their fingers interlacing as they settled into the peaceful quiet of the drive. She watched the rolling Montana landscape unfold outside the window, so vastly different from Jamaica yet bringing a profound sense of peace. She felt as if she were finally home.

As they pulled up to the front of the ranch house, the kids barely waited for the SUV to come to a complete stop before they tumbled out, rushing toward the two elderly figures standing on the porch. Their grandparents enveloped them in hugs and kisses, the love spilling over. Noel felt the familiar tug of emotion, her heart warming at the sight.

"Come on inside," Margaret urged gently, beckoning them all toward the house.

Noel glanced down and sighed. Seeing Landon's raised brow, she explained, "I'm grungy, never showered after everything this morning, and quite honestly would love to find my bed and sleep for about two days."

He slung his arm around her shoulders and inclined his head toward the house. "First of all, you're beautiful, but I understand how you feel. We'll finish this, and then you can get home."

"Yes, but there's a lot to go over here, right?"

He looked down and held her gaze, then nodded slowly. "Yeah. I'm sure Margaret will have the kids, so be prepared to go over exactly what happened with Pamela and the entire last couple of days with Stan."

She took a deep breath and plastered on a wide, deliberately exaggerated smile. "Oh, goody," she said, feigning enthusiasm.

He laughed, pulling her a little closer with a gentle squeeze. Together, they followed the others into the warmth of the ranch house, ready to face the final pieces of this journey, hand in hand.

27

The moment they stepped into the warmth of the ranch house, Landon wasn't surprised to see Margaret gently ushering Tad and Penny upstairs, her voice soft but commanding as she fussed over them. He could hear her words of comfort, promising clean clothes and warm showers as she called for the housekeeper to tend to their laundry. Her maternal touch seemed to envelop the children, offering them the security they hadn't felt from their mom.

Standing nearby, Thurston extended a firm, heartfelt handshake to Landon, then turned to Noel, his gaze filled with gratitude that words couldn't quite convey. Landon noticed the same raw emotion in Thurston's face that he'd seen in Stan's back at the airport—a profound, unfiltered relief mixed with something unbreakable, a kind of respect and quiet awe.

"I can't thank you enough," Thurston said, his voice thick with emotion. He cleared his throat, trying to steady himself. "Please, come into the study. Stan and I need to hear everything—without the chance of the kids overhearing."

Landon placed a gentle hand on Noel's lower back, guiding her in front of him as they entered the study. He glanced around, finding it exactly as he'd expected—a sanctuary of warmth and dignity. The walls were lined with bookshelves filled with worn volumes, each one likely holding its own history in this house. A large window framed a view of the vast ranch, stretching endlessly under the Montana sky. The wood floors, softened by thick green-and-maroon rugs, grounded the space, while a comfortable sofa against the far wall seemed to invite honest conversations. A double desk sat between the windows, a sturdy piece that had clearly served both Stan and Thurston for years.

Stan indicated they should take the sofa. He and his father turned the two cushioned, wooden chairs from in front of their desks to face the couch. Once settled, Margaret entered. She smiled, and then her gaze landed on Thurston. "I had our cook prepare something light to eat for everyone. Do you think you'll be long, honey?"

"Why don't you ensure the kids eat once ready? We'll have something when we've finished."

Her lips tightened as she blinked several times, then quickly wiped at an errant tear. Thurston jumped to his feet and wrapped his arms around her. "Now, now, Margaret. The kids are home safe."

She exhaled shakily, brushing away a tear that had slipped free. Her gaze turned to Noel, a look of both strength and vulnerability in her eyes. "If you don't mind, I'd like to speak with you later, to learn what I can do to help Tad and Penny through... all of this."

Noel nodded, her voice soft but steady. "I promise we'll talk before I leave. I'll make sure you know everything I can share to help them."

Landon stole a glance at Noel, taking in the exhaustion etched on her face and the subtle tension in her shoulders, yet still seeing the compassion and determination that drove her. Despite the toll of the past few days and the physical and emotional exhaustion weighing her down, she was still here, willing to give more of herself. A surge of admiration welled in him, mixed with something deeper—an ache he wasn't ready to name. He simply took her hand in his and squeezed it gently, letting her feel his quiet support.

As soon as Margaret left, Stan leaned forward, his voice low and firm. "I want everything," he said, his words filled with an urgency he could barely contain. "I need to know what my children went through, what happened, what their mother did—or didn't do. Leave nothing out. Please." His gaze flickered between Landon and Noel, a man ready to face whatever truth they brought to light, no matter how painful, because his love for his children demanded it.

Landon looked over at Noel. "I'll let you speak about what all happened, and then I can add my thoughts and conversations with Pamela, Tad, and Penny."

He nodded, then faced Stan and Thurston. "Most of this information you know from LSIMT keeping you in the loop with everything we encountered once we arrived at the resort where Pamela had a house. I will say that she appeared distraught—"

"Hmph," Stan grunted.

Landon didn't acknowledge the interruption but continued. "We questioned her, the housekeeper, Horticia, and Roger—"

"Goddamn fuckin' leech," Stan snarled.

"Stan, they'll get finished a helluva lot faster if you keep your comments to yourself," Thurston chastised.

Stan nodded, but before Landon could continue, Noel said, "Mr. Fugate, I know this is so hard for you to hear. But, at that moment, I can truthfully tell you that Pamela was very upset. Now, what other emotions was she feeling? I can't be sure. But she was desperate for the kids to be safe."

He nodded, then mumbled, "I'm sorry. Please continue."

"We waited until our people could ping the call that came in and comb through the CCTV footage in the area. Since they were taken from the beach and immediately walked through the jungle to get to their vehicle, we didn't want to waste time. Once we had the area and knew the storm was coming, Noel and I went after them. They were held about twenty miles away from the resort."

"You went, too?" Stan asked Noel, his eyes wide.

"I thought being there when Landon rescued them was important."

Stan winced, pain lacing his face as well as his tone. "Thank you. Jesus, thank you."

"Goddamn," Thurston muttered.

Noel twisted her head slightly to catch Landon's eye, and she nodded. Beginning again, he said, "Noel and I made it to where the children were being held. There were a few buildings, two uninhabitable, and I identified the one they were held in. They were upstairs, the three men downstairs." He could see Stan and Thurston barely hanging on, so he pushed past the details. "The men were dealt with quickly and efficiently, and we got to the children. They were frightened but unharmed."

Stan's gaze shifted sharply from Landon to Noel, his eyes filled with worry and the need for reassurance. As Noel nodded, his shoulders relaxed, and he seemed to breathe just a little easier.

Landon kept his voice steady yet compassionate. "By then, we were in the storm, but we got back to our vehicle. A mudslide closed off the road leading back to the resort, and as we drove in the other direction, trees fell over the road. My people were able to locate a small shack that may have been used as a barn at one time, but it offered us a respite from the rain and wind. We spent the night there. It may not have been what the kids were used to, but Stan..." He paused, a note of admiration in his voice. "You should be very proud of them."

Stan appeared to hang on every word.

"Noel talked with them, and again, despite being very frightened, they were also resilient. The four of us chatted, and then the kids fell asleep, and it wasn't long before we also slept. The following morning, we returned to the road but left our vehicle. We hiked down toward the mudslide because that's where my people who'd managed to fly in would meet us. Again, Penny and Tad were troopers during the entire time. They did everything we asked and were excited to get back."

Silence fell, thick with emotion, as Stan absorbed Landon's words, a profound gratitude evident in his expression. At last, he nodded, his voice catching slightly as he said, "I can't express what this means to me, to all of us." He raised a hand, stopping Landon and Noel before they could respond. "I know you'll say it was just part of your job. But taking care of my children's emotional needs, helping them feel safe—that's above and beyond, and we'll never forget it."

"It was my pleasure to be able to help," Landon said.

Noel leaned forward, her voice gentle. "I feel the same. Your children are wonderful, and I talked with them on the way to their mom's house, again once we arrived there, and more on the airplane. I feel very comfortable with how they're dealing. I will strongly suggest that they receive counseling because there can be long-term reactions to the trauma, but I can discuss that with Margaret when she joins me."

"You are right, of course, that we had been in constant contact with your boss, Logan Bishop, and our longtime family attorney, who's a close friend. And we appreciate the calls you have provided between us and the kids. Again, the two of you have exceeded anything we could expect in such a crisis. What I need to know now is about Pamela. Not just what she knew and when she knew it, but how she responded to the kids when they were brought back."

Noel looked at Landon, giving him a subtle nod to proceed.

Landon took a deep breath, choosing his words carefully. "By the time we arrived, Horticia had informed Pamela that the kids had been taken from the beach, but the local police were stretched thin, focused on preparing for the storm. The storm shifted north, sparing the island the worst, but it created chaos for them all the same. They handed the case over to me quickly."

Stan and Thurston were listening intently, their eyes pinned on him.

"As Noel said earlier, Pamela was distraught, begging us to find the children. Since neither of us has any previous history with her, I cannot attest to her mental state or her actions. When we returned, she greeted the children and fussed over them but didn't question them about what happened." He offered a pointed glare. "Roger was interested in what the kids overheard. Horticia was there but in the background. My people discovered phone contact between Roger and Horticia from the last time Pamela had brought him to the island. Our suspicions were aroused."

"Are you telling me that their mother's fuck buddy was the one who had my children kidnapped?" Stan's face was red and mottled as he roared his fury.

Landon maintained his composure and nodded. "Roger knew that half a million dollars was being brought to the island for Pamela. He convinced Horticia to find someone to participate for a cut of the money. Horticia's cousins, along with a friend, must have easily agreed and took the children. Roger escaped and is now hunted by the Jamaican police, who have Horticia in custody."

"He's still out there?" Thurston asked, his eyes narrowing.

Landon lifted his arms with palms up. "With the tropical storm, the police are doing their best. But if he tries to come back into this country, he'll be stopped and arrested. Our FBI has been contacted by the Jamaican police as well as my boss."

"And Pamela?" Stan bit out.

"By this morning, Pamela was… distracted. She'd already attached herself to a new man she'd met… or perhaps someone she knew before. An older gentleman with a resort house nearby. She said goodbye to the kids, knowing there'd be no payoff, no papers to sign. When we left, she was with him."

Stan's expression twisted with a mixture of pain and anger. He ran a hand over his face, his jaw tight. "The only good things I ever got from that woman were Penny and Tad. Otherwise, she's been nothing but a waste."

Thurston leaned forward, his chest heaving with emotion. "And Mike?" He closed his eyes for a moment and shuddered. "Christ, I can't believe Mike is gone. He was part of this ranch most of his life. Part of our family for that long."

Noel glanced over at Landon, her lips pressed together and pleading in her eyes. He nodded and swallowed deeply. "Mike was good for the kids to see when they got back. They were excited, and it was evident he was relieved. He walked outside and a few minutes later had a heart attack. Noel saw him from a window and alerted the rest of us. I worked on him until the ambulance arrived. I received the call from the hospital not too long after that he had died."

Stan rubbed his hand over his face, his eyes blinking back the gathered moisture. "We're taking care of everything. His body will be sent to us, and we're dealing with what needs to be done."

"The kids were asking about that," Noel said softly. "I gave them accurate answers without giving too much detail."

"Thank you," Stan said, then his shoulders heaved with a great sigh. "Seems like that's all I say to you, but honest to God, you have my thanks."

Just then, footsteps sounded outside the study, and Margaret peeked through the doorway. "I wanted to let you know that the kids are downstairs at the table having something to eat. As soon as you're finished, I'd love for you all to join us."

Thurston stood, wrapping his arms around his wife with a gentle strength. "I think we're finished here," he murmured, his voice carrying a profound relief. "Sitting with the kids for a while will be good."

Stan also took to his feet and thrust his hand out, once again shaking both Noel's and Landon's hands. "If you follow my mom and dad, we'll be pleased to have you join us."

As Landon and Noel rose to follow, Landon's hand found the small of Noel's back once again. At that moment, a silent promise passed between them, grounding her, anchoring them both as they stepped out to join the family, ready to share in the joy of being safely home.

Soon, they were gathered around the spacious, sunlit kitchen table, the atmosphere infused with warmth and the scent of freshly made food. The kitchen was modern but cozy, with soft wooden cabinets, polished countertops, and a large window that framed a stunning view of the backyard. Beyond, the sprawling ranch stretched out, with mountains towering in the background, casting their peaceful shadows over the land.

Even though he'd eaten on the plane, Landon realized how hungry he was. Margaret had prepared a perfect meal of roast beef and sharp cheddar sandwiches on homemade sourdough, creamy potato salad, vibrant fresh fruit, and slices of golden, flaky homemade pie. He devoured his plate, glancing up to see Penny and Tad doing the same, their spirits visibly lifting with each bite.

He sat across from Noel, initially disappointed not to be beside her, but now grateful for the view. She was eating very little, though she kept her smile bright, effortlessly drawing laughter from the children and calming Margaret's frayed nerves. Still, he noticed the dark circles beneath her eyes, the occasional flicker of strain behind her smile. She was running on pure will, and he could feel her exhaustion in his bones.

He wanted to suggest they leave, but Margaret had requested a private moment with Noel after the meal. The kids, full and a bit more relaxed, begged to see their horses, and Stan invited Landon to join them on a short walk to the barn. He hesitated, reluctant to leave her even for a moment, but Noel looked up and gave him a warm, genuine smile. With a wink and a promise in his eyes, he turned and followed Stan and the children outside.

It was heartening to see Penny and Tad in their familiar surroundings, shedding some of the tension of the past days. But he was still restless, his thoughts always drifting back to Noel. After a short while, he saw her and Margaret emerge onto the deck, and without a second's hesitation, he returned to her side.

Then came the farewells, filled with handshakes, tight hugs, and murmurs of gratitude. When it was time for Penny and Tad to say goodbye, both kids clung to him, their eyes misty with tears.

"Remember," he whispered softly to each of them, "I couldn't have asked for better companions on this rescue. One day, you'll look back and remember your strength, not your fear."

Tad managed a shaky smile, squeezing Landon's hand with surprising firmness, while Penny wrapped him in a sweet, lingering hug. Noel had her own heartfelt goodbyes with each of them, her voice tender, her words comforting. Together, they walked toward their vehicles, flanked by the family who'd watched over them with pride and love.

Landon stood at her door once Noel had slid behind the wheel of her small SUV. He noticed her glance, a hint of something unspoken in her eyes. He leaned down and whispered, "Just follow me."

They drove down the long ranch road, and as they

reached the large wooden sign marking the entrance to Fugate Ranch, he pulled over, parking beneath the shadow of the sign. She stopped behind him, stepping out with a curious smile as he came around and wrapped her in his arms. They stood there for a long moment, silent, their embrace deep and wordless as they let the weight of the last few days melt away.

Finally, she leaned back, her eyes soft as she looked up at him. "I'm so glad you did this, Landon. I hated the thought of such a public goodbye."

He smiled, brushing a strand of hair from her cheek. "Noel, no way was I letting you go without a moment alone."

They stayed wrapped in each other's arms, savoring the closeness, until he looked down, his gaze tender. "I know you're exhausted, but you were incredible back there. Just what everyone needed. I hate that you have to drive home alone, as tired as you are."

She shrugged, a hint of a playful smile returning. "You have a longer drive than I do." She laughed, shaking her head. "Although, I have no doubt your stamina's a bit better than mine right now."

He resisted the urge to make a teasing remark about exactly how long his stamina could last with her. Instead, he let his thumb gently trace the back of her hand as he spoke his true intention. "I'm going to follow you back to your place."

Her eyes widened slightly, surprise mixing with gratitude. "Landon, you don't have to. I don't want you to go out of your way—"

His voice was gentle but insistent. "I just want to

make sure you get home safe. Please, let me do this for you."

She laughed, wrapping her arms around his waist, her smile lighting up her face. "If a gorgeous man I happen to like very much offers to see me home, I'd be crazy to say no."

He bent down, brushing a soft kiss across her lips, savoring the simple, sweet moment. "Good to know."

"I'll pull in front, and you can follow me."

He continued to nibble on her lips, mumbling, "Can't wait to have you in my arms again." With that, they climbed into their vehicles, and with a lighter heart, he followed her down the road.

28

Noel pulled into her apartment building's parking lot, and a thrill ran through her as she watched Landon stop in one of the visitor spots. For the entire drive, she'd had to resist the constant urge to check her rearview mirror, ensuring he was still behind her. And now, here he was.

How has this become my life? she wondered. For a professional dedicated to children's rights, her world had been full of courtroom battles and advocacy. But somehow, in the past few days, she'd been swept into an alternate reality—a world of security specialists, high-stakes danger, threats, and a one-night stand that, it seemed, wasn't just for one night.

Now, she had no idea what to expect. *Would he want to come in? Would he want to stay for a drink?* She let out a soft laugh at herself, thinking of her "drink" options—just water, orange juice, diet soda, or a local pale ale.

Before she could overthink, he was there beside her

door, smiling in that quiet, reassuring way. She fumbled for her purse, grabbing her phone as she stepped out.

"I'll get your bag," he offered, reaching in the back seat to grab her small overnight case and lifting it with ease.

"Thank you." She started to take it from him as soon as he had it in his hand but hesitated, still not wanting to say goodbye. Looking up into his face, she hoped for a sign of what he might want. He wasn't making any moves to dump her case and leave, so she ventured, "Would you like to come up?" The words slipped out before she'd finished thinking them through, but he smiled, and she was instantly glad she'd offered.

"Yes. Absolutely, Noel." His smile widened instantly.

With her bag in one hand, his other hand rested lightly against the small of her back as they walked, a simple touch that sent sparks through her, so subtle yet intentional. Something about the gesture—a blend of warmth and protection—had her heart racing in ways she hadn't thought possible.

"Are you okay?" he asked gently as they climbed the stairs to the second floor.

A blush crept across her cheeks, and she managed a small laugh. "Yes, just… thinking too much," she admitted, reaching for her key. She opened the door, stepping into the neat space she'd thankfully cleaned before the trip. "Would you like something to drink?"

"Water would be good," he said, setting her bag by the door.

"I also have orange juice or pale ale from a local brewery."

"Are you going to have anything?"

She walked over and placed her purse on the small table beside a window between the kitchen and living area. "You know, I think I could have the beer."

His smile warmed, and he dipped his chin. "Make it two."

He followed her as she walked into her tiny kitchen, grabbed the two beer bottles from the refrigerator, and popped the tops.

"I don't need a glass," he said. "Straight from the bottle is fine and less for us to clean later."

They stood together in her cozy living room, the quiet intimacy of the moment wrapping around them like a blanket. Lifting their bottles, they tapped them together, the soft clink mingling with their breathing and her pounding heartbeat. The room was bathed in the soft glow of early dusk, the sun dipping low in the sky, casting a warm, amber hue over everything.

She wanted to offer him a chance to spend the night and drive back to his place in the morning, but an awkwardness lingered. They were back in the real world now, far from the adrenaline-fueled days they'd shared. Was their connection just a fleeting spark from an intense, high-stakes experience?

She took a slow sip of her beer, her gaze drifting over him. "It's strange," she finally murmured, her voice soft. "Just… being here, with you, like this. I wasn't sure if it would feel the same, you know?"

Landon bent over to set his beer bottle on the coffee table, then slid her bottle from her fingers and placed it next to his. She looked up in surprise as he stepped closer. His hands curled around her fingers to hold her tightly. Drawing their clenched hands up, he pressed them close to his heart. "If you're tired and want me to leave, just say so. My feelings won't be hurt."

"I am tired, but I don't want you to leave. I want you to stay. I mean, if you'd like to—"

"I absolutely want to stay," he said, his gaze not wavering.

"You can stay as long as you want. If you spend the night here, you'd be more rested to drive back to your place tomorrow." She winced, hoping she didn't sound desperate.

His grin widened. "I like the way you think. But here's the thing—this," he said, gesturing between them, "this isn't something I want to let go of. I don't want this to just fade away because we're back to our normal lives."

With the smile staying firmly on his face, she relaxed. "You said I was in my head earlier, and you were right. The way you and I met and started a relationship was completely out of the ordinary for me. And once we got back here, I suddenly had no idea if we were simply together because of the bizarre situation we found ourselves in."

He squeezed her hands, still holding them to his chest. "I promise that this is new for me too."

She laughed and cocked her head. "So you don't usually pick up women during your intense assignments?"

"Never. I'll admit that I've had friends who found

their significant other during assignments. But for me? This is new, too."

"Then I'm glad you're here in my home."

His gaze drifted around her space. She tried to see her apartment through his eyes—colorful pillows on the dark blue sofa and matching chair. The TV was on a low console she'd found in a discount store, along with the coffee table. She'd sanded and repainted them in rustic cream. There were framed pictures on the wall, some of her family over the years—others, scenes that offered more splashes of warm color. She hefted her shoulders. "I like it. It's home." Her gaze moved back to him. "It's not a forever place, but a perfect right-now place. I hope it'll be comfortable for you tonight."

"If you think I'm staying here just to have a restful layover, then I need to convince you that I'm staying here because I want to spend time with you."

Her breath hitched as his words sank in. She could see the sincerity in his eyes, the way he looked at her as if he saw all of her, even the parts she hadn't yet revealed. "Oh."

Landon laughed and wrapped his arm around her. "No pressure. No expectations of sex. Just a chance to spend some quiet downtime with you where we're not racing through the jungle or hiding out from a storm. Although, I wouldn't object to another shower with you."

"Yes," she said, her voice breathy with anticipation. "In fact, we should take care of that now." Hesitating, she crinkled her nose. "I should warn you that, unlike the resort house guest suite, my shower is over the bathtub. I'm not sure it's big enough for—"

He stepped closer, his hand lifting to cup her cheek. "Noel, what we have is more than a one-night stand. As much as I love having sex with you, right now, that's not what you need. And I'm not such a horndog that I can't take a shower without us having sex." His lips quirked on one side. "I can't guarantee that biology won't kick in, and my cock will be good and ready as soon as I see you naked in the shower. But I have control over my actions. And we are not going to have sex now. When in the shower, we'll take care of each other, pile up on your couch, finish our beer, watch a movie, and then head to bed and sleep. I know you need that, and I want to take care of you."

His words moved through her, settling deeply inside, finally resting near her heart. She breathed in, then let it out slowly, her gaze never leaving his face. "You do realize that makes you almost perfect, don't you?"

He lifted a brow. "It doesn't make me absolutely perfect?"

"I like to leave room for improvement." She laughed.

He chuckled and rolled his eyes. She grabbed his hand and started toward the hall, skidding to a stop. Looking over her shoulder, she scrunched her nose. "I just realized you don't have your bag. Go get whatever you need from your vehicle, and I'll start the shower."

"Good thinking. I totally forgot about my bag after thinking about you naked in the shower."

She playfully slapped him on the arm and watched as he darted out of her apartment. By the time she'd carried her bag to her bedroom, dumped the dirty clothes into her laundry basket, and grabbed a T-shirt, sleep shorts, and clean panties, he was already back.

She had not falsely claimed about the limited space bathtub shower. He didn't seem to mind as he helped wash her hair, and she sudsed his body. He also hadn't lied when his cock stirred and looked ready to play. Her gaze wandered over his entire body, marveling at the naked beauty presented in front of her. Lean muscles. Hard abs. And an impressive erection. "I can… um… take care of that, you know," she offered.

He shook his head but grinned. "I can't believe I'm turning down the chance for a blow job from you. Any man with a gorgeous woman, especially one as sweet as you, would consider themselves lucky to have your lips wrapped around their cock. But the relationship we're building will be one of trust."

She considered protesting, feeling more refreshed after her shower and more than a little tempted to put intimacy back on their evening agenda. But as she combed through her damp hair, a yawn escaped. Landon was right—exhaustion clung to both of them. And the thought of a quiet, cozy evening, snuggled up with him, simply talking and unwinding in front of the TV, sounded unexpectedly perfect.

They settled into the living room, finishing their beers and adding a simple snack of cheese, crackers, deli meats, and crisp apple slices to share. Their conversation drifted to light, easy topics, both of them too tired to wade into anything deep. She was delighted to find out he loved not just action films but had a soft spot for old mysteries.

"When I really want to relax," he admitted with a grin, "I put on animal documentaries."

Her jaw dropped in mock surprise. "Oh my God, me too! I think I might've just fallen in love with you and decided we need to have all the babies!"

He laughed, tugging her close to brush his lips over hers. The kiss was warm and lazy, stealing her breath and making her consider a shift in the night's plans. But he pulled back, his thumb tracing her cheek. "Let's clean up and get some rest."

They tidied up their snack, and he took a moment to check that the apartment was secure. When they finally climbed into bed, she flipped on the TV, finding an animal documentary on Caribbean wildlife. As soothing footage of crystalline waters and vibrant fish filled the screen, Landon turned toward her, his eyes thoughtful.

"Would you ever want to go back?" he asked softly.

She looked over at him, a little surprised. "Go back?"

He nodded toward the screen. "To the Caribbean? Maybe Jamaica or another island if that holds too many memories?"

She traced her lower lip with her tongue. "I'd like to," she said at last. "It was breathtaking, and I only had a few minutes to soak it in—the white sand, the warm water on my feet. The color of the ocean..." She paused, remembering the perfect blue that had stretched endlessly before her. "It was like the Montana sky on the clearest day, that brilliant shade you can hardly believe is real. Looking out over the water, I felt...

peace." She let out a soft laugh. "So yes, I'd like to go back someday. But who knows when or if I could afford it."

He watched her with a quiet intensity. "Would you go alone? Or would you want company?"

She met his gaze, holding it as she weighed her answer. The warmth in his eyes, the way he was looking at her—it was impossible to be coy. "If I had someone I cared about, then yes, absolutely. But if it were just a tour group... no. I prefer the company of someone I trust, someone special." She let her words hang in the air, feeling them linger between them like a whispered promise. "But I'm not afraid of being alone, either."

He didn't say anything, just pulled her closer, his arms circling her as if to silently convey everything he felt. It was fine with her; she'd rather savor the moments they had now than dwell on a future that might not come.

They lay together, comfortably entwined, watching the soothing scenes of coral reefs and dolphins until her eyelids grew heavy. She barely registered him turning off the TV and switching off the bedside lamp before he curled around her, his arms holding her close. Her last memory was his soft, deep voice, murmuring, "Good night, sweet Noel. I'll catch you in the morning." She drifted off with a smile on her lips, feeling safe and cherished as sleep claimed her.

She woke, feeling cocooned in warmth. She smiled while still blinking her eyes open to the early morning light. Landon's arms were wrapped around her, one holding her breast and the other pressed against her tummy. His erection was nestled against her ass, and she immediately felt her core clench.

She started to speak, but as his hand on her breast kneaded the flesh and his fingers rolled her nipple, no words came forth. Her brain had emptied with all the electricity firing along her nerves.

"Morning, baby."

His deep greeting sounded next to her ear, and she felt the rumble from his chest as it pressed against her back.

She leaned her head back and twisted slightly, giving his lips access to her neck.

He accepted her silent invitation and began kissing from her jaw down over her neck, sucking gently at the fluttering pulse. His hand on her breast now moved between the two, still kneading, tugging, eliciting moans. "Morning," she managed to mutter between groans.

The hand he had pressed on her tummy slid lower, and she was grateful she'd slept without panties. His thumb circled the swollen nub as his fingers glided through her wet folds. She lifted her leg, giving him easier access.

She reached behind her, her fingers trailing along his taut ass, then sliding between their bodies to cup his balls. Now, the groan that sounded out in the room came from him. Moving her hand slightly, she wrapped it around his engorged cock, feeling pre-cum already leaking from the tip.

"Oh God, I want you," she gasped. She had an unopened box of condoms in her nightstand, always wanting to be prepared just in case. She had no idea if he would trust them. "I have protection in the drawer if you don't have any with you. Don't be surprised that the box hasn't been opened. I rarely need them, and I always keep an eye on the expiration date and buy a new box. Honestly, I haven't looked in a while and hope the expiration date hasn't passed."

"I'll check." His hand left her sex, and she immediately missed the feelings his talented fingers elicited. He reached over her, pressing her body into the mattress as he pulled open the nightstand drawer and rummaged around. His hand must've landed on the correct box because he pulled it out, held it up, and she heard a sigh of relief.

"They're good, babe."

"Oh, thank God!"

He chuckled again, and she loved the feel of his laughter against her back. He shifted enough to get his hands free, rolling the condom on. "You on top?"

She grinned widely and nodded. "Absolutely. I'd be fucking overjoyed to ride you!" She scrambled to her knees as he rolled on his back, his cock bobbing up. She took him in her hand as she straddled his lap. She now wished she'd wrapped her mouth around his erection before he sheathed himself, but seeing him ready had all neurons firing in her body. His hands were on her hips, his fingers digging into her ass as she lifted and then plunged. She used to read her mom's historical romances and had to fight a giggle at the idea of his sword being slid into the scabbard.

His hands reached for her breasts, but she should have known he would have been aware of everything when he asked, "What the hell are you laughing about?"

As she lifted and settled over his cock, finding a rhythm as his hands tweaked her nipples, she admitted, "Just comparing you to the old romances my mom used to read. I have to tell you, real life is a hell of a lot better."

A grin spread over his face. "Good to know."

By now, his erection stretched her, dragging against her inner core as his hands expertly played with her breasts in a way that had her almost weeping for joy. It didn't take long for her to know her orgasm was imminent, and she desperately wanted them to come together. "I'm close, so close. Please, please…"

Her plea was almost incoherent, and she wondered if he knew what she was begging for. But his intuition was spot-on as he continued helping her by sliding his hands back down to her hips and lifting her slightly. He worked his hips as he plunged upward.

She watched in fascination as his face grew red, the muscles in his neck corded, and the vein was prominent. But he didn't close his eyes, and neither did she. With her hands firmly planted on his shoulders, her breasts dangling in front of his face, and her hair creating a curtain around them, their bodies moved together in unison until she shook as her release tightened her core, squeezing his cock.

He groaned at his release, and her eyes clenched shut as the tremors moved from her head to her toes. Unable to hold herself upright anymore, she flopped down on him, eliciting a grunt as her chest hit his. They lay, panting, her body slowly cooling until his cock slowly slipped from her sex.

"Jesus, babe. I've never come so hard. I saw fireworks. Lights flashing. Maybe even a glimpse of heaven when I came with you."

She laughed, her body moving with his. "I think that's the sexiest thing anyone's ever said to me," she admitted. She lifted and looked down at his face. "And for what it's worth, I've never had anyone like you."

They kissed, languid and long, until he finally groaned, "I need to deal with the condom."

She rolled to the side and watched as he pulled the condom off, tied it, then left the bed to walk his gorgeous ass into the bathroom. She stretched her arms over her head, feeling alive, sated, and happier than she could remember being in a long time. She hoped the feeling lasted.

29

Landon drove to work later that day, and his mind filled with thoughts of Noel. He'd only stopped by his house long enough to change into clean clothes. He hadn't spent the whole night with someone in a very long time and wasn't ashamed of feeling glad that she hadn't either. It felt easier to start something without the residual emotions of a recent someone. Waking with her this morning had been how he'd like to start each day.

But then, in truth, it hadn't all been about the sex. His concern yesterday started from the moment Mike collapsed to the terror he'd felt when a man held a gun on Noel. It continued on the plane flight back to Montana, and wanting to protect her when they were at the Fugate Ranch. Last night, he just wanted to care for her—ensure she was fed and rested. Spending the night was a privilege. Sex before he left was a bonus.

Soon, he was at the compound. He greeted Mary and returned his equipment to Bert, offering thanks for having the foresight to make sure he'd been well taken care of. He greeted the Keepers as he walked into the main workroom, knowing some were in the field on other missions. Moving to Logan, he shook his boss's hand and asked, "Anything new?"

"Devil and Frazier have filled us in on everything beyond your report," Logan said. "We've checked with the Jamaican police, and they have Horticia under arrest and they're still actively searching for Roger. Word is, he may have taken a boat from Jamaica to one of the islands. Pamela didn't return to the resort house, spending last night with her latest fling. With the children's safe return to Stan, our part of the mission is officially complete."

Landon's eyes narrowed. "And what about the person who sent Mike to kill Pamela?"

Logan's gaze held steady. "Officially, that falls outside our mission parameters, especially since the Fugates, who hired us, haven't been told anything yet. "But," he added, "we're aware there are risks if it gets out that Mike shared something with Noel before he died. We won't leave that loose end hanging for her... or for you."

Landon tilted his head back, closing his eyes as he absorbed the information, steadying his breathing. He knew Logan wouldn't leave any of the Keepers vulnerable, nor anyone they cared about. Dropping his chin, he looked back at him. "I'm sure it's already been reported to you, but I want you to hear it directly from me. I've started a relationship with Noel. It's new, but I want her protected."

Logan's lips quirked upward, and his nod carried a hint of amusement. "Devil *may* have mentioned this to us."

Landon turned, giving Devil a dry, pointed look. "Relationship counselor and matchmaker, huh? You're one crazy bastard."

Devil's laughter echoed through the room, joined by the others as they shared a rare moment of levity. "What can I say? I'm a man of many talents."

As the laughter faded, Landon walked over to Devil and Frazier, getting back to business. "What's our progress?"

Sadie swiveled her chair to face him. "It's more tangled than we thought. We're combing through Mike's calls and emails. Recently, most of his communication was with Stan and Thurston, but there's a good amount from Margaret about the kids. And going further back, he was actively managing a plethora of details on the ranch."

Todd snorted. "Plethora."

Sadie shot a narrow-eyed gaze at him before tossing a pen at his head. "That means a shit-fuck-ton, for those of you with limited vocabularies."

The others chuckled at the levity as Todd ducked the flying pen.

She continued, "We're also scanning for coded messages that might have slipped through. And I'm digging into the cell towers that may tell us who he talked to on his burner phone."

Landon swung his head around to look at Logan, his face set with resolve. "I know whatever we find can simply be turned over to the Bureau, and nothing may happen. That's fine with me. All I care about is that no one comes after Noel."

Logan nodded his agreement, and Landon sat down at his station. He began the mundane assignment report that needed to be completed, along with his timesheet and expenses for Mary. He wanted to ditch the paperwork and just start helping the others. But having worked for the government, he was used to protocol. Even with LSIMT, accountability had to take place. After years working for the FBI, he was used to the activity and completed his reports quickly.

After a lunch brought in from the local bar, he looked down as his phone vibrated and smiled. "Hey, Noel. How are you?"

"I'm fine. Actually, after this morning, more than fine." She laughed, and his cock stirred.

He considered taking the call outside or moving the conversation to a more professional topic. He didn't mind his cock looking forward to being with her again, but he didn't want to be tenting his pants around his coworkers.

"Are you at work?" he asked.

"Yes, just checking in. I've finished writing my report and am going to court tomorrow for the meeting with the judge about Pamela."

Even though Pamela was a shit mom, Noel didn't take her duties lightly. Nor was she so cavalier that she wouldn't be bothered about her decision. "How do you feel about your report and recommendations?"

She hesitated, then sighed, and he could already see her actions and mannerisms in his mind. Tension lines would bracket her downward-turned mouth, and her shoulders would slump for a moment. Then she'd steel her spine and be resolute. Her words didn't surprise him.

"If I hadn't been in Jamaica, maybe I wouldn't feel so strongly, but... after seeing everything firsthand, I'm firm in my recommendation. Limited supervised visitation for Pamela. Always with someone else present."

I think you're doing the right thing," he said, his voice low with conviction. "At least, that's my opinion, for whatever it's worth."

"I don't mind your opinion, Landon," she replied with a soft laugh.

His mind flashed with more of what he'd like to contribute, but he kept his tone steady. "So... when can I see you again?"

"Anytime you want," she replied easily.

He'd asked her the same question that morning before he left her apartment and had received the same answer. He hadn't been sure if the hours between then and now had made a difference, but there was no coy pretending with Noel. She said what she thought and gave honest answers. He appreciated that more than she could realize. "I'd love to see you tonight, but I know things might be tight with your report and the early meeting tomorrow."

She groaned. "You're right. I'm wrapping up the

report today and meeting with my supervisor this afternoon to finalize my recommendations. Then tomorrow's the court date. I've also heard the Fugate family's attorney wants a copy of the report this evening—they're pushing for Pamela's visitation rights to be restricted."

"Sounds like Stan and the family aren't holding back."

"Absolutely not."

He hesitated, then plunged ahead. "We're looking into the situation with Mike, trying to find out who sent him after Pamela. It's technically outside our mission… but it doesn't sit right with me."

She went quiet, understanding the implications immediately. "Whoever that is… if they realize Mike told me something before he died, it could come back on me, couldn't it?"

He sighed, wishing he could shield her from even the thought of danger. "Yes. I hate the idea of you being alone tonight. Why don't I come down and stay with you?"

Her gentle laughter filled the line, easing his worry. "Sweetie, I'll be fine. I'll lock up, finish my reports, and settle in. Don't worry."

"Noel…" he said, still reluctant, but she laughed again, light and untroubled.

"Okay, Landon. If you happen to show up, I sure as hell won't kick you out!"

He chuckled, the tension in his shoulders finally easing. "All right, babe. I'll see you tonight."

When he disconnected, he glanced up to find the

other Keepers grinning at him, their expressions unashamedly amused. Shaking his head, he barked, "Back to work, all of you."

Laughter sounded out in the room, and even though everyone got back to what they were doing, he couldn't keep the smile off his face.

30

PENNY

Penny walked out of the barn and hurried to catch up to Tad as he strolled toward the house. Glancing ahead, she whispered, "Looks like we have an audience." She nodded toward the patio, where her grandparents and dad stood watching them with a quiet intensity.

"Did you know Grandma almost slept in my room last night?" she whispered.

Tad snickered, rolling his eyes. "Dad kept waking me up, checking on me. And I'm pretty sure Grandpa did, too."

Penny fell silent for a moment, thinking it over. "I know they're scared after what happened to us," she said softly, kicking at the ground as they walked. "But I don't feel scared. Not since Landon and Noel got us out of there. It's weird, though, right? You'd think that I'd have nightmares and wake up crying. But everything happened so fast. And you were with me, so I never felt alone."

"Yeah," Tad agreed, shrugging. "I was scared, but I

kept telling myself they wouldn't hurt us. They just wanted their money."

"I thought you were brave," she admitted, twisting her head to glance up at her twin.

A snort erupted. "No more than you. I mean, other than being scared of what might happen, when I think back, we were kind of badass the way we did what Landon said to do to escape."

Her eyes widened as she nodded. "Once he got to us, it was like being in the middle of an action movie!"

By then, they'd reached the patio. Penny noticed her grandma holding a platter of cookies, and her stomach did a happy flip. Within moments, she and Tad were seated outside, bathed in sunlight, munching on chocolate chip cookies with glasses of cold milk. Still, she couldn't shake the feeling that something serious was about to be said—the way her dad and grandparents kept looking at each other with those deep, worried lines on their faces. A small twist of nervousness tightened her stomach.

She exchanged a glance with Tad, and finally, she couldn't keep it in. "Daddy, you're making me nervous. It's like you want to say something, but... you're scared to."

Stan chuckled, shaking his head slightly. "You always were good at picking up on things," he said, his voice soft. His gaze moved from her to Tad, his expression pained yet relieved. "These past few days... they've been harder than I can even put into words. At first, we were angry with your mother for taking you without my consent and making all those demands. But when we heard you'd been taken from her…" His voice cracked, and he closed his eyes, swallowing as if to steady himself.

Penny felt a surge of emotion she wasn't used to seeing in her dad. She'd seen him happy, angry, even sad once or twice, but this raw fear was something new. She looked over at Tad and saw the same realization mirrored in his eyes. Their family was relieved they were back, but she didn't understand just how deep the worry had run.

Stan opened his eyes, his expression determined. Leaning forward, he clasped his hands on the table. "Ms. Lennox suggested you both might benefit from talking to someone—a counselor. She talked with you about it already, but your grandmother made some calls, looking into her recommendations. We found a group nearby that we think might be a good fit. But since you're both old enough to have a say in this, we want to involve you in the decision. You might feel more comfortable talking to a woman or a man, someone younger or older. You can see the same person or choose different counselors."

She exchanged another look with Tad, nodding in silent agreement. "That sounds good, Daddy. I liked talking to Noel… I think I'd be more comfortable with a woman. Someone not super young, but not, you know, super old, either." She paused, then gave her grandma an apologetic smile. "Grandma, I know you were checking in on me last night. I'm sorry you were so worried."

Margaret sighed, reaching over to squeeze Penny's hand. "Oh, sweetheart. I couldn't help it—I had to be sure you and Tad were safe and sound. And don't you apologize. None of this was your fault."

Tad nodded, turning to his grandmother. "I didn't even hear you, Grandma. But I knew Dad was checking in on me a lot."

Stan's lips curved into a small smile. "Guess I'm not as stealthy as Grandma." He looked over at Tad, his gaze gentle. "Do you have any thoughts on a counselor?"

Tad shrugged thoughtfully. "I liked talking to Noel, too. I don't think it needs to be a man. I have you and Grandpa for that. But maybe it'd be nice to talk to the same person as Penny, so they only have to hear the story once, you know?"

Stan let out a deep sigh, visibly relieved. "Good. That's good."

"Daddy?" Penny asked hesitantly. She bit her lip, feeling a lump form in her throat. "What will happen with Big Mike? Will there be… a funeral?"

"Of course, sweetheart," Thurston answered, his voice warm and steady. "We're taking care of everything."

Penny nodded, exhaling slowly. "It felt… I don't know, good, I guess, to have him there when we got back to the resort house. By then, we already liked Landon and Noel a lot. But seeing Big Mike felt like having a piece of home with us." She looked down, her eyes stinging as memories of Big Mike flooded back.

Margaret squeezed her hand again. "It's all right to talk about him, sweetheart. He was like family, and he loved you both dearly. Losing him hurts deeply, but…

we're all so grateful to have you home. That joy keeps us going."

Penny glanced at Tad, and he nodded in silent agreement, his face serious. "That was the first time I've ever seen anyone... die," he murmured.

Margaret winced, and both Stan's and Thurston's faces tightened. Penny nodded, not saying anything, but she could feel the weight of his words.

"I know it was terrifying," Margaret said softly. "We would've done anything to keep that from happening or to shield you both from it."

Stan's gaze softened, his eyes glistening. "If I could've kept Big Mike from harm or spared you from witnessing it... I would have. I'm so sorry."

Tad's eyes drifted over to Penny as he spoke. "But you know... at least he had Noel with him at the end. She was calm, speaking to him so gently. Whatever she said seemed to bring him peace."

The table grew quiet, and Penny expected the adults to nod in understanding. But instead, her granddad's brow furrowed, and her dad's eyes widened slightly. Margaret sat up a bit straighter, looking between them.

"Did Big Mike... talk to Noel?" Stan asked, his tone cautious.

Tad shrugged. "I don't know."

Penny added, "We couldn't hear what he was saying. But he kept trying to speak until Noel leaned down close to him. After that, he just... relaxed. His face looked peaceful."

"That was the last time we saw him," Tad said softly.

Margaret cleared her throat, the calm in her voice

returning. "Well, now that we've had our snack and discussed some options, I have a few phone calls to make. Thurston, I know you and Stan have work to do in the barn. Kids, we'll have lunch ready in about an hour." She rose, pressing a kiss to each of their heads before heading inside.

"We checked on our horses already, Dad," Tad said.

Penny stretched, feeling some of the tension leave her shoulders. "I think I'll spend the afternoon reading. We're going back to school soon, and I want to be prepared."

Tad nodded in agreement, and they both rose, walking around the table to hug their dad and granddad. As they headed back toward the house, Penny glanced over her shoulder, catching the solemn exchange between her father and grandfather, their expressions unreadable.

31

Noel walked out of the judge's office with the Fugate attorney at her side. She stole a quick glance at him and offered a polite, almost weary smile, her emotions tightly controlled.

"Are you alright, Ms. Lennox?" he asked, his voice low and calm, as though he'd spent years perfecting the art of speaking gently.

"Yes, Mr. Barton." She managed to keep her tone steady, though the strain of the day tugged at the edges. "These cases... the outcomes never sit easy with me, but I understand their necessity." She paused, searching for the right words. "Actually, I've never had a case quite like this. Usually, when I recommend supervised visits or limited parental rights, it's because of clear-cut abuse or neglect. But with Penny and Tad... they've been cared for by their mom in the past. Not perfectly, maybe, but they were safe and their needs met. But Pamela's recent actions put the children at risk."

Mr. Barton nodded, a soft sigh escaping him.

"Pamela would certainly never win any mother-of-the-year awards." He hesitated, his tone softening as he added, "Please, call me Roy."

"And I'm Noel," she replied, feeling a bit of the tension ease as she offered her first genuine smile since leaving the judge's chambers.

"Oh yes, I've heard your name quite a bit these past few days," he said with a knowing smile, holding open a door as they passed through another corridor.

She knew he wasn't just their attorney but also a good friend of the family. She brushed a stray lock of hair behind her ear. "I've enjoyed spending time with Penny and Tad, though I wish the circumstances were different."

A fond look crossed his face. "I've known those kids since they were born. I've been the family's attorney for years, actually. My father was the Fugate lawyer before me, when Margaret and Thurston took over the ranch. Stan and I even went to college together," he added, a faraway look settling in his eyes. "I remember Pamela from those early days."

"Oh…" Noel didn't know how to respond. The layers of history between him and the Fugate family ran deep.

He chuckled, the sound tinged with both humor and regret. "Pamela was… well, let's just say she should have come with a warning label. But Stan was completely mesmerized by her. She knew how to play the part of the perfect girlfriend, but there was always more beneath the surface."

Noel nodded as they made their way down another

long, echoing hall in the courthouse. "The judge asked me to take on this case, which is how I ended up in Jamaica." She let out a slow breath, her lips pressing together. "I never anticipated things to turn out this way… the security agent I was with used a term… FUBAR, I believe."

Roy laughed as they walked outside and down the steps. "I'm familiar with that, and it seems apropos."

Noel lifted her hand to say goodbye, but to her surprise, Roy hesitated. "Would you care for a cup of coffee?" he offered, gesturing across the street. "There's a little bakery nearby. It's small, but I'd like to at least offer coffee."

She nearly declined, the urge to retreat into solitude strong. But she could feel the weight of the morning still lingering, and the thought of coffee—and maybe a sweet pastry—sounded like exactly what she needed. "That would be lovely," she replied, her smile softening as she met his kind eyes.

They crossed the street at the corner light, their steps in sync as they made their way toward the cozy coffee shop. The scent of freshly baked bread and freshly ground coffee greeted them as they stepped inside, and Noel felt a small surge of comfort wash over her. The shop was mostly empty, and the lull between breakfast and lunch made it easy to find a quiet corner table where they could speak without interruption.

Roy stirred his coffee, glancing up with a thoughtful expression. "As relieved as I am that Penny and Tad were brought home so quickly," he began, his voice soft, "I can't shake the sorrow that Mike didn't make it back with them."

Noel felt a pang in her chest at his words. She hadn't realized Roy knew him, but upon reflection, it would make sense if Roy was the attorney for the ranch. "I didn't get to know him very well," she admitted, her voice gentle. "But I could see how much he cared for Penny and Tad. When we finally found them, he was overwhelmed, just... so relieved to have them safe."

"I know that filled his heart," Roy said, nodding while sipping his coffee. "He was a little older than Stan and me, but as a longtime fixture at the ranch, he wanted to make sure the kids had a familiar face down there. Pamela had told Stan that if he showed up, she might not sign the papers." He shook his head. "God, what a..."

"I know what you mean," she murmured. "I didn't spend much time with Pamela, but I wasn't... impressed. She seemed genuinely upset about the kidnapping, but I couldn't shake the feeling that something was missing."

Roy's mouth curled into a wry smile, and he gave her an appraising look. "You're very... professional in your choice of words, Noel."

A small laugh escaped her, and she met his gaze, a hint of warmth between them. "Perhaps. But you knew her on a personal level. I think you're the one holding back here, Roy."

His eyes lingered on her, and a trace of amusement mingled with admiration. "Touché," he replied, lifting his cup before taking another sip. Setting it down, he leaned in slightly. "Forgive me if I'm being too forward, but Margaret spoke to me after the kids were returned. She mentioned you were with Mike when he had his heart attack?"

Noel hesitated, the weight of what the kids had seen settling heavily on her. Her hand tightened around her coffee cup, and she let her gaze drop, gathering her thoughts. She took a slow sip, hoping to buy herself just a moment to find the right words. "Yes," she finally replied, her voice quiet but steady. "I saw him from the upstairs balcony. He was on the phone, and just as he finished the call, he collapsed. I ran down, shouting for help as I went. Someone called emergency services, and Landon started chest compressions."

Roy's expression remained steady, but his eyes held a hint of sadness. "And you stayed with him through all that?"

"Yes," she murmured, her voice soft as the memory washed over her. "He was still conscious. I held his hand and kept talking to him right until..." Her voice faltered briefly. "Until he lost consciousness as the paramedics arrived."

Roy's gaze didn't waver, his hand steady on his coffee cup. "Did he say anything? Was he able to share his thoughts with you?"

Noel took a deep breath, pondering her words, not wanting to reveal too much while offering solace to Mike's friend. "He just wanted some peace, I think. You could see it in his eyes. He seemed... worried... not really afraid, but concerned."

Roy nodded, his hand reaching across the table to pat hers gently. "And you were able to give him that peace?"

"I hope so," she said, a gentle, bittersweet smile tugging at her lips.

Roy's face softened, and he squeezed her hand lightly before letting go. "He was a good man. I'm sure he was comforted by having a kind voice and a... pretty face by his side at the end."

She felt warmth rise to her cheeks, but she smiled back, appreciating the kindness in his words. "Thank you. That whole trip felt like a nightmare. I was so relieved to return to Montana."

Her phone buzzed, the vibration pulling her from the memory. She glanced at the screen—a meeting reminder. She'd spent longer here than she'd planned. "It was truly lovely meeting you, Roy. But I need to head back to the office."

Roy rose, offering a firm handshake. "It would be nice if we only ran into each other at the Fugates' holiday parties from now on. They certainly know how to put out an amazing spread. But I hope we don't cross paths again over another case."

"Agreed," she said with a smile, slipping her hand from his as she stepped out into the sunshine. She hurried to her car, feeling a strange mix of emotions—a subtle relief from the case closing intertwined with the lingering heaviness of recent events.

As she settled into the driver's seat and started the engine, Noel dialed Landon. He picked up quickly, and she couldn't keep the smile from her face. "Hey, Landon.

I'm on my way back to the office. Gave my report to the judge, and I'm almost certain he'll rule in Stan's favor for full custody, with Pamela's rights reduced or revoked."

"I'm glad that part's over for you. It's been a hell of a week," he replied, his voice warm and steady.

She sighed, tension melting just a bit. "You can say that again. I met Roy Barton, the Fugates' attorney. We had coffee afterward. He's known the family for years… even knew Mike."

"Did he ask about Mike?"

A beat passed before she answered. "Yeah. The kids must've told their dad and grandparents that Mike spoke to me just before he… passed. I know we hadn't planned on sharing that yet, but… now it's out there."

A sigh on the other end. "Damn. We'd hoped for more time to gather intel on who might have sent Mike down to Jamaica with orders to target Pamela."

She gripped the steering wheel a bit tighter. "I know. Anyway, I'll be home before you get back tonight. I'm heading to an afternoon meeting, so my phone will be on silent."

Landon's voice softened. "Can't wait to see you, babe."

She grinned, her heart feeling lighter. "Same here. Bye." She disconnected, the warmth from his words lingering as she drove toward her office, a quiet smile staying with her the whole way.

32

Landon turned and said, "What can you dig up on Roy Barton, the Fugates' attorney?"

Sadie didn't even blink before tapping away on the keyboard.

"What's up?" Devil asked.

Landon looked at Devil, noting he also had Logan's and Frazier's rapt attention. "Noel just left the courthouse," he began, his voice low but steady. "She filed her recommendation with the judge, and the Fugates' attorney was there. They struck up a conversation, and it turns out Penny and Tad mentioned to their family that Mike spoke to Noel before he died. The family passed that tidbit along to their attorney."

Devil's eyes narrowed. "Did he sound suspicious?"

Landon shook his head, trying to piece it together. "Not that she noticed. He didn't raise any red flags with her, but he's definitely someone to keep on our radar. Right now, I don't trust anyone in the Fugate orbit who hated Pamela."

Sadie piped up from her computer, a grin tugging at her lips. "Royster Barton," she said, unable to resist a smirk. "If my name were Royster, I'd go by Roy too."

Devil chuckled, and Landon couldn't help but roll his eyes, though his own tension remained. "What do we know about him?"

Sadie's expression shifted, and she quickly dove back into her research. "Roy Barton's a well-known attorney. Works at the firm his father founded, no complaints, lawsuits, or investigations on him. He lives alone in Bellehaven, that upscale subdivision outside Helena. Think golf courses, big but tasteful houses, restrained wealth."

"Man, I'd like to have *restrained wealth*," Devil muttered with a grin, though his humor only barely covered the interest in what they could dig up on Roy.

"Sadie, can you pull up any correspondence between Barton and Mike?" Landon asked, his tone sharpening. Devil's smirk faded, and he turned his focus back to his screen, fingers flying over the keyboard.

Just then, Todd strode in, his normally composed face hard. He didn't waste any time. "We got the results back from the liquid sample found in Mike's toiletry kit," he announced. "It's digoxin. Medical name, but it's basically derived from Foxglove. Every part of that plant is toxic. It can trigger a heart attack."

Landon clenched his fists, the revelation settling in like a dark weight. "It could look natural, especially somewhere like Jamaica, and no one would question Pamela dying of a heart attack." His voice was a rough whisper. "And when her body would be sent back, the

Fugates would just want closure—no one here would push for an autopsy. They'd pay for Pamela's return and bury her."

Devil nodded grimly. "But who gave it to Mike? Which Fugate ordered Mike to poison Pamela?"

Frazier's brow furrowed as he hesitated, then exhaled sharply. "We found an unknown number that called Mike the day before your flight and once again on the morning of your departure. Then it hit his phone again after you arrived. I haven't yet been able to narrow down where a call from the burner came from."

"Any way to trace the unknown number?" Landon's voice was taut with anticipation.

Sadie leaned forward, her fingers tapping rapidly. "Not immediately, but I can get the call origin using Logan's new software."

Landon couldn't sit still. He moved to stand behind her, his focus locked on her screen. "And?"

Sadie's brow furrowed as she worked, then she glanced up, her eyes glinting with intensity.

"Chill out, Landon. This will take a while."

He knew she was right, and while patience was usually one of his virtues, he found that when it came to Noel, he couldn't dislodge the knot in his gut to make sure she was protected.

An hour later, Sadie finally swiveled around and reported, "Two of the calls were placed from downtown Helena... right near the courthouse. Roy's office building is near there."

A surge of frustration twisted in Landon's chest, and he rubbed the back of his neck, trying to ease the tension. "That's still circumstantial. We need more than proximity."

Sadie's fingers flew across the keyboard again, her jaw set. "Okay, okay, I'm working on it."

Time crawled, then she finally turned to face him and the other Keepers staying late to see how this would play out.

"The last call, the one placed after you arrived in Jamaica and the family was notified about the kids being taken… pinged from Bellehaven."

A hushed silence fell over the room as the weight of this new detail sank in. "Goddamn," Devil murmured. "That's some fuckin' good software."

"Yeah, and while it still doesn't give us the proof we need, we're much closer."

Logan joined Landon, his expression grim. "Do you think one of the Fugates might've put this in motion? Maybe Thurston or Stan? Maybe Margaret? Pamela was becoming a problem for them, and it's possible they decided they'd had enough. Could they have approached Roy to set Mike up for this?"

Landon considered it, his mind racing through the options. "Margaret? I can't see her being involved, but then she'd probably do anything to protect her family. But as for the others… hell, I just don't know. Stan hates his ex-wife, and Thurston would protect the ranch at all costs."

"It wouldn't be the first time a family attorney was used to take care of *problems*," Logan said.

He checked his watch, feeling the pressure of time and wanting desperately to warn Noel. "Let me call her," he said, dialing her number. The phone rang, but it immediately went to voicemail. He cursed under his breath, then left a message, his voice steady but with an urgency he couldn't hide. "Noel, just wanted to update you. We're becoming suspicious of Roy Barton. Evidence suggests he might have been the one to contact Mike regarding Pamela. We don't have solid proof yet, and we're not sure if any of the Fugates were involved, but be careful. I'd prefer you don't see him alone again." He ended the call, gripping his phone tightly.

"Had to leave a message?" Devil asked, watching him closely.

"Yeah, but I'll talk to her tonight. She needs to know not to be alone at the Fugate Ranch—or anywhere near Roy."

"Bingo!" Sadie shouted, snapping everyone's attention her way. Her wide-eyed gaze swept the room. "Roy Barton's elderly mother passed away last year. He was her primary caregiver—and she was on digoxin."

Landon's jaw tightened, and his lips thinned into a hard line as he pressed them together. "Who the fuck is yanking his chain? Which Fugate? Or all of them?" He exhaled sharply, his fists tightening at his sides. "I'm going to head to Noel's place now."

Todd turned to his computer, already pulling up the tracking program. "She's still wearing the tracker. I can see she's north of Helena, on the main highway."

Relief softened Landon's shoulders for a second. "That's good. She must be on her way home. Keep following her. I'll feel better when she's in my sight. " He left out that he wouldn't feel safe until she was also in his arms.

Todd's expression turned grim as he tracked the signal. "Wait. The signal is off the highway, now closer to Bellehaven."

The air left Landon's lungs, and he gripped the back of Todd's chair, his pulse spiking. "Oh God. Check her phone!"

Sadie's voice rang out. "She got a call from Roy Barton... ten minutes ago."

The room shifted into action instantly. "Cole!" Logan barked. "Get the bird ready. Landon, take Devil and—"

"And me!" Frazier called, already sprinting toward the equipment room. Landon didn't hesitate. Within minutes, they were geared up and heading for the helicopter, where Cole had it primed for takeoff.

"ETA?" Landon shouted over the whir of the blades as they lifted off.

Cole's voice came through the headset, steady and reassuring. "I can have us landing at the Bellehaven tennis courts in twenty minutes."

Landon gritted his teeth, his gaze fixed on the horizon as they sped through the air. Every second felt like a countdown, every unanswered call to Noel's phone like a dagger twisting deeper. He kept redialing, his grip tightening on his phone as each call went to voicemail. He prayed, hard and fast, that she wasn't picking up simply because she couldn't hear it—that it wasn't already too late.

33

Noel felt a rare lightness as she drove home, a smile tugging at her lips at the thought of seeing Landon again tonight. If she tried to explain to anyone how she could be so crazy about someone after knowing them less than a week, she wouldn't be able to do it. She could describe how he makes her feel when he turns his smile toward her. Or maybe the way he listens carefully, interested in what she has to say. Perhaps because he treats her as an equal, not someone to patronize. She could describe how his deep-set gray eyes stared intently at her, causing all other thoughts to flee from her mind.

She laughed and shook her head. "All I know, girly, is he is someone that I finally met, and I want to see where the relationship can go," she muttered to herself as she pulled out of the parking lot.

She meant to check her messages when she left the meeting, but since it ran extra long, she hurriedly shut down her computer, grabbed her phone, and headed out. Her fingers had just touched the radio when her phone rang. A quick jolt of hope ran through her, imagining Landon's voice on the other end. She glanced at the screen, her heart sinking a bit at the unknown number. Still, it could be something important—she had cases waiting for her attention. "Hello?"

"Is this Ms. Lennox?"

"Yes, speaking. Who's this?"

"This is Roy Barton, the Fugate family attorney. We met earlier today."

"Oh, of course. What can I do for you?"

He hesitated, his voice taking on a polite but rushed tone. "I just got home and realized one of the forms requires your signature. I know we discussed full custody for the Fugates with only supervised visitation for Pamela, and they're eager to have everything ready for the judge in the morning. But I noticed one of your reports has an unsigned page."

Noel frowned. She prided herself on meticulous work, never missing signatures or details. "I was sure I signed all the documents before filing. But if it's missing, I can meet you first thing in the morning at your office."

"Actually," he said, his voice softening, "I'm at home now. I thought, if you're nearby, you could swing by? I'll be traveling for business early tomorrow, so I was hoping to send everything electronically tonight."

She glanced at the time, realizing she was closer to Bellehaven than she'd thought. "I'm actually in your area now. I don't mind stopping by to save us both the trouble tomorrow. What's the address?"

"It's very easy." He chuckled as he rattled it off.

"I'm turning off the exit that will take me to Bellehaven."

"How fortuitous! You're about ten minutes away. I'll see you then. Thank you so much for everything," Roy said before they disconnected.

A small voice inside her suggested calling Landon, but she pushed it aside. This was a quick formality. A few minutes, and she'd be back on the road.

The drive to Roy's house took less than ten minutes. The Bellehaven subdivision was polished and quiet, the houses tucked behind manicured lawns and shadowed by thick trees. When she parked in the driveway, he stepped outside to greet her, dressed down in jeans and a navy polo, a far cry from his courtroom attire. He looked almost unassuming and relaxed as he waved her inside.

"Thank you so much for making the time, Ms. Lennox," he said warmly, gesturing her into the foyer, where he already had the file open on a small side table. "I didn't want to delay the filing, and it seemed best to get it done tonight."

She moved closer, taking in the familiar report and flipping to the page he'd mentioned. Her fingers paused over the paper. Something about it seemed off—she could swear there was a faint smear, as though the original ink had been tampered with. Her signature wasn't there, yet the document looked… different.

She hesitated, feeling his gaze on her. He offered a small, placating smile. "I don't blame you for double-checking."

Her eyes scanned the text, noting that it was worded exactly as she'd written. Finally, she signed her name at the bottom, flipping through the remaining pages to make sure all was in order. Satisfied, she handed the pen back with a polite smile. "I think that's everything. I'm sorry I missed it earlier."

He waved away her concerns, smiling widely. "It's no problem at all! I'm sorry I can't offer you dinner. Would you like a drink?"

"Oh no, thank you. I'm just heading home."

"I hope I haven't kept you from your plans."

"Not at all."

"Well, enjoy your evening." He hesitated, then smiled. "I have just opened a lovely white. It's a Skalkaho from the Hidden Legend Winery. Please allow me to offer you a small glass. I don't want to impair your driving, but a small glass, perhaps. It would be lovely to toast our success in removing Pamela from the Fugates."

Noel blinked at his invitation, surprised at his choice of words. She paused, a faint unease tugging at her, but quickly brushed it aside and offered a polite smile. "I've never been to that winery but have had their wines before. Just a very small glass, though."

Following him into the spacious, well-lit kitchen, Noel couldn't help but admire the luxurious decor. Granite countertops gleamed under the soft lighting, and a half-filled wineglass sat on the counter beside the open bottle. She slid onto one of the barstools at his suggestion, feeling its comfort and style as her eyes took in the rest of the space. From here, she could see a family room beyond, its stone fireplace and expansive windows making her wonder what view it offered during daylight.

"You have a beautiful home," she said as he poured a fresh glass and handed it to her.

"Thank you," he replied with a smile that hinted at pride. "I've been here about six years. The neighborhood's ideal—quiet, with friendly neighbors, though we rarely see each other. I enjoy a bit of social interaction, but solitude is a luxury."

He slid the freshly poured glass toward her, and she wrapped her fingers around the stem. "I know what you mean. I only live in an apartment now, but it's fairly quiet. I'd love to buy a home, but I haven't found exactly where I want to live."

"Where are you from?"

"Born and raised in Montana."

His eyes widened, and he smiled. "A homegrown woman."

She laughed and nodded. "My parents still live in the home where I was raised."

He lifted his glass and sipped the wine, and she followed suit. She took a cautious sip, letting the wine's crisp, dry flavor linger on her tongue. "This is delicious," she murmured, though it was drier than she usually preferred.

"I often think people are pretentious regarding wine… or any alcohol. I firmly believe in finding something you enjoy and then enjoying it! It doesn't matter if it's expensive or cheap. Life's too short to worry about labels."

"Absolutely," she replied, relaxing slightly as she took another sip. But the wine seemed to taste more bitter with each sip, and she hesitated. She didn't want to be rude, but the dryness wasn't quite her style.

He glanced down at her glass and offered a little smile. "You're being very polite, but I'll bet you prefer sweet wine, right?"

A blush rose to her cheeks, and she nodded sheepishly. Before she could politely decline more, he moved to another cabinet and pulled down a different bottle.

"I have something you must try," he announced, eyes glinting with enthusiasm. "This is a mead from Hidden Legend—one of their signature honey wines."

"I've never had mead."

He looked over his shoulder as he pulled down a new glass. "Oh, you're in for a treat," he replied, turning to her with the glass in hand.

He seemed so excited, it was infectious.

"In Greek mythology, mead was known as the nectar of the gods," he stated with a wink. "This is the winery's King's Mead. It's a delightful honey wine with a sweet flavor."

She took a tentative sip, surprised by the burst of flavor. "Oh, my gosh. This is incredible," she said, her eyes widening.

Roy nodded, clearly pleased. "I thought you'd like it. Mead is an ancient drink—thought to be the world's first alcohol. It's fermented honey."

She took another sip, savoring the taste, imagining it would make a wonderful holiday drink. "I can see why it's called the nectar of the gods."

"It's thought that mead actually predates other alcohols. It is considered the father of all alcoholic beverages. It is fermented honey, and the oldest records come from China, almost eight thousand years ago."

She took another sip, fascinated with his knowledge. "What else is in it besides fermented honey?"

"At its core, it is fermented honey and water, but it is combined with grains, spices, fruits, and sometimes hops. It's often called honey wine."

"Oh, I can imagine spices in this would be delicious at the holidays."

He nodded with enthusiasm. "I have a few flavored versions of this—pomegranate, orange ginger, even elderberry," he continued, swirling his glass. "I bring out the spiced one during the holidays. There's something truly comforting about it in the winter."

Lost in conversation, she finished her glass without realizing it. When she glanced at her watch, she was startled to see nearly an hour had passed. "Oh, I really need to get going," she said, sliding off the stool, but a wave of dizziness made her pause. Her hand shot out to steady herself, and she cursed under her breath. She hadn't expected to feel this unsteady.

Roy's eyes flashed with concern as he took a step forward. "Are you alright?"

Noel forced a smile, swallowing back the growing nausea and unease. "I'm fine. I think the mead just… caught up with me." Her words slurred slightly, and a prickling sensation crept down her spine as she felt his eyes linger a little too long.

"Of course," he replied smoothly, that same polite

smile never leaving his face. "Would you like to use the restroom before you go? It's just down the hall, to the right."

Relieved to escape his gaze for a moment, she thanked him and made her way to the powder room, gripping the walls slightly as the room tilted again. She shut the door, steadying herself against the counter and staring at her reflection. She felt strange, more than just tipsy—like the alcohol was coursing through her veins faster than it should.

She splashed cold water on her face, trying to clear the fog in her mind. Her hands shook as she reached into her purse, relieved to find her phone. Her pulse spiked when she saw the screen filled with missed calls and messages from Landon. She tapped on the first voicemail, her heart sinking as his voice filled her ear.

"Noel, I just wanted to let you know that we are suspicious of Roy Barton. Evidence points to the possibility that he may have been the one to contact Mike about Pamela…"

A cold chill ran down her spine. She could feel her breath hitching as she tried to process his words, her mind slowly processing as she looked at the door. The affable, easygoing Roy she'd been sipping mead with a few minutes ago was potentially a dangerous man.

Hands trembling, she stared at the blurry screen and texted. **Jus got you messages At Roy's houssse Leaving**

She hit send, even knowing the words were just as wonky as her vision. Steeling herself, Noel opened the door and took a shaky step into the hallway. She fought to keep her expression neutral, hoping her pounding heart wasn't visible in her eyes. Her vision blurred slightly, and she blinked rapidly, forcing herself to focus as she made her way toward the foyer. The house felt eerily silent, and her stomach twisted when she noticed Roy wasn't in the kitchen.

She continued toward the front door, each step a battle as she tried to ignore the spinning room and her fading strength. As she neared the entryway, she spotted him standing just inside the door, leaning slightly out and listening, his face turned toward the distant sound of a helicopter.

She forced herself to walk calmly toward him, hoping he wouldn't turn around until she'd managed to slip by. But before she could get close enough, he spun around, his eyes locking onto hers with a glint that sent a jolt of fear through her.

"Oh, there you are," he said, his smile tight. "It was lovely to share a drink with you, but I know you need to be on your way. I won't keep you any longer." His voice had a strange, rushed quality as if he was eager to get her out of the house.

"Yes... thank you," she managed, trying to move past him. But just as she stepped toward the door, his hand shot out, grabbing her arm with a force that made her gasp. He shoved her back, slamming the door shut behind him.

Her heart hammered as she struggled to keep her balance. "Roy, what... what's going on?"

He didn't answer, his grip tightening painfully as he dragged her back toward the kitchen. "Dammit!" he cursed.

She stumbled, her legs heavy and unsteady, barely able to keep up as he pulled her along. Panic surged through her, every nerve on high alert. "Roy! Let go! What the hell are you doing?" She tried to pull away, but her strength felt sapped, her body not responding the way it should.

The pleasant, easygoing man she'd met earlier was gone, replaced by someone cold and unrecognizable. His eyes were hard, his face twisted into a grimace as he pulled her into the kitchen. "You're not driving anywhere now. I'll make sure you get exactly where you need to go."

She tried to back away, but he caught her again, pulling her in front of him. He pulled out his phone. Punching in a number, he said, "Change of plans. She can't drive on her own. Get here, and we'll take her in her car. Same plan, just altered."

Her heart lurched at his words, their meaning hidden, but the harsh tone of his voice let her know that whatever he planned, she wouldn't like the outcome. As her gaze dropped, she caught sight of a large kitchen knife nearby on the counter. She wanted to reach for it but froze as his fingers wrapped around the handle. Her eyes went wide, and she held her breath, paralyzed by fear.

"I know Mike must have talked to you. He was too good a man to die without wanting some kind of absolution."

"It... it was you that sent him to k... kill Pamela," she said as she clutched the counter while the room still spun.

"And that knowledge will die with you. Anyone you told will just have secondary information. Not credible in court, my dear." He inched closer, the knife now lifting toward her.

And then, suddenly, a loud crash shattered the tension—a window breaking nearby.

34

The flight to Bellehaven felt like an eternity to Landon. Every second that ticked by without a response from Noel was another punch to his gut. Why was she at Roy Barton's house? He scrubbed his hand over his face, forcing himself to shove aside the barrage of questions and focus on what mattered: getting to her. Keeping her safe.

Sadie discovered that Roy had called Noel when she was on the road. *He must've lured her there with something —some questions or a legal need for the Fugates' case.* It was the only thing Landon could think of that would make her deviate from traveling home to go to the attorney's house.

Sadie radioed, "According to her lighthouse necklace tracker, she's still there."

Yeah, but that doesn't mean she was unharmed.

Cole set the helicopter down on an expansive grassy area next to the Bellehaven tennis courts. Logan had notified their FBI contact, alerting them to the severity of the situation, but Landon didn't care about the bureaucratic red tape. He'd tear through it himself if it meant getting to Noel faster.

As soon as they touched down, he, Devil, and Frazier alighted from the bird and, with night vision goggles, raced to the back of the park area to get to Roy's house quicker than along the road.

As he raced through the shadows with night vision goggles, Cole stayed behind to meet with the FBI and secure the perimeter. Landon pushed forward, heart pounding as they reached the edge of the trees overlooking Roy's property. It was immaculate, with neatly trimmed hedges and meticulously arranged flower beds. His eyes were locked on the house, searching, desperate.

The three Keepers crouched, assessing the structure. The large back window offered a clear view of the family room, and to the left, a wide kitchen window illuminated the space beyond. Landon's heart nearly stopped when he saw Roy's hand on Noel, gripping her arm as she swayed, her movements unsteady. A few wineglasses on the counter suggested she might have been drinking, but he knew Noel. She was careful. Whatever Roy had given her, it had been with intent.

"I have the kitchen," Frazier said over the radio, his voice steady and calm.

"Front door," Devil confirmed.

Landon moved like a shadow, sliding up to the patio doors that separated the kitchen from the family room. His eyes flicked to Noel, taking in her glazed, wide-eyed look. Her body swayed slightly, and he felt a spike of white-hot rage, imagining what Roy could have slipped into her drink. She looked terrified but too dazed to escape.

"Going in," Devil said before he kicked open the front door, the sound echoing through the house.

Roy whipped around, instinctively pulling Noel closer, his hand grabbing a large kitchen knife. Before Landon could blink, Frazier took his shot, shattering the patio doors and creating an opening. Landon surged forward, adrenaline and fury propelling him through the broken glass.

He locked onto Roy, his weapon raised, every nerve in his body taut. Roy's grip was bruising as he held Noel in front of him, his hand now holding the knife too close to her. Noel's dilated eyes darted to Landon as fear filled the space.

Landon ripped off his night goggles, keeping his weapon fixed on Roy. "Drop the knife and step away from her," he commanded, his voice low and lethal. "And tell me what the hell you gave her."

Roy hesitated, feigning innocence as he carefully laid the knife on the counter. "We were simply having a drink," he said, his tone overly smooth. "How dare you burst into my house and threaten me!"

"Lan...don?" Noel's voice was faint, barely a whisper. She was blinking, struggling to focus, and it sent a fresh wave of fury through him.

Landon gritted his teeth, stepping closer. "What did you give her?"

"We were simply drinking, and she's unused to mead," Roy said.

"Let her go, now," he said, his voice like steel.

Roy's lips pinched together.

Landon's eyes narrowed, and he advanced, his tone slicing through the tension. "We know you had a stash of drugs you kept after your mother passed. The same drugs you used to give her."

Roy's mask faltered, his eyes widening for just a split second before he forced a smirk, tightening his grip on Noel. Her head lolled slightly, and Landon's stomach churned at the sight.

"And we know you contracted Mike Westerly to poison Pamela Fugate. You think we haven't pieced it together?"

Roy sneered. "You wouldn't understand. Some things are family matters."

"No," Landon replied, his voice low and laced with fury. "The only business here is getting Noel out of this house."

Roy's grip on Noel slackened just slightly as his resolve wavered. It was all Landon needed. He lunged forward, grabbing Roy's wrist and twisting it sharply, forcing him to release her. Roy stumbled back as Landon pulled Noel into his arms, one hand protectively around her shoulders.

"Noel," he said softly, cradling her against him, his voice gentler now as he ignored Roy's blustering protests. "What did you drink? I need you to remember."

She blinked up at him, dazed and pale, glancing toward the counter. "I... I had a few sips of white wine and... and honey wine," she murmured, her voice shaky. Her eyes, wide and unfocused, met his. "Something's... wrong, Landon."

Landon's gaze snapped back to Roy, and he took a menacing step forward, voice like ice. "You made a mistake, Barton. We have evidence of the calls you made to Mike in Jamaica, and the poison vial? It has your fingerprints." He was bluffing—fingerprint results hadn't come back yet—but he was banking on Roy's reaction. He inclined his head toward the wineglasses and bottles. "And you haven't gotten rid of the evidence here."

Roy's composure crumbled, his breathing ragged, eyes flicking to the wineglasses on the counter. "I'll wait until my lawyer arrives," he snapped, though his voice was unsteady.

"You go ahead and lawyer up," Landon replied, his mouth spreading into a feral grin. "But if anything happens to Noel because of you, I'll come after you myself." His voice dropped to a dark, dangerous edge. "Now, tell me what you gave her, or I swear you'll regret it."

Roy faltered as Noel sagged against Landon, her legs giving out beneath her. "It was just... something mild. To make her sleepy," Roy stammered, his hands raised in surrender.

She looked up at Roy. "You gave me something... make me sleepy and... then tried to get me to drive... home?" Her gaze was bleary, her hand weak as it gripped Landon's arm.

Another sound came from the front, and Cole

walked in with a bevy of FBI agents and local police. Landon recognized his friend, Agent Everett Tomey.

"We found your man," Everett said, his voice like steel. "At the entrance to your subdivision. Man has a record... easy hire for whatever you need. The one you hired to run Ms. Lennox off the road, Barton. He's talking—willing to make a full confession to save himself."

Roy's face drained of color, his jaw tightening as he gritted out, "I'm not saying anything else."

Landon shifted, lifting Noel securely in his arms. His anger burned hotter as he met Roy's eyes. "You can play silent all you want, but you're telling me right now what you put in her drink."

Roy's face was tight, but he blurted, "Sleeping pills. She only had a small amount of a prescription for sleeping. Enough to make it easy for her to have a car accident if someone ran her off the road."

Everett nodded, and the FBI agents rushed forward and quickly arrested Roy.

"Landon... I feel... sick," she murmured, her voice barely above a whisper.

"I know, sweetheart. I'm here." His tone softened with every word. "I have you now. You're safe."

Devil was already on the phone with LSIMT, asking about the drug she'd been given.

"I'm so sorry, so sorry," Noel muttered as Landon held her so tightly her face was smooshed against his chest.

"It's not your fault," he said, heading to the door.

"He said I needed to come by... sign some papers that I... needed. Didn't look right to me. Then... he offered... wine, and we talked... he seemed nice."

"You didn't get my messages," Landon groaned.

"No... not until I was trying to leave." Her brows lowered. "I'm... sick and tired... all this... stupid stuff... happening..."

"Devil, we've got to go to the hospital," he yelled, hurrying to the front door.

Devil said, "They can do a toxicology report, but it helps us to know what she was given. I'm getting the bottles and glasses for them to fast-track the evidence."

Everett hurried alongside Landon. "There's an ambulance already outside. He told me to come in with no signs."

He carried her bridal style, then turned just as he heard Devil ask, "Which Fugates knew about this? Who was in on the plan to kill Pamela?"

Noel lifted her head, looking at Roy. Landon didn't think Roy was going to answer. "Not wasting time here."

Suddenly, Roy shouted, "None of them! Stan is a fucking loser when it comes to his ex-wife. I told him years ago she was a gold-digging bitch. When they divorced, I thought we'd be rid of her, but she kept coming back, dragging her claws into the family." His chest heaved, his eyes flashing with a sick satisfaction. "The only way the Fugates could ever be free of her was if she was dead!" He thumped his chest with a twisted pride. "I was the one to protect the family. Mike agreed with me. He despised her just as much."

The FBI was still talking to him, but Landon had heard enough. He turned and stalked out, placing Noel in the back of the ambulance and then climbing in with her.

"Meet you there," Devil said.

Landon offered a chin lift, and that was all. He turned to look at Noel, giving her his complete focus. She gave a sleepy grin and held his hand as the paramedics started an IV.

"Come on, baby. Stay with me," he said, leaning close. As the words left his lips, he realized he meant them in every way possible.

35

As dawn broke, Noel stood by the window, gazing at the sprawling mountains painted in the soft morning light. The world felt still, the quiet beauty of the scene washing over her, and for a moment, the tension in her shoulders melted. She held her cup of tea close, breathing in its warmth, savoring the comforting heat as she took a sip. It was cool enough to drink, the perfect balm for her frayed nerves.

With a deep sigh, she turned away from the view, letting her mind drift back over the past few days' events. Her chest tightened as she recalled the dizzying sequence of fear, anger, and disbelief. The hospital's toxicology report had confirmed what Roy had admitted—he'd slipped a small amount of temazepam into her drink. Enough to make her disoriented, groggy... vulnerable. But his plan had hinged on her finishing the dry wine, where he'd added the most. When she'd only sipped it and turned to the honey wine, he'd had to improvise. If she'd driven off that night, she'd likely never have seen the morning.

A shudder ran through her, and she took a slow, steadying breath, grounding herself in the present. She was safe now. Landon had stayed by her side, a solid anchor, steady and unyielding.

The memory of that hospital night lingered—the weight of Agent Tomey's questions, the realization that the plan had been darker, colder than she'd first thought. But nothing had struck her harder than the visit to the Fugate family. Telling Stan, Thurston, and Margaret that their attorney and close friend had betrayed them so deeply was like tearing open an old wound. They'd been horrified when they learned that Mike, a trusted family employee, had agreed to kill Pamela, the mother of Stan's children.

Noel had been so pleased that none of the Fugates had been involved that she hadn't fully prepared for how hurt and angry they were, although, in hindsight, it made sense.

"You're telling me that Mike was going to poison my children's mother while they were in the house?" Stan roared.

Tears ran down Margaret's face, as she shook her head, shock mixed with fear evident in her eyes. The lines deepened on Thurston's brow.

They had asked questions, and Noel and Landon filled them in on what they knew. Once the Fugates discovered Roy had drugged her and planned on her demise, they were even more shocked. It was decided that they wouldn't tell Penny or Tad anything at this time. And by the time the twins got home from school, Noel and Landon were composed enough to offer heartfelt greetings and promises to come back to visit.

Now, two days later, she was staying at Landon's place, a quiet refuge where she could breathe and let the last of the fear ebb away. She glanced around his house, surprised at how warm it felt for a single man's home. It was large, with wide windows and open spaces that bathed the rooms in light. The same view of the mountains from his bedroom window had greeted her when she'd woken, a sight so stunning it was almost enough to quiet the uneasy memories.

Noel glanced back toward the bedroom, wondering if Landon was still asleep. She'd slipped out of bed quietly, surprised he hadn't stirred. She couldn't help the faint smile that played on her lips. Even when he was fast asleep, she felt his presence like a protective warmth.

"Hey," he said, and she jumped, her gaze snapping to see him leaning against the refrigerator just inside the kitchen.

She smiled and walked straight to him, setting her tea onto the counter as she went. He opened his arms as she neared just like she knew he would. Snuggling close, she rested her head against his chest as her arms snaked around his waist. "Hey, back," she murmured.

"You left." His accusation was spoken softly and mumbled against her hair.

She smiled and squeezed her arms. "I was surprised you let me go."

"I knew when you left and figured you needed some time to yourself."

She leaned back to peer up into his face. "That's very perceptive."

He grinned and kissed her nose. "You haven't had a moment alone in days. Your parents came, and the Keepers stopped by. Mary, Vivian, and Lenore came over and brought food."

"I think Mary, Vivian, and Lenore were doing more than just bringing food. They are absolutely wonderful, but I'm pretty sure they were checking me out. You know... *Is she worthy to be with a Keeper?*"

He chuckled. "You might be right, but there's no doubt about that. I'm more worried about being worthy of you."

Her arms squeezed again. "I think we're perfect together."

"Agreed." Now, he bent farther to place a soft kiss on her lips.

"Oh, and just so you know, Lenore and Sisco's daughter is trying to give us a kitten."

Landon burst into laughter. "She can't part with any of them, so I have no idea why she is trying to find a new home for one." As their mirth eased, she held his gaze and said, "I like your friends, Landon."

"That's good. They like you."

She sighed. "My life has always been boring." Seeing his lifted brow, she said, "Shooting someone, running through the jungle during a storm, sleeping in a shed, having someone hold a gun on me, hearing the confession of sorts from a dying man who was going to be a murderer, being poisoned and a knife pulled on me with a plan to kill me... Landon, I'm tired of all this stupid stuff. It's ridiculous!"

He chuckled, and she felt the rumble from deep in his chest as his gaze held hers. "I admit, all that is nuts, but the way you've handled it, sweetheart, is what makes everyone think you're perfect for me."

Eyes wide, she shook her head. "Are you telling me that we can't go back to my boring life?"

"I think we've had our fair share of excitement. Now, you and I can settle in for boring if you'd like. Just as long as we're together."

Her top teeth pinched her bottom lip. "We've only been together for a week."

"Do you know how you feel about me?"

She nodded. "Yeah. I'm crazy about you, but then maybe I'm just crazy."

He laughed and shook his head. "Noel, all I know is that I want you right where you are—in my arms for as long as you'll let me hold you."

She placed her head on his chest again. "Good. Because right here is where I want to be."

Don't miss the exciting new LSIMT on the horizon!
Devlin

ALSO BY MARYANN JORDAN

Don't miss other Maryann Jordan books!

Baytown Boys (small town, military romantic suspense)

Coming Home

Just One More Chance

Clues of the Heart

Finding Peace

Picking Up the Pieces

Sunset Flames

Waiting for Sunrise

Hear My Heart

Guarding Your Heart

Sweet Rose

Our Time

Count On Me

Shielding You

To Love Someone

Sea Glass Hearts

Protecting Her Heart

Sunset Kiss

Baytown Heroes - A Baytown Boys subseries

A Hero's Chance

Finding a Hero

A Hero for Her

Needing A Hero

Hopeful Hero

Always a Hero

In the Arms of Hero

Holding Out for a Hero

Heart of a a Hero

For all of Miss Ethel's boys:

Heroes at Heart (Military Romance)

Zander

Rafe

Cael

Jaxon

Jayden

Asher

Zeke

Cas

Lighthouse Security Investigations

Mace

Rank

Walker

Drew

Blake

Tate

Levi

Clay

Cobb

Bray

Josh

Knox

Lighthouse Security Investigations West Coast

Carson

Leo

Rick

Hop

Dolby

Bennett

Poole

Adam

Jeb

Chris's story: Home Port (an LSI West Coast crossover novel)

Ian's story: Thinking of Home (LSIWC crossover novel)

Oliver's story: Time for Home (LSIWC crossover novel)

Lighthouse Security Investigations Montana

Logan

Sisco

Landon

Devlin

Hope City (romantic suspense series co-developed with Kris Michaels

Brock book 1

Sean book 2

Carter book 3

Brody book 4

Kyle book 5

Ryker book 6

Rory book 7

Killian book 8

Torin book 9

Blayze book 10

Griffin book 11

Saints Protection & Investigations

(an elite group, assigned to the cases no one else wants…or can solve)

Serial Love

Healing Love

Revealing Love

Seeing Love

Honor Love

Sacrifice Love

Protecting Love

Remember Love

Discover Love

Surviving Love

Celebrating Love

Searching Love

Follow the exciting spin-off series:

Alvarez Security (military romantic suspense)

Gabe

Tony

Vinny

Jobe

SEALs

SEAL Together (Silver SEAL)

Undercover Groom (Hot SEAL)

Also for a Hope City Crossover Novel / Hot SEAL…

A Forever Dad

Long Road Home
Military Romantic Suspense

Home to Stay (a Lighthouse Security Investigation crossover novel)

Home Port (an LSI West Coast crossover novel)

Thinking of Home (LSIWC crossover novel)

Time for Home (LSIWC crossover novel)

Letters From Home (military romance)

Class of Love

Freedom of Love

Bond of Love

The Love's Series (detectives)

Love's Taming

Love's Tempting

Love's Trusting

The Fairfield Series (small town detectives)

Emma's Home

Laurie's Time

Carol's Image

Fireworks Over Fairfield

Please take the time to leave a review of this book. Feel free to contact me, especially if you enjoyed my book. I love to hear from readers!

Facebook

Email

Website

Made in the USA
Columbia, SC
10 June 2025